The Clown Prince of Paris

D1713680

JAMES DUDLEY

DEDICATION

To Tom Clancy and Vince Flynn, two of my favorite authors who both left us far too soon.

ACKNOWLEDGMENTS

A big "thank you" goes out to everybody who helped make this book possible; to all my friends who served as sounding boards for these crazy ideas of mine, to Clarissa Yeo of Yocla Designs for creating the cover art, and to Amazon for providing the platform.

CHAPTER ONE

A cool autumn breeze blew across the still, peaceful waters of the Seine River as the sun set on a clear Paris evening. Along the cobblestone path by the water's edge, Natalia Petrova strode forward at a determined pace, feeling the freshly fallen leaves crunch underneath her stiletto heels. Her face and hair were obscured by an oversized hat, and a freshly-baked baguette protruded from her handbag, helping to create the illusion that she was nothing more than an anonymous bachelorette walking home with her groceries. Off in the distance, she could hear the distinct sounds of the music and merriment that so often filled the air in this city of artists, romantics, and revelers. Natalia blocked out these distractions, for hers was a life of subtlety and deception, and tonight, she was on a mission.

In the dull, mechanical glow of the streetlamps, she carefully watched her reflection in the water until she was certain that she had not been followed. While this came as a relief, on a certain level she couldn't help but feel slighted that the French security services did not seem to consider her worthy of the level of surveillance that a diplomatic official from the Soviet bloc could otherwise expect. As a cultural attaché, her official duties mainly consisted of planning receptions, leading tours, and giving lectures to school groups, none of which would arouse much suspicion. However, as with most things in the shadowy world in which she worked, these duties were merely a cover for her actual role as a clandestine officer in the KGB. As she drew near one of the stairways that led to the street level above, she found her colleague Boris Bryzgalov leaning against the wall, stamping out his cigarette when he noticed her approaching. He was posing as a vagrant, but the disguise was not terribly far removed from his usual unkempt and slovenly appearance. Natalia dropped some coins in his outstretched hat to help sell the cover as they talked.

"I've been watching the route for an hour; it's all clear," Boris said.

"Thank you, it shouldn't take long."

Boris wiped his brow, a look of exhaustion in his eyes. "I hope it doesn't take long. I'm getting tired of standing here with all the pigeons and ducks. They're really quite foul."

Natalia shot him an icy glare that was as cold as the Russian winter itself.

"You get it? Foul…because it sounds like fowl? And they call birds fowl?"

Natalia rolled her eyes. "Boris Mikhailovich, if you weren't such a dependable comrade, I would have you sent to Siberia for that."

"But alas, in all these years of working together, I

have never let you down once," he said.

Natalia glanced back towards the river as an evening mist began to set in. "You know what to do if you see anybody. Keep your eyes open and I'll see you at the reception."

His instructions clear, Boris stayed behind to keep watch while Natalia walked a few meters further to stand underneath one of the bridges spanning the river. Once there, she stepped down to the water's edge, put her hands in her pockets, and waited. She had explored almost all the secret nooks and crannies of the city at the behest of the *Rezident*, as the chief of the KGB station at the embassy was known, but this particular mission had come directly from Moscow and the desk of General Kharlamov himself. After a few minutes of waiting, a small motorboat appeared with a solitary man at its helm. He shut off the power and let the boat coast towards her position, its small wake sending ripples to disturb the peaceful water ever so slightly.

"Do you know where I can find a good crème brûlée?" she called out when the boat was near enough.

"I prefer the crepe suzette," the boatman responded, completing their prearranged code phrase.

He pulled the boat as close as he could to the shore and opened the concealed cabin where a second man had been hiding. Without speaking a word, the second man stood up and jumped ashore and then the boat departed as quickly as it had come.

"Welcome to Paris, Viktor Ivanovich," Natalia said.

Viktor Ivanovich Bazarov nodded in reply. With his square jaw, neatly trimmed blond hair, and imposing physique, he was a propaganda artist's model of the perfect Soviet man. His reputation preceded him, having been one of the Red Army's most feared snipers during the Battle of Stalingrad before moving on to work directly for General Kharlamov on special assignments. Whenever or wherever the General had a problem, Viktor could make it go away.

Natalia reached into her handbag and produced a folder. "We are now commencing the first phase of Operation Arctic Fox. Inside you will find directions to the safe house from which you may base your operations. The local chapter of the French Communist Party has volunteered to provide whatever manpower you may require."

Viktor opened the folder and flipped through the pages, skimming through the writing as quickly as he could. Unlike Natalia and Boris, whose diplomatic status granted them the protections of immunity, he was in the country illegally and therefore had to proceed with more caution.

"What's the condensed version?" he asked as he looked up.

"The Montravia negotiations have brought all the players in our game into one place. We have learned that the Western intelligence agencies are working with the Montravians to plan a covert mission called 'Operation Corner Kick.' We must identify who is involved, find out what they have planned, and prevent them from achieving it," Natalia said.

Viktor tucked the folder inside his suit coat. "I'll take care of it." He had the casual yet brutal efficiency of one who could kill someone on his lunch break and then finish eating his sandwich like nothing happened.

"I'll be in touch," Natalia told him as he turned to walk away. "Let me know if you need anything, but don't use the embassy line."

With the skill of a seasoned operator, Viktor stealthily slipped away into the night. When he was gone, Natalia turned and nodded to Boris, who slowly packed up his things and walked away. She then lingered for a few minutes before departing in a different direction. After a circuitous route involving several different modes of transportation, she finally arrived back at the Soviet Embassy with mere minutes to spare.

While Natalia's KGB duties consumed the bulk of her time and energy, she was also required to perform her official duties as a cultural attaché for the sake of her cover. One of those duties was hosting classy embassy receptions, and one such reception was about to begin. As quickly as possible, she retreated to her office and barricaded herself inside to get changed. When she emerged, the transformation was complete. She was wearing a royal blue evening gown that perfectly accentuated her eyes, and her long blond hair was done in an elegant updo that was previously concealed by her hat. As she stepped into the lobby, she bumped into Boris, who looked like a completely different man in his neatly pressed dinner jacket and black tie.

"Wow, you look just like Grace Kelly," he said. "I didn't think you could pull it off."

"And you look like a sober, serious man, which I really didn't think you could pull off."

Boris grinned as he revealed the flask that was tucked away in his pocket. "Don't worry, that won't last long."

She smiled and shook her head as they began to walk. "I'm probably going to need some of that to get through talking to these guests."

"Natalia Sergeevna, that does not sound very diplomatic. You should be honored to share the culture of the Motherland with these esteemed guests."

When they turned the corner to enter the ballroom, Natalia found that all her preparations had come together quite nicely. A long table was set up in the middle of the room with silver dishes of hors d'oeuvres on a finely knit tablecloth. The well-stocked bar was tucked away in the corner, and the hardwood floors were polished enough to see one's reflection in the light of the glass chandeliers. Many of the guests had already arrived, and from what she could tell, they seemed to be enjoying themselves.

After a long swig of vodka to steel herself, Natalia prepared to begin the excruciating but necessary duty of making small talk with the guests. She hated all the awkwardness, fakeness, and flattery, but it was all part of the role she had to play. Boris had already slipped away, probably chasing after some Swedish receptionist, leaving Natalia to fend for herself. Sensing a window of opportunity that may not be open for long, she made a dash for the food table, hoping to take what she wanted before she inevitably got roped into conversation. She almost made it. The food was nearly within arm's reach when she found herself trapped in an eclectic circle with Sir Alastair Thorncliffe, an experienced British diplomat, Howard Duckworth, a wealthy American industrialist, and Raymond LaFleur, a well-known French director of critically acclaimed arthouse films.

"My compliments, Natalia, this is an outstanding event," Alastair said with the kind of polished politeness that only a seasoned diplomat could muster.

"Thank you, Sir Alastair." With his thinning gray hair, thick -rimmed glasses, and intellectual mannerisms, he had the outward appearance of a stereotypical British schoolmaster. However, Natalia knew that there was much more to him than met the eye. It was fairly well-known in certain circles that he was actually a high ranking member of MI6, Britain's Secret Intelligence Service. She found it a bit odd for adversaries in a war to be exchanging pleasantries over cocktails, but this was a different kind of war and there were different kinds of rules.

"This is what I love about Communists," Howard Duckworth interjected. "Even when their own people are starving, they still manage to throw great parties for us."

Not in the mood for a political debate, Natalia simply glanced down towards his massive beer gut. "Well I am glad to see that you, for one, are in no danger of starving."

Howard responded with a hearty laugh as the other men joined in on the needling. Natalia smiled, knowing that Howard would not be laughing if he had any idea how many of his employees were currently selling technologies to the KGB.

Next, LaFleur cast a lecherous eye in her direction. "You look hungry though, Mademoiselle. I think you could really use a nice long baguette."

"But even the rats in the sewers would have no use for old and soggy baguettes," she responded.

Howard and Alastair laughed hysterically while LaFleur hung his head in shame, looking as if he was going to get radiation sickness from the sheer force of the burn. As Natalia gracefully excused herself from the circle, the crowd began to stir as the guest she most dreaded talking to stepped through the doors. Princess Sophia Maria Teresa von Landenberg was the heiress of the exiled monarchy of Montravia, and she had made the most of her exile, becoming one of Paris's most popular socialites and fashion icons. Tonight, she was wearing a long black dress with white velvet gloves and a string of pearls, and her dark hair was adorned with a silver tiara. She casually strolled through the floor with a martini glass in one hand and a cigarette in the other, knowing full well that every eye was on her.

Natalia braced herself as the Princess approached. They had met several times before at events like this and were not particularly fond of one another. However, diplomatic formalities required that their dislike could only be expressed through one-upmanship and back-handed compliments.

"Natalia, it is a pleasure to see you as always," the Princess said.

"The pleasure is all mine."

"You really did an excellent job with this party. It reminds me of when I was little and I wasn't old enough to attend state banquets. I would hold my own party in the basement with the servants' children, and it looked just like this."

Natalia bit her lip as she smiled as politely as possible. "Well in the Soviet Union, there are no servants, for we are all equal."

The Princess gulped down the rest of her martini

and handed Natalia the empty glass. "Then you wouldn't mind taking this then." She then handed over a very generous tip. "And here you go, darling, buy yourself some decent shoes."

Natalia gritted her teeth as she watched Princess Sophia slink away. Montravia had been a constant thorn in her side, but it was merely a mouse in the paws of the Russian bear.

CHAPTER TWO

The bright glow of the fluorescent bulbs burned Tommy Malloy's eyes as he paced in front of the long mirror in the dressing room of the Club Poutine, anxiously awaiting his scheduled stage time. As the hour grew nearer, a thick layer of sweat built up underneath the increasingly heavy fabric of his tuxedo, and the uneasy feeling in his stomach moved ever closer to nausea. He had performed on stage many times in his career as a comedian, but this particular spotlight was going to be a little bit brighter than the rest.

Tommy's comic skills were first honed on a much simpler stage ten years earlier, entertaining his fellow GI's in English dance halls during respites from the frontlines. Eventually, he got the opportunity to perform opening acts for more famous comedians visiting on U.S.O. tours, which gave him the connections he needed to help break into the business. After the war, he made his name performing stand-up in seedy clubs across America, eventually making his way to Hollywood, where he landed some small roles in big movies and big roles in small movies. It was more than enough to make a decent living, but not nearly enough to make him a household name. But now, a new level of stardom awaited him as he began a two-week run of headline shows in one of Paris's hottest clubs. If it went well, the doors would be flung open to bigger performances and bigger roles that could propel him into to the ranks of A-list stars. It was a lot to take in for the son of a South Philadelphia shipyard worker.

Looking for something to calm his nerves, Tommy walked over to the stereo in the back corner of the room and flipped through the pile of vinyl records beside it. He made his selection, and then sat down to listen to Tony Vespa's new album *Buongiorno from Livorno*, finally feeling a bit of relaxation thanks to the Brooklyn-born crooner's smooth and melodic voice.

"Hey, that's a good song. Do you know who sings it?"

Tommy looked up and waved as Tony Vespa himself strutted into the room. "Humble, as always." The two performers had started from the bottom together, working their way up from some of the sleaziest backwater clubs to their current levels of success. Their careers were in many ways intertwined, and they had even appeared in three B-movies together.

"We should coordinate our tours like this more often. This is fun, especially in a place like this," Tony said.

Tommy stood up and stretched. "So you've been outside then?"

"It is one classy joint out there. It's not like the clubs we've played at back home. And you should see the broads! Real high class, society dames, somebody even said there's a princess!"

"Is she single?"

"Far as I know."

Tommy stared off wistfully. "Imagine that, a guy like me becoming a prince. Prince Thomas the First, it even has a nice ring to it."

"There's a better chance of the Phillies winning the World Series next year."

"Well then I'm going to be pretty busy next year between my royal wedding and the World Series parade."

Tony shook his head and laughed. "That may be the funniest joke you've ever told."

Tony walked over to the liquor cabinet, poured two shots of whiskey, and handed one to Tommy.

"To Tommy Malloy, the craziest mick in Paris."

After they downed the shot, Tony turned to walk back outside.

"Better get back to my seat. But wait, are we still doing that bit at the end?"

"Yes we are," Tommy said.

Just as Tony was stepping out of the dressing room, Louis Poutine stepped in. France's most popular comedian had just applied a new coat of wax to his signature mustache and was ready to introduce the show in his namesake club.

"You're on in five minutes, Tommy."

Tommy took a deep breath. "I'm nervous, Louis."

Louis smiled calmly. "Just remember, no matter where you are, a stage is just a stage and a microphone is just a microphone. This is no different from any other place you've performed. And besides, a lot of the crowd might not speak English, so they won't even know if you make a mistake."

"Thanks, Louis, that actually helped a lot." Tommy's French was passable enough to get by, but he was only comfortable doing comedy in his native tongue.

Louis glanced down at his watch. "It's that time. I'll see you out there."

With nothing left to say, they walked through the hallway that led to the stage. Tommy stopped and watched from backstage as the lights in the club went dim and Louis strode out towards the microphone. Tommy absentmindedly put his hands in his pockets as he looked on, and his nerves were steadied when he felt the presence of the two good luck charms he carried with him during every performance. One was a small medal of Saint Thomas that his grandmother had given him before he left for the war, and the other was a 1933 baseball card of Chuck Klein, the Philadelphia Phillies' star outfielder who had been his boyhood idol. He closed his eyes and focused as the crowd cheered wildly for Louis's arrival.

Louis smiled and waved until the cheering subsided, then the audience grew quiet when he began his introductory remarks.

"Ladies and gentlemen, it is a great honor to welcome you all to Club Poutine. From my humble beginnings as a silent film star oh so long ago, to the global stardom I enjoy today, it has been my great privilege to share the gift of laughter with all of you. Through all the dark times our great city has endured, it is our sense of humor that sustains us and brings us together."

Raucous applause made Louis pause for a moment before he moved on.

"Tonight, you are in for a very special treat. Ten years ago, I performed a U.S.O. show for American GI's and one of their own performed the opening act. I knew from that moment he was going to be a star, and sure enough, we were making movies together just a short time later. Now, I have invited him back to bring his career full circle. Not only is he a great comedian, but he has become like a son to me. Ladies and gentlemen, please give a warm welcome to the greatest American invader since Eisenhower, Mr. Tommy Malloy!"

Tommy took a deep breath, smiled as big as he could, and then waved to the crowd as he ran out onto the stage. He reached out for the microphone, but intentionally fumbled it onto the ground in a show of feigned clumsiness. He then awkwardly dove after it and floundered and flailed across the stage until he finally stood triumphantly with the microphone in his grasp. It was shameless slapstick and the crowd loved it. With a dramatic flourish he then proclaimed, "Lafayette, I am here!"

The crowd cheered wildly, seeming to appreciate the versatility of a comic who could combine lowbrow physical comedy with well-placed historical references.

"Good Evening Paris! It's great to be back. The last time I was here was during the war and let me tell you, the food has gotten a whole lot better since then. We finally got rid of all those sour Krauts."

The crowd burst out in laughter, and Tommy felt a rush of energy now that he had found his groove.

"I love it here in France, but you have some of the weirdest history. Did you know the French Revolution started on a tennis court? What a racket that was! And then they went and put a guy like Robespierre in charge? Those people must have really lost their heads."

During the ensuing pause for laughter, Tommy scanned the crowd to see what he was working with. The room was filled with round tables, each finely decorated with white tablecloths, wine glasses, and desserts. Each table sat about four or five people, and the crowd featured a fairly eclectic mix. There were wealthy Parisians socialites, fellow artists and creative types, traveling businessmen, GI's on liberty from nearby NATO bases, and a beautiful brunette in the back corner who he assumed had to be the Princess.

Heeding Louis' advice about the language barrier, the remainder of Tommy's material was lighter on wordplay and heavier on universal slapstick and physical comedy. With an occasional interspersed pun, he proceeded through a series of gaffes and gags using various props, each slightly more complicated and audacious than the last. Much to his relief, the crowd seemed to love every minute of it.

When the act was nearly finished, Tommy walked down from the stage, a lone spotlight following him as he walked through the crowd and towards a table in the back.

"Now you've all been a great audience, except for one little thing. Mr. Tony Vespa is in the house, and he hasn't laughed all night. What seems to be the problem, sir?"

Tony rose and took the microphone, feigning

anger. "My problem is that you are a no-good son-of-a-bitch!"

The crowd laughed nervously, awaiting Tommy's retort.

"You sir, have a dirty mouth. Perhaps you need to wash it out."

Tommy grabbed a nearby pitcher of water and splashed it in Tony's face, much to the delight of the crowd.

Tony scowled as he shook himself dry. "You comedians are all the same; all you ever do is whine about it."

He reached for a glass of red wine and poured it over Tommy's head, to the sounds of even more laughter.

Tommy stood firm. "You sir, do not appreciate good comedy. Do you know what I say to people like you? Let them eat cake!"

He reached for a nearby slice of cake, smashing it in Tony's face. Tony then rolled up his sleeves and wildly chased after Tommy, recklessly swinging his bawled fists. Tommy greatly embellished his motions as he fled, dodging under tables and chairs and startling unsuspecting guests. The audience loved every second of it, nearly falling out of their seats as they doubled over with laughter. As the staged feud continued all over the floor, Tommy and Tony shared a knowing nod. The show was an undeniable success, and the city was theirs for the taking.

CHAPTER THREE

A police escort led the way as the black Mercedes limousine carrying Prince Hans Friedrich slowly but steadily maneuvered through the morning traffic. The Prince was sitting in the rear of the vehicle, leafing through the pages of his notebook in preparation for his scheduled remarks. He was a man of the old aristocracy, extensively schooled in courtly manners, the classics of language and literature, and the fencing and riding skills of a bygone era. He had slowed down considerably in his advancing age, and what remained of his hair had long since turned to grey, but on this day, he felt like a young man once more.

"How did that sound, Rolfe?" the Prince asked as he finished rehearsing his speech for the fourth or fifth time.

"It's going to be magnificent, Your Highness."

The Prince's young steward, Rolfe Schrodinger, was proving to be indispensable. He had served the Prince for the past three years while finishing his university studies, but his family had served the

House of Landenberg for nearly three hundred.

"Well, it looks like we're here," said the Prince.

The limo pulled over and stopped by the curb in front of an office building leased by an organization known as the "Friends of Montravia." It was a gathering point for the large and growing community of Montravian ex-patriots residing in France, and was seen as the unofficial base of Montravia's government in exile. Its walls were lined with portraits of the country's previous monarchs in chronological order, and the overall decorating scheme conveyed the sense of fair-minded professionalism that Montravians were known for.

The Prince walked through the reception area and up a stairwell, offering handshakes to the appreciative staff that rose to greet him. Finally, he arrived at the building's main conference room, which was crowded beyond its capacity. Every Montravian within a hundred mile radius was squeezed inside, and the event had also been opened to the press. When the Prince approached the doorway, the tension inside was palpable. He paused at the door as Rolfe stepped forward and announced his presence.

"Ladies and Gentlemen, His Royal Highness Prince Hans Friedrich of Montravia."

Everyone in attendance rose from their seats in accordance with protocol, and the press's cameras began to flash. The Prince walked towards the center of the room towards a podium that bore his royal seal. When he got there, he looked out at the crowd, feeling knots in his stomach. He had made his fair share of public appearances; it was an important aspect of his job description after all, but this was probably the most politically consequential address he would give since his coronation thirty years prior. As he looked down at his papers, his eyes were still flashing green from all the cameras. He took a moment to acclimate himself to the room, then took in a big gulp of air and began his remarks.

"Ladies and gentlemen, friends and citizens of Montravia, and our distinguished guests from the press, it is an honor and a privilege to speak before you today. Most of you are very familiar with the history and culture of our country. We have long been considered by many to be one of Europe's hidden gems. From the picturesque skiing villages on the slopes of the mountains, to the glistening blue waters of the harbor, to the charming medieval architecture of the capitol, it is a place of unforgettable beauty. It may be small, but it has a large place in our hearts."

He reached for the next page of his notes, feeling more comfortable now that he was getting into the flow of things.

"For over 400 years, the Royal House of Landenberg has presided over a peaceful and prosperous principality, maintaining our position as a center of arts, culture, and business. Since 1924, I have had the great honor of serving the people of Montravia as their Prince. I was determined to maintain this history of peace, but unfortunately events elsewhere in the continent conspired against us. In 1938, our nation was politically absorbed into Germany as part of the *Anschluss*. I did not desire this change, nor did the people of Montravia, but with our small size and very limited defense forces, we were powerless to stop it. I was not willing to pledge the Nazi regime the loyalty they demanded, so the monarchy was forced into exile, first in London, and then here in Paris.

Since the end of the war, the political systems of Europe have undergone massive changes. The West has embraced democracy, while the East has turned to Communism. Meanwhile, the former Axis powers remain under Allied occupation. Much like Germany, Montravia has been divided into American, British, French, and Soviet occupation zones, with provisional governors appointed to administer each zone. This situation is not ideal, but it was a necessary aspect of the post-war rebuilding."

The Prince paused for a moment. Most of the crowd probably already knew all that, but now it was time for the breaking news.

"However, over the past several months, high-level diplomatic negotiations among all the interested nations have been conducted right here in Paris. With the generous assistance of the French government, as well as the Soviet, American, and British delegations, a more permanent solution has been agreed upon. I am pleased to announce that on the 25th of October, the aforementioned nations will formally sign the Treaty of Montravia, which will officially terminate the Allied occupation and restore the sovereign government of Montravia. Next week, I will stand before you no longer as an exiled pretender, but as your true and rightful Prince."

The Prince could hear the excited whispers in the crowd after his latest revelation. He was back in the game, and it felt great.

"As Europe divides between the competing alliances of NATO and the Warsaw Pact, Montravia has pledged in this treaty to maintain a policy of neutrality. My hope is that by doing so, we may be an even-handed mediator that can play a key role in promoting peace and cooperation throughout the world. Many of us have seen this continent ravaged by war twice in our lifetimes, and I will do everything in my power to ensure that it does not happen again. If you are committed to justice, peace, and fair play, you will have a friend in Montravia. Thank you."

Having finished his speech, the Prince turned and walked out of the room, ignoring both the wild cheers of his compatriots and the frantically shouted questions of the press. With Rolfe following close on his heels, he walked straight outside back to the limo, fully aware by the reactions that he had just dropped a bombshell.

Once they were safely inside the car, the Prince finally exhaled. "So how did I do?"

"You were superb, Your Highness, it was a wonderful beginning to a new era," Rolfe said.

As the limo took him back to his residence, the Prince glanced out the window, taking in the view of the Eiffel Tower extending over the rooftops. He had developed quite a fondness for the city that had become his home in exile, but he was very anxious to return to his real home. After a short drive through the city, they arrived at the town home where he had made his temporary residence. It was no royal palace, but he made the most of it. He stepped into the foyer, where Rolfe took his coat and hat and hung them in the closet.

The Prince took his time as he strolled through his main hallway, trying to calm himself back down after the adrenaline rush of the speech. Along the way, he paused to look at the family portraits that hung on the walls. A portrait of his father, who had safely guided the country through a policy of neutrality in the First World War, was the first one that a visitor would see. Hans Friedrich admired his example, and hoped that he would have approved of his current courses of action. The Prince's own official portrait was directly across on the other side, hanging adjacent to one of his late wife Princess Catherine. Following them were the portraits of his true pride and joy, his three daughters. The eldest, Sophia, lived here with him in Paris, a fact that gave him much joy, if not a little bit of consternation. Meanwhile, the younger sisters were currently attending British boarding schools.

He sent Rolfe to fetch some tea and biscuits as he walked into his study. It was a high-ceilinged room with wood paneled walls, a prominent grandfather clock, and shelves full of leather bound books. Comfortable leather chairs and a mahogany coffee table sat atop an oriental rug in front of the fire place. When he arrived, he found that Sir Alastair Thorncliffe was sitting by the fireplace waiting for him while Princess Sophia was doing her best to keep him entertained.

"So the reporter asked me how I enjoyed my trip to Manchester, and I told him, 'It was a really delightful city,' but then he insisted, 'No, this is off the record, what did you really think of Manchester?' So I said, 'Well in that case, it was positively ghastly.'"

Alastair doubled over in laughter, then immediately paused and looked up when he noticed the Prince's entrance.

Sophia excitedly rose to greet her father. "Papa! How did the speech go?"

"Exactly according to plan," he said as he plopped down into one of the chairs.

Sophia glanced at the grandfather clock. "Oh my, I really must be off."

"Where are you off to today?"

"An exhibition opening at the Louvre."

The Prince sighed. He never could keep track of her socialite lifestyle. "I thought you were going to the comedy show?"

"That was last night."

"Oh right, how was it?"

She chuckled. "It greatly exceeded my expectations. Well, I didn't really know what to expect, to be honest, but I dare say that Tommy Malloy is a comic genius."

She kissed her father on the cheek and departed the room as Rolfe returned with a tray bearing a teapot, two cups, and a plate of biscuits. Once the tea was poured, Rolfe left the room once more as Alastair and the Prince got down to business.

"So you gave the speech, exactly as we discussed?" Alastair inquired.

The Prince nodded. "Do you still think it was the right move?"

"Yes I do," Alastair assured him. "The Soviet delegates have agreed to the treaty, presumably with the full support of the government in Moscow. However, we must be wary of the power struggle that lies behind the scenes. There are factions in Moscow that still cling to the goal of seeing Montravia go Communist, and we cannot be entirely certain just how much influence they have. Now that the terms of the Treaty are out in the open, we have effectively forced their hand. The Soviet government can no longer go back on it, at least not publicly."

The Prince nodded, taking it all in. "So I don't know the full extent of your government's involvement in this whole situation…"

"And trust me, the less you know, the better."

"But do you think that these hardliners in Moscow might take some sort of…covert action to derail the agreement?"

Alastair shrugged. "It's possible. If they do, they only have one week left to do it."

The Prince took a deep breath. "So in other words, this is going to be an interesting week?"

"Yes it will," Alastair said as he puffed on his pipe. "Yes, it will."

CHAPTER FOUR

Thanks to the magic of makeup and wigs, Natalia looked at least forty years older as she stepped outside, walking with a cane to complete the ensemble. The disguise was so convincing that she could almost feel the arthritis in her joints and osteoporosis in her bones. While a simple change of wardrobe was often sufficient to disguise oneself from strangers, it was an entirely different proposal to disguise oneself from friends and colleagues.

It initially seemed strange that General Kharlamov had contacted Natalia directly with his orders to work with Viktor and uncover the Western spy ring rather than utilizing the regular chain-of-command. However, as she read the full content of the orders, the reasons why became clear enough. The General had identified that there was a leak in her office, and identifying it would be the first major lead in discovering their adversaries' plans. There were only a handful of potential suspects, so Natalia and Viktor divided them up and set forth to investigate them one by one. Tonight, she was following Boris, hoping to establish that he could be safely crossed off the list.

Boris's evening began quietly enough, eating a sandwich at a local café before enjoying a couple pints of beer at a nearby pub. From there, he walked a few blocks and then went underground to board the Metro as Natalia discreetly followed. A few short stops later, Boris left the train, blending in with the crowded pack of commuters. Natalia followed from a distance as he walked up the stairs and back out into the city. After a brisk walk down a busy street, he was standing at the entrance of the Alexander Nevsky Cathedral.

With its familiar three-barred crosses sitting atop golden onion-shaped domes, the cathedral appeared to be a little slice of Russia that managed to end up in Paris. It was a Russian Orthodox church, constructed in the previous century to serve Paris's growing community of Russian emigres. Natalia found it somewhat odd that Boris had come here, as she had never known him to be a pious man, but perhaps he was merely feeling homesick or nostalgic.

Natalia looked on as Boris walked through the doors, and then waited a few minutes before following him in. The inside of the church was dimly lit and mostly empty, as there were no services currently going on. The distinctive scent of incense lingered in the air, and the sound of her footsteps echoed against the cold stone walls. Beautifully painted icons filled the walls, the eyes of the ancient saints seeming to silently observe everything that occurred within.

Boris walked down the center aisle and then took

a seat in one of the front pews on the right side. He sat there for quite some time, seemingly very deep in prayer. Natalia took a seat near the rear of the church, pretending to pray as she watched him intently. Finally, she saw what she was looking for, and what she had really been hoping not to see. In a motion so quick that she would have missed it if she blinked, Boris reached underneath the pew and attached a small metal container to the bottom. It would have looked like nothing to the untrained eye, but Natalia knew a dead drop when she saw one. It was one of the primary methods by which spies conveyed information to one another.

After making his drop, Boris stood up and left the church by a side entrance. Natalia remained in her seat and kept watch until a second man appeared and sat down in the same pew where Boris had been. Just as she was expecting, the man slid his hand underneath the pew and slipped the container into his pocket. Natalia snapped a picture of the man on a miniature camera and then stood up to leave, beginning to accept the grim reality of the situation.

She now had no choice but to report Boris's transgressions and leave him to the mercies of Viktor. After leaving the cathedral, Natalia returned to the Metro station and took a ride back to her neighborhood, disembarking two stops early to walk the rest of the way. Years of counter-surveillance training had instilled in her the importance of varying one's schedules and routes. Along the way, she stopped by a produce stand to buy her groceries for the week. Her shopping lists were never very long, given that she lived alone and spent almost all of her waking hours at work. She picked out a hearty selection of vegetables, fruits, and meats, as well as a copy of a newspaper. Being fluent in French and English in addition to her native Russian meant that she could perform such transactions with the familiarity of a local. With her purchase complete, she lingered a while to eavesdrop on conversations. It was a simple method that was often one of the best ways of obtaining new information. However, most of the conversations she gleaned seemed to revolve around the prospects of Stade Saint-Germaine, one of the local professional football clubs.

She took a few more turns down various side streets, taking a route that was far from direct. Finally, she arrived in the quiet block where she kept her modest apartment. It was part of a square concrete building, completely indistinguishable from those around it. Her neighbors were mostly quiet and kept to themselves, which was the way she liked it.

Inside the drafty room, she set her groceries down on the counter. It was a small and simple place that was often eerily quiet. She wished she could buy a cat for some form of company, but she did not have the time or energy to commit to taking care of one. The furniture was simple and practical, and a plain grey carpet covered the floor. The walls were decorated with a few prints of Impressionist art she had picked up at local museum shops, as well as a Time Magazine cover from 1942 that featured her idol, the composer Dmitri Shostakovich, serving as a firefighter during the war.

When the groceries were put away, she pulled off her wig, poured herself a glass of vodka, and sat down to read the newspaper. The headlines were covering Prince Han Friedrich's speech about the Montravia

Treaty, but it was nothing that she didn't already know. As she flipped through the pages and reached the lifestyle section, she came upon an article about an American comic named Tommy Malloy performing at the Club Poutine. She paused for a moment and stared at the photo of him smashing a cake in a famous singer's face while the audience in the background laughed hysterically. Was this what passed for humor in the West?

Having seen enough juvenile frivolity, she finished her drink and then walked over to the aging piano that she had purchased second hand. She flipped through her book of music, and decided to practice *Rachmaninoff's Piano Concerto No. 2*. Music was an important way to relieve stress for her, but it had once been much more than that. As a young girl, she dreamed of one day becoming a classical pianist. As a teenager, she was accepted to the Leningrad Conservatory, where those dreams were set to become reality. However, she was only just beginning her studies when the war came.

The armies of the Third Reich launched a massive invasion of the Soviet Union in 1941, and for over two years her home city was subjected to a brutal siege. Wanting to do whatever she could to help the Motherland, young Natalia would sneak her way around the city, mapping out German troop positions and eavesdropping on their plans. It didn't take long for her reports to catch the attention of Soviet commanders.

General Kharlamov in particular found Natalia's contributions invaluable. He incorporated her into his command, gradually giving her larger and more complicated missions. She rose through the ranks as the tide of the war slowly turned, making invaluable contributions to the cause. As the Great Patriotic War gave way to the Cold War, the General personally recruited her to pursue further training and become one of his most valuable assets in this new form of conflict. That road had brought her here, living mere blocks away from the grand theatres and concert halls she had once dreamed of performing in, but living the much different life than fate had in store for her.

She finished the piece and sat motionless, staring back at the half-empty vodka bottle on the table, wondering if it was some sort of allegory or metaphor for her life. The only thing she knew for certain was that big things were happening, and Paris was about to get a lot more dangerous.

CHAPTER FIVE

The first raindrops of an evening thunderstorm were beginning to bounce off the sidewalk when Harry Thompson stepped off the city bus, regretting that he forgot to bring his umbrella. He was a man of average height and average build, wearing a charcoal business suit with a matching fedora and carrying a black leather briefcase. He was virtually indistinguishable from the legions of men in any major city that would fit his exact description, which was exactly the way he wanted it, for anonymity was the cloak that guarded him.

A fluent French speaker and experienced world traveler, Harry knew Paris inside and out. He first visited the city on one of his first missions as an OSS officer in the spring of 1944, making a rendezvous with the French Resistance on a reconnaissance mission ahead of the Allied invasion. His skills and reputation grew as the OSS became the CIA and wartime allies became Cold War enemies, and now he had come full circle. He was back in Paris, and once again he was working for his wartime commander, Sir Alastair Thorncliffe.

On this particular evening, Harry was on his way to meet one of his most valuable sources, who had requested a face-to-face meeting. He first met Boris Bryzgalov late one night at a seedy bar, where the eccentric Russian had gotten into a tight spot while attempting to hustle a game of billiards with a local criminal gang. Harry stepped in to smooth things over and pay Boris's debts. Boris was very grateful, but as most things went in their business, Harry made it clear that he expected some "quid pro quo," unless, of course, he didn't mind the KGB finding out about his gambling habits. Boris went on to exceed all expectations in holding up his end of the bargain, providing the West with indispensable eyes and ears inside the Soviet Embassy.

The latest microfilm that Boris dropped at the Alexander Nevsky Cathedral was the most valuable yet; providing shocking revelations about ongoing KGB operations. Now that Boris wanted to meet in person, Harry could only excitedly speculate on what else he may be able to reveal. For the location of their meeting, he had selected the Club Poutine. Public performances like this were ideal for secret meetings, as they were crowded, noisy, and dimly lit. Furthermore, one of his work colleagues had seen the opening performance of the current show, and had reported that it was actually very funny.

Thirty minutes before show time, Harry purchased two tickets, leaving one at the window for "Lars Svenson," the assumed name that Boris would sometimes work under. He walked through the lobby, scanning the people in the crowd as they entered, mingled, and made their way to their seats. Seeing no signs of Boris or of any unwanted surveillance, he took a seat at an empty table in the back left corner of the theatre. He draped his suit coat over the back of the chair next to him and placed his hat on the seat, clearly indicating that the seat was being saved.

Trying hard to maintain his situational awareness, Harry glanced around at the surrounding tables, taking careful stock of who was present. Two tables over to the left, he noticed the singer Tony Vespa taking a seat, surrounded by the usual celebrity entourage. A group of businessmen took the table to the front, and the table to the right was occupied by journalists who were there to write reviews of the show. Harry's table remained empty, and he grew ever more anxious as he awaited Boris's arrival.

When the hour of show time approached, the lights dimmed and Louis Poutine took the stage, delivering his opening monologue as the emcee. Harry shifted uncomfortably in his seat; tardiness was a frequent issue for Boris, but it still made him uneasy even if it was expected. Back on the stage, Louis stepped aside from the microphone as he concluded his opening remarks, "And now, please give a warm welcome to Tommy Malloy!"

Harry stood and applauded along with the rest of the crowd, happy to show support for his fellow American. As Tommy launched into his act, Harry pretended to pay attention, laughing and clapping along with everybody else while his eyes continuously scanned the room. One could not survive as long as he had in his business without developing an innate sense for when something just wasn't right about a situation, and that sense was now in overdrive. It was entirely possible that Boris was simply running late or had been held up, but Harry was becoming increasingly worried that other factors may be at work.

The crowd around Harry roared with laughter as Tommy Malloy clumsily tripped across the stage, catastrophically dropping the comically large stack of ceramic plates he had been attempting to carry. The cacophony of sounds dulled Harry's senses, and masked the approaching footsteps of the blond man in a business suit who presumptuously sat down in the open seat next to him.

"Excuse me, that seat is saved for my friend," Harry said.

The blond man crossed his legs and lit a cigarette. "Yes, your friend Boris Bryzgalov." He took a long puff of smoke. "I am afraid he will not be able to attend tonight. He is otherwise detained, and I dare say he is no longer your friend."

Harry's mind raced to make sense of the situation. It was now apparent that Boris's cover had been blown, and now the Soviets were attempting to exploit the situation to their advantage. While he had been in similar situations before, he knew of only one KGB officer who was audacious enough to go about things in this manner.

"Viktor Bazarov," he said aloud as he shook his head in disgust.

Viktor nodded in acknowledgment. "Your reputation precedes you as well, Harry Thompson. 'The Philadelphia Phantom,' is that what they call you?" He leaned forward, speaking in an ominous tone. "You and I have been playing the same game for years, this deadly chess match of ours. One day I move a bishop to Budapest, the next you land a knight in Rome, and we each plan our next moves carefully, never knowing where the next piece will fall."

As Viktor paused, they could hear Tommy's voice continuing with his jokes. "I love doing this show here in Paris because they let me do the whole performance. I tried to do a show in Berlin last week, but they said I had to cut it in half!"
The audience roared with laughter, appreciative of the geopolitical humor.

Muffled by the sounds of laughter, Viktor spoke once more. "You see, even that clown is a part of our game, with his own role to play. But now, it appears you are in checkmate. It would seem your role in this game has come to its end."

"Save the monologues for your Shakespeare class," Harry responded. "Let's just get this over with. So you caught Boris, but you came here to talk to me, which means that I have something you want and you're using his life as a bargaining chip. So what are your terms? What do you want from us?"

"Oh no, I am afraid you have misunderstood the situation. I am not here to negotiate another silly move in our great game. I am here to remove you from the game."

Viktor waved his hand and two other men approached to join them at the table, one tall and gaunt with a hooked nose, and the other short, round and stocky. Harry recognized them as Jacques Trebuchet and Pierre Brodeur, members of the local Communist Party. He had always suspected they were taking orders from Moscow, but he never realized they were in this deep. Their faces glared at Harry, watching his every move. He could also see other groups of men moving about, taking up positions near the exits.

"I know what you're doing here in Paris, and I know about Operation Corner Kick," Viktor said.

Harry started to stammer in protest, but Viktor cut him off, "Don't insult me with denials, for it is known."

Harry slumped back in his chair, trying desperately to keep his mind alert as he fought off the feeling of utter defeat washing over him. When he first realized he had been played, he felt crushed, as if his carefully constructed house of cards had just come crashing down on top of him. But he quickly pushed these thoughts aside, his survival instincts frantically searching for some hope to cling on to.

Harry looked across the room at the crowd of people innocently enjoying a comedy show, blissfully unaware of the deadly game being played in their midst. Then he took a deep breath and turned to face his opponents once more. Viktor could make all the chess analogies he wanted, but there was only one rule that mattered in America; it ain't over 'til it's over.

Viktor looked Harry in the eye as he explained, "I have been instructed to offer you the following terms: you will receive a pardon for your crimes and full recognition as a Hero of the Soviet Union. You will be given an estate in Moscow and two weeks' vacation each year at a luxury dacha on the Black Sea. All we require is your defection and that you provide us with the identities and objectives of the other agents involved in Operation Corner Kick."

Harry was not swayed. "I'd rather die than work for you bastards."

"I predicted that you would respond as such, and don't worry, we have come prepared to fulfill your request. You probably noticed that my men are covering every exit. You can rest assured that you will not be leaving this club alive."

With the stakes made clear, Harry took careful stock of the situation. The odds were stacked against him, but some factors still worked in his favor. While he may be trapped and outnumbered, he was still at a public performance with a large crowd around him. As long as the show was still going on, a glimmer of hope remained.

"Isn't it customary to let a condemned man have one last cigarette?"

"Yes, of course, I am not the thoughtless brute you take me for," Viktor said.

Viktor offered Harry a cigarette and leaned forward to give him a light. Harry's muscles tensed, waiting for a window of opportunity to knock the lighter out of his hand, which would hopefully ignite a fire. But Viktor seemed to anticipate the move, holding the lighter close to his chest and protecting it with his left elbow.

Harry leaned back and inhaled a deep puff of smoke. He needed another idea, and time was quickly running out. He looked towards the stage, where Tommy Malloy was in motion, walking down into the crowd with a microphone in hand. Tommy strolled across the floor, stopping next to Tony Vespa's table, just two tables over from Harry. Harry watched this intently; a new factor was being introduced to the situation, and he was fairly certain that Viktor had not planned for it.

"You have all been a great audience, except for one little problem," Tommy announced. "Mr. Tony Vespa is in the house and he has not laughed all night. What seems to be the problem, sir?"

Tony stood and responded, "My problem is that you are a no good son-of-a-bitch!"

Tommy reached for a pitcher of water to fling. "You sir, have a dirty mouth. You need to wash it out!"

Sensing an opportunity, Harry let his impulses take over. He shot up to his feet and loudly exclaimed, "Tommy Malloy isn't funny at all! He's a stinkin' bum! They oughta' throw him out on Skid Row!"

The rest of the audience laughed, assuming it was part of the show. Meanwhile, Tommy and Tony exchanged puzzled looks, taken aback at the unexpected audience participation.

"It looks like we got a wise guy over here," Tony improvised.

Tommy turned to face Harry. "Nobody likes a wise guy!"

Harry felt a jolt of excitement, now he was getting somewhere. "Nobody likes your face!"

The audience laughed at the insults while Viktor squirmed uncomfortably in his seat, seeming to sense that the situation was slipping out of his control. Determined to escalate things further, Harry lifted up his chair, calling out Tommy and Tony as he brandished it as a weapon. "Come on you punks, let's see what you got!"

Tommy and Tony approached cautiously, seeming to improvise in the hopes that the audience wouldn't realize that this wasn't supposed to be part of their routine. Harry was beginning to step forward as if to throw the chair when he noticed Viktor standing up in his peripheral vision. But Viktor was not quick enough. Harry swiftly spun around, bringing the heavy wooden chair crashing down over his head. Viktor stumbled backwards as Jacques and Pierre leaped to his assistance. Seizing his opportunity, Harry charged forward, shoving Tommy to the ground as he ran past, and then leaping on top of the next table he found. He surveyed the scene from the higher vantage point, noticing that several unintended fist fights were already breaking out. He kicked over several glasses of wine, and then jumped and dove on top of the irate businessmen he had just spilled on, randomly throwing punches and elbows at anyone within his reach.

Within moments, the club had erupted into an all-out melee. Punches and kicks were flying, drinks were being spilled, chairs and tables were being broken. Nobody could clearly tell who exactly they were fighting or why they were doing it, but in the heat of the moment, they were giving way to their baser instincts. Harry was at the center of it, doing his best to get lost in the shuffle. It was pure chaos, and chaos was the only ally Harry Thompson had right now.

CHAPTER SIX

Tommy stumbled his way back to his dressing room and closed the door behind him. He had finally escaped from the violent ruckus outside, and it was only just now beginning to subside. When he turned on the lights and looked at his reflection in the mirror, he looked much more like a Skid Row resident than a professional performer. His hair was disheveled, he had multiple bruises, and his upper lip was swollen and bleeding. He had lost his bow tie, his dinner jacket was torn, and his white shirt was stained with blood and spilled wine, and also missing several buttons.

Hecklers were a constant annoyance in the life of a comedian, but he had never experienced anything quite like this. He tried to recollect what had happened after the initial incidents, but it was a blur of various fragmented images; an exchange of blows with a tall ugly Frenchman, the heckler leaping on top of a table, Tony managing to slip out the front door and hail a cab, Louis Poutine taking the stage and pleading for order. It began with a simple act of heckling, but it turned into pure pandemonium.

Tommy slumped down in his chair, reaching for a bottle of whiskey with which to drown his sorrows. The show must always go on, but he was going to have to purge this night from his memories before he got back on the stage again. His run in Paris began with such promise, but now it was in danger of ending in disaster. He glanced at a local newspaper's review of his opening show, which had been effusive in its praise, claiming that Louis Poutine, the long-reigning King of Comedy, had discovered a worthy prince to be his heir. They even dubbed Tommy "The Clown Prince of Paris." Tomorrow that same newspaper would probably be calling him an unruly Yankee ruffian who can't put on a show without trouble.

A faint rustling noise emanated from the costume closet in the back of the room, and Tommy turned to see a well-dressed but disheveled looking man stumble out to reveal he had been hiding there. Tommy stared at this curious appearance, and then sprang to his feet as he recognized the face of his heckler. He felt his blood boiling with rage; this man had quite possibly ruined the biggest break of Tommy's career, and he wasn't about to let him get away with it. He grabbed the man by the lapels and shoved him against the wall.

"You crazy bastard! What the hell do you think you were trying pull out there?"

The man reacted quickly, using Tommy's strength and aggression against him. In a few swift motions, he escaped Tommy's grasp and pinned his arm behind his back. Tommy struggled futilely to break free as the man spoke quietly but firmly in his ear.

"Now you listen to me and you listen good. My name is Harry Thompson. I am an American working for our government. The KGB is here in this club and they are trying to kill me. I apologize for ruining your show, but everything I did out there was necessary to give me the cover to escape."

Tommy took a step back as Harry released him. He sat back down, not sure what to make of this new development.

"Now there's a story I haven't heard before."

Harry went on to explain as much as he could comfortably divulge about his own identity and mission as well as those of his adversaries. It was a lot for Tommy to process. He had seen a lot of crazy things in his life, but now he had truly seen everything.

"So that's a pretty crazy story, but what do you want from me?"

"Just one small favor, I need you to get me out through the performers' entrance," Harry said.

"They had men watching the exits, but they probably didn't think of that one. Would you be willing to do that for me?"

"Yeah, I'll do it." Tommy stood up and put the bottle away, stretching and jumping to shake out his stupor.

"So anyway, what made you think you could trust me in the first place?"

"You don't stay alive for long in my business without being able to read people."

"Oh yeah? And how do you read me?"

Harry looked him up and down, seeming to

evaluate as he went. "Expensive tux, designer shoes, you've been working in some very wealthy circles. But you still put your cummerbund on incorrectly, which shows that you were never really comfortable in those circles. You come from a working class background and feel more at home there. You made the sign of the cross before you took the stage, so I'm guessing you went to Catholic schools and have a pretty clear sense of right and wrong. You charged right into the brawl out there, so I know you're tough. You're not afraid of the unknown, and you don't back down from a challenge, but you have some issues with authority. You were definitely in the service, possibly a paratrooper, definitely junior enlisted. Overall, you're the type of guy I wouldn't mind having next to me in a scrape, even if you are from *South* Philadelphia."

Tommy was taken aback but just how accurate most of the assessment was. "Wait...does that mean... are you from the Northeast?"

Harry nodded.

"Let me guess...Archbishop O'Riley?"

"Class of '38," Harry confirmed.

Tommy extended a handshake, finally starting to warm up to this strange man and his incredible story.

"South Catholic, class of '42."

"My senior year we played you guys in the Catholic League final."

"And you lost," Tommy reminded him. Their respective high schools enjoyed a healthy athletic and academic rivalry that mirrored the relationship between their Philadelphia neighborhoods.

"So, about that performers' entrance?"

"Right, follow me."

43

Tommy cracked the door open and peered outside, then walked through and motioned for Harry to follow. They walked through the dimly lit hallway and down a little-used and well concealed stairwell.

Tommy constantly looked over his shoulder, making sure nobody was watching them. A familiar feeling of tension and anxiety came over him, something he had not felt since the war, when he had to help clear a Belgian village full of German snipers, never knowing when the next one would strike. They walked through another door and finally out into the dark and quiet alley behind the club. The rain had stopped, but a thin mist still hung in the air. As quickly as possible, Tommy and Harry jumped into the back seat of the black BMW that the club had provided.

"Back to the hotel," Tommy told the driver as he started the car.

They rode in silence for the short journey of several blocks to the Hotel Villeneuve, the upscale establishment where Tommy had been staying. There were only a handful of cars on the road at this hour, and an eerie calm masked the danger that they knew was lurking out there, somewhere. The car pulled up to the front entrance, and they got out and stood by the doorway as the car pulled away.

Harry shook Tommy's hand. "Thank you, I really appreciate the help."

"So what are you going to do now?"

"Probably lay low for the night, and then take the first train out of town in the morning."

"Do you have a place to lay low?"

Harry paused to consider his options.

"Come on, just stay in my room for the night."

Harry protested, "I can't ask that of you, I've pulled you too far in to this as it is."

"Come on, I can't just leave you out here like this," Tommy insisted.

After some more back and forth, Harry finally relented, and they walked briskly through the hotel lobby. They took the elevator up to the third floor, and Tommy led the way to Room 321, where he slid in the key and opened the door. When the door closed behind them, it was safe to talk once more.

"I still can't believe this is all happening. I mean, just look at us, two Philly boys this far from home, mixed up in all this," Tommy said.

Harry kicked off his shoes and reclined on one of the two twin beds. "It's a crazy world isn't it?"
Tommy took a seat on the other bed, his body starting to remember that it was hungry. "Hey, you know what I could really go for right now? A real Italian hoagie from Mr. Barzini's shop."

Harry's ears perked up. "The one on Chestnut Street? I love that place!"

This launched them into long conversation reminiscing about memories of home; the school trips to the Liberty Bell, the strict discipline of the nuns that taught them, Christmas light shows at the Wanamaker store, Phillies games at Shibe Park, and those horrible rumors about the Athletics moving to Kansas City. The life of a comedian was often a lonely and nomadic one, and it was always great to make a new friend, but especially one from back home. Philadelphians had a special kind of loyalty to their city that people from other places just never understood. It was that type of bond that allowed two men who had only just met each other already feel like they were lifelong friends.

When the conversation began to wind down, Tommy's mind turned to food once again. He was quite hungry, but he feared that most nearby places had already closed for the night and he didn't want to stray too far away, so he resigned himself to settling for a cigarette instead.

"Do you smoke?" he asked Harry as he reached for his pack.

"No thanks," Harry responded. He was folding up his suit and starting to get ready for bed.

Deciding to be considerate, Tommy stepped outside to smoke. He paced down the hallway, walked past the doors of his probably sleeping neighbors, and stopped to sit in the stairwell. His head felt like it was spinning as he tried to make sense of everything that had just happened. In the span of a few moments, he had gone from performing on one of the biggest stages of his career, to the middle of a chaotic brawl, to being a player in an international spy plot. It was hardly just another day on the road. After a good long smoke, he inhaled the last of the fumes and flicked the butt out the window. There would be plenty to think about tomorrow, but now, it was time to get some sleep.

Tommy walked back to the room, feeling weary, overwhelmed, and ready for some much needed rest. When he got there, the door was slightly ajar. He thought he remembered closing it, but he must not have shut it all the way. His eyes were struggling to stay open as he pushed the door open and stepped inside, but he was suddenly jolted wide awake by the shocking sights inside.

The room had been completely ransacked. The

lamps were broken, his suitcases had been thrown open, sheets and clothing were strewn about, and most of the drawers had been pulled out of the dresser. He took a few more steps forward and saw a sickening sight; Harry's body was face down on the bed, a long knife still protruding from his back. There was blood splattered everywhere.

Tommy felt a sense of panic wash over him. He no longer felt like a comedian; it was now 1944 again; he was back in the warzone, and his survival instincts were kicking in. He quickly searched through the bathroom and closets, but saw no signs that Harry's attacker was still in the room. Next, he ran over to Harry and checked for a pulse. There was none; he was already dead. Whatever game Harry had been playing, its stakes were made dangerously clear, and Tommy was now square in the middle of it.

As he glanced around the room, Tommy noticed that there was a pen lying close to Harry's hand and a notepad of paper sitting on top of the nightstand. A small letter "T" had been scribbled on the top sheet, as if to grab Tommy's attention. He was about to reach for it and investigate when he was distracted by a sudden noise. There was a thunderous stomping of running footsteps outside in the hallway, and it was quickly drawing closer.

He grabbed ahold of the knife and assumed a defensive position, ready to give a proper greeting to whoever might be coming through that door. The door swung open in a blurry blaze of blue as a group of police officers came charging into the room, loudly barking orders. Tommy breathed a sigh of relief and dropped the knife when he realized it was them and not the killer. However, that relief soon turned to panic again when the leading officer started to restrain him.

"Wait, what are you doing? I'm not the killer!" Tommy protested.

"Monsieur, you are under arrest for murder," the officer said as he shoved Tommy's face down into the bed and pinned his arms behind him.

Reacting impulsively, Tommy used his best wrestling moves to wriggle free and slip out of the officer's grip. He stood up to face him, took a mighty swing, and connected with a powerful right hook. The officer stumbled backwards, clutching at his nose. This gave Tommy all the space he needed as he ran straight to the window, threw it open, climbed over the sill, and looked down. It was quite a jump from the third floor, but as the other officers closed in behind him, he had no other way out. He closed his eyes and leaped, landing with a painful thud in the dumpster below.

The force of the impact made Tommy grimace. The garbage bags beneath him had absorbed a lot of the force, but it was still quite a fall. He could hear the police shouting in the room above, and then heard their footsteps again as they began to run for the exit. He looked around at the stinking piles of garbage, wondering what kind of trouble he had just gotten himself into.

CHAPTER SEVEN

Tommy grimaced in pain as he stretched out his arms and legs, knowing that he would have to move as soon as possible. Despite its welcoming confines, the dumpster would obviously not suffice as a place to hide. The police had seen him jump, and were presumably on their way down. With mere seconds to go until they reached him, Tommy wracked his brain, desperately trying to think of his next possible course of action. Jumping off the balcony was the easy part; the hard part was only beginning.

The first possibility was simply to let the police capture him. Tommy knew he was innocent, and eventually the facts of the situation would have to come to light and the misunderstanding would be cleared. However, that option was also fraught with risk. The police had found him at the scene of a murder holding the murder weapon. What if they considered it an open and shut case and didn't bother with a deeper investigation? The police probably weren't feeling very sympathetic towards him after he punched one of them in the face and fled the scene. Furthermore, he was in a foreign country, an ocean away from his support network and any attorney who could assist him. No, turning himself in was out of the question. Tommy Malloy was now a fugitive, and his only option was to run.

As Tommy struggled to find his footing and stand up, he was knocked right back down by an incoming garbage bag.

"Ahhh, you son-of-a-bitch," Tommy muttered under his breath.

"Oh, I'm sorry. I didn't know there was anybody in there," said the man who had just thrown the bag. He leaned over the edge to investigate, and Tommy recognized him as one of the maintenance workers from the hotel. He was a young man of about Tommy's size, and the nametag on his uniform shirt read, "Thierry."

"Say, what exactly are you doing in there anyway?" Thierry asked as he looked at Tommy.

"Wait a minute, you're Tommy Malloy! I'm a really big fan. I heard you were staying here and I was hoping I would get to meet you. But, if you don't mind me asking, what exactly are you doing in the dumpster?"

Tommy had to improvise quickly. "I...I was visiting one of my mistresses...her husband came back early and I had to escape."

Thierry grinned. The French seemed to love those kinds of stories.

"But listen," Tommy said, "Things got really ugly up there...it's a long story but the police are after me and I need to run and hide fast."

Thierry nodded sympathetically. "And may I be of any assistance in this matter?"

Now Tommy finally had an idea. "Yes, there is something you can do."

Thierry listened intently as Tommy explained his idea, and he seemed to like the sound of it. With time quickly running out, he offered a sturdy hand to help Tommy climb out of the dumpster. Then, the two of them broke into a full sprint as they darted around the corner of the back alley and ducked into an unoccupied out cove by the hotel's service entrance. Once there, they hastily exchanged their outfits. Tommy put on Thierry's work uniform, complete with his cleaning equipment and master set of keys. Thierry, meanwhile, had squeezed into Tommy's tux. They were roughly the same size, so the clothes fit relatively well. As they finished their exchange, they could hear the shouts and whistles of the police coming from around the corner.

"Just like we discussed," said Tommy. "All you have to do is casually walk out of here. The police might stop you and ask some questions, but they'll be able to tell that you're not me."

Thierry steadied himself. "I can do that. Then I'll walk home and get my other uniform and I'll come back here as soon as I can."

The two men shook hands and wished each other luck as Thierry departed. Tommy then used Thierry's key to open the service door and slip inside the back entrance to the hotel. He found himself in an industrial looking passageway that led to the main lobby. To his right, there was a closet that was filled with cleaning supplies. Hoping to effectively sell his act, Tommy grabbed a broom and began to sweep the floor. While he hoped the police wouldn't think to look inside the service area, he wanted to be as convincing as possible if they did. As he diligently cleaned the floor, it felt a bit reminiscent of basic training, when he and the other recruits had to endlessly sweep the barracks until it met the drill instructor's standards.

As Tommy pushed the dust into neat piles, the door to the lobby swung open. A police officer stuck his head inside, shining a flashlight through the room. "Excuse me, we are looking for a murder suspect. Have you seen any suspicious people or activities?" he asked.

Tommy shook his head. "No, nothing here, but I'll keep my eyes open."

The officer continued his cursory search for another minute, then thanked him and moved on. Tommy felt an incredible sense of relief. He wasn't sure how well his disguise would conceal him, but the factor that worked in his favor was that people usually saw what they expected to see. If he was dressed as a maintenance man, and acting as a maintenance man, they would simply assume he was the maintenance man.

Feeling momentarily safe, Tommy sat down and concentrated, trying to replay all the events from the fracas in the club until now and somehow make some sense of it all. When the image of the murder scene was etched in his mind, he recalled an important detail that had been pushed aside; the notepad on top of the nightstand. The top page was marked with only a letter "T," but what if there was something written on the other pages? If Harry has used his last dying breaths to write it, it was probably pretty important and probably had national security implications.

The more Tommy thought about it, the more he realized he was going to have to go back for the notepad. Sure, he could always just quietly slink away into the night, but then where would he go from there? If he wanted to clear his name, he was going to have to find the real killer, and to do that, he was going to need all the evidence he could get. It was also personal, as he felt he owed it to Harry to help bring whoever had done this to justice. Furthermore, his patriotic feelings were stirred. If he could do something for his country and help stick it to the Soviets, he was going to do just that.

Against the wall of the service closet, Tommy found a wheeled cart that was made to transport cleaning supplies. He loaded it up, opened the door, and walked out into the main lobby, pushing the cart ahead of him. He kept his head down as he walked across the floor, trying not to draw any attention to himself. Several police officers were searching the premises, and one was jotting down notes as he asked the concierge at the front desk a series of questions. They paid Tommy no heed as he passed by them, seemingly in the midst of his custodial duties.

Tommy pushed the up button for the elevator, and thanked his luck once more when the elevator was empty. He pushed the cart inside and rode it up to the third floor. Once there, he slowly made his way through the hallway, quietly observing the scene. A police officer was standing guard outside the door of Tommy's room, looking rather bored with the duty he had drawn. Tommy approached cautiously, then stopped the cart when he reached the adjacent room and used his master maintenance key to open the door. He gave the officer a silent nod, each of them feeling empathetic about the other's job.

The room was unoccupied and nothing appeared to be out of place. So far, everything was breaking Tommy's way. Pressing his luck, he walked straight to the connecting door that attached this room to his room and pressed his ear against it. Hearing nothing, he unlocked the door and slowly pushed it open. A detective was inside, scouring the room for evidence, and he seemed surprised to see Tommy's appearance.

"Cleaning staff?" he asked.

Tommy nodded.

"You'll have to come back later. This room is closed for a police investigation."

"Oh ok, I'm sorry," Tommy said. It was a disappointing setback, but at least the disguise was holding up.

Tommy stepped back into the adjoining room and began to vacuum the carpet, giving him an excuse to stay there and providing a helpful source of background noise. A few minutes later, he could hear a door closing next door, seeming to indicate that the detective was taking a bathroom break. Recognizing that this was a golden opportunity, Tommy tiptoed through the connecting doors, leaving the vacuum running to cover the sound of his footsteps. He made his way around the first bed and approached the nightstand. When he got there, the notepad was exactly where he remembered it. He slipped it inside his pocket just as he heard the unmistakable sound of a toilet flushing. He darted back through the connecting doors, knowing there was no time to spare. Ideally the detective would then take the time to wash his hands, but given what he knew of French hygiene habits, he had to assume otherwise.

When the detective finished up in the bathroom, Tommy was already back on his side of the connecting doors, working the vacuum once again. Alone in the room with the noise to cover him, Tommy pulled out the notepad to have a look. The first page still had a letter "T" on it, and the next three pages were empty. On the fifth page, the words, "Operation Arctic Fox, October 25" were written in very shaky handwriting. Whatever that meant, it seemed like it would be very important that he passed it along to the right people.

Having achieved his first objective, Tommy shut off the vacuum, packed up the cart, and walked back out into the hallway. He was almost at the elevator when he heard a voice calling after him.

"Hey, you there, wait up!"

Tommy grimaced as he froze in place. It had all seemed too easy so far, which was probably a bad thing. He looked over his shoulder and was surprised to see that he was not being summoned by a police officer, but by an overweight middle-aged man in a bathrobe.

"I've been trying to get service for the past hour, it's about time I found somebody," the man said, huffing to catch his breath. "I figured an upscale place like this would take better care of its paying customers. Do they even know who I am? I am Howard Duckworth, innovator extraordinaire, and captain of industry."

Tommy sighed, knowing it was tourists like this that gave Americans a bad name. He was very tempted to respond with a "Do you know who I am?" of his own, but thought better of it given the circumstances. He resigned himself to helping the man, not wanting to get Thierry in trouble on his account if Duckworth complained to higher-ups. Accepting his fate, he turned the cart around and followed Duckworth back to his room.

"It's the toilet," Duckworth said when they reached his room. "I ate too much caviar at the Soviet Embassy the other night and it really did a number on my system. I've never had problems with American toilets, but this little French thing just clogged up like the Hoover Dam."

Tommy grabbed a plunger, held his nose and hoped for the best. A few plunges later, the toilet was finally restored to working order. When the job was complete, Tommy walked back to the elevator and made his way back down to the service area, thankfully free of interruptions this time. Thierry was waiting for him, wearing another set of his work uniform, and ready to finish the rest of his shift.

"Glad to see it worked. It was an honor to be able to help you, Mr. Malloy. I'll make sure your luggage is mailed back to you once the police are finished searching," Thierry said.

Tommy reached out and shook his hand. "Thank you, I really appreciate everything you've done."

He started walking towards the service exit, but Thierry called him back.

"Wait, you forgot something. You left these in the pockets of your other pants." He held out the Chuck Klein baseball card and the St. Thomas medal.

"Thanks again," Tommy said with relief. Luck

was smiling on him at the moment, but he was going to need a whole lot more of it.

CHAPTER EIGHT

Tommy slipped out the service entrance and snuck through the back alley, staying close to the wall to hide in the cover of the shadows. He concentrated on the situation as he went, trying to decide on his next course of action. For now, the police seemed preoccupied with searching the hotel and its immediate surroundings, but it would probably not take them long to realize that he had fled the scene. Therefore, his first goal had to be getting away from the immediate area as quickly as possible.

Having established his immediate goal, Tommy then tried to take stock of what he was up against. It seemed logical to assume that the KGB people Harry was trying to escape from at the club were also responsible for his murder. He tried to piece together his blurry memories of the brawl with the bits of information Harry had told him. The big blond Russian who had been sitting next to Harry seemed to be the ringleader. According to Harry, this man was named Viktor and he was somebody you didn't want to run into. The other two Frenchmen from the table, Jacques and Pierre if he remembered correctly, seemed to be Viktor's immediate sidekicks. And apparently there were also several other henchmen that he never got a good look at. These trained killers were probably already looking for Tommy, along with the entire Parisian police force. It was just another night in the life of a traveling comedian.

The night had grown quiet as the hour grew later, and the sound of every footstep would echo though the walls. When Tommy finally reached the main street at the end of the alley, he pressed himself against the wall and peered around the corner to take in the scene. There were no pedestrians out and the only vehicle on the road was a city bus, lazily rolling to a stop near a marked bus stop. Tommy remembered that the hotel's front desk had an ample supply of bus schedules and maps of the city, and cursed himself for not thinking to take copies. Nevertheless, this was still his best opportunity to get away and he was simply going to have to ride the bus and see where it took him. He looked both ways and then sprinted across the street, feeling a dose of nostalgia for the many times he had to furiously chase down his school bus as a kid. Just as it was about to pull away, he lunged towards the door, frantically waving his arms. The bus driver rolled his eyes as he pushed the door back open.

The driver was a tired-looking man of around sixty-five who took Tommy's fare without looking too closely. It seemed that the night shift did not agree with him and he would much rather be home in his bed. When Tommy stepped aboard, he took a window seat near the middle of the bus and tried to discreetly look around to get his bearings. The only other passenger was a small elderly woman, sitting alone as she silently worked on knitting a scarf. Tommy wondered what somebody her age was doing out this late, but then he concluded it was more likely that she had effectively "lapped" the night; it was now so late that she had already woken up to begin her morning.

As the bus pulled away, Tommy looked out the window at the sleeping city. Just a few hours ago Paris had seemed ready to embrace him as one its favorite adopted sons. Now, all he wanted was for the city to keep him hidden away where it kept its secrets. He thought back to the message on the notepad. He was obviously meant to pass it on somebody who would know what "Operation Arctic Fox" was, but who would that be? Harry had never specified exactly who he worked for, but it had to be the CIA or something like it. The CIA usually had people at embassies, so he probably just had to talk to somebody at the U.S. Embassy. That seemed easy enough, now he just had to figure out how to get into a heavily guarded building as a wanted fugitive.

The bus paused once more at the next stop and another man came onboard. He was wearing a black and white striped shirt, black pants with suspenders, and a black bowler hat. His face was painted white, indicating that he was, in fact, a mime. He shuffled to the back of the bus to take a seat, lugging his bag of props along with him. Tommy stifled a laugh as he watched, feeling as if the situation had become a real life version of one of his jokes. *An old lady, a mime, and a fugitive comedian walked onto a bus…*

The bus rode on quietly as late night gave way to

early morning and the city began to show the first signs of waking up. The sun was beginning to appear, the bakers were arriving at their shops, and the newspaper men were beginning their deliveries. Tommy sat in silence the whole way, not wanting to draw attention to himself. The old lady sat silently as well, concentrating intently on her knitting. The mime also sat in silence, as speaking was strictly verboten for mimes. They continued on their lonely journey until a few stops later, when another man boarded the bus. He was short and stocky, and had a very impatient expression. In a huff, he paid his fare and grabbed a seat near the front of the bus, across the aisle and several rows up from where Tommy was sitting. He constantly fidgeted in his seat and looked at his watch, as if he was running late for something important.

The man looked strangely familiar, and Tommy stared at him until he figured out why. When he made the mental connection, Tommy slumped down in his seat and tried to conceal his face. He was certain that this man was Viktor's sidekick Pierre, the one he had grappled with during the theatre brawl. Tommy was stuck now; he could not leave the bus because he would have to walk by Pierre's seat in order to do so. For now, he was simply going to lie low and hope that Pierre didn't notice him.

For the next several minutes, the strategy worked. Tommy kept a low profile as the short man's eyes shifted between his watch, the bus driver, and scanning out the window. However, when they reached the next stop, the old woman stood up and approached Tommy's seat, attempting to ask him for directions. She spoke in a regional dialect pretty far removed from the elementary French Tommy had learned in school, and he had great difficulty understanding her. He squirmed uncomfortably and spoke in hushed tones as he tried to answer her, hoping he could somehow avoid drawing the attention of the other passengers. But that was too much to hope for. As the old lady walked back to her seat, Pierre turned his head, his eyes seeming to linger on Tommy. Their eyes locked in recognition; it was fight or flight time.

Tommy stood up and assumed a defensive position, challenging his opponent to make the first move. The veneer of a comfortable celebrity life could not erase the inner toughness of a boy who had made his bones on the streets of Philadelphia and gone toe-to-toe with the Nazis all over Europe. Whatever was about to hit him, he was ready for it.

Responding to the challenge, Pierre balled his fists, lowered his head, and charged with the reckless abandon of a bull running through the streets of Pamplona. Tommy wisely used this aggression against him, holding his position until the last possible moment, and then dodging quickly to the side as Pierre lunged at him. Pierre fell forward into the seat, landing on his face with a thud. Tommy managed to avoid the brunt of the blow, but there was still enough of a collision to knock him off his balance.

Pierre recovered quickly, ramming Tommy's nose with the top of his head as he jolted upwards. As Tommy stumbled back, Pierre charged forward with a flurry of punches. Tommy slowly retreated into the aisle, absorbing the punches as he increased the distance between them to lessen the blow. When Pierre began to tire, Tommy seized the opportunity and launched a furious counterattack, landing a quick succession of punches to the face and body. Pierre began to lose his balance, and Tommy sprung forward with a thunderous kick that left him sprawling in the aisle. Pressing the attack, Tommy jumped on top of him and mercilessly pummeled his face until Pierre went out cold.

Once Pierre was out, Tommy began to lose his balance as well because the bus was starting to swerve erratically. He looked to the front and saw that the bus driver was having difficulty steering and seemed to be slipping out of consciousness. The stress and shock of the situation seemed to be too much for him to handle. Letting his instincts take over, Tommy ran to the front, lifted the driver out of the seat, and sat down to take the wheel himself. He motioned to the mime, who came forward and began to administer first aid to the driver. Tommy had never driven anything bigger than a station wagon before, and he found the steering and maneuvering to be quite challenging.

At the next intersection, Tommy steered the bus in a wide right turn, hearing some angry honks as the back of the bus swerved into the next lane. As best as he could, he tried to follow the posted map of stops and keep the bus on its course. Just when he started to feel he was getting the hang of things, he heard a noise behind him as Pierre began to stir. Keeping one hand on the wheel, Tommy stood and formed a fist with the other. He maintained this perilous balance, trying to keep his eyes on both Pierre and the road, until Pierre suddenly slumped back down, unconscious once more. The old woman stood over him with a grin, brandishing the heavy purse she had just very effectively used as a weapon. Tommy couldn't keep himself from laughing as he pulled over at the next stop, opened the door, and rolled Pierre out into the street.

When the sunrise began to appear over the horizon, Tommy finally reached the last stop on the route. When he opened the door, the old lady nonchalantly walked off with only a quiet "Au revoir." He could only imagine the stories she would surely be telling her friends at whatever senior citizen activity she was going to. By this time, the driver had recovered and insisted that he was perfectly capable of returning the bus to the depot on his own. The mime, who seemed to know what he was doing when it came to first aid, gave a thumbs-up and a nod when the driver climbed back into the seat, then picked up his bag and walked off. Continuing to make things up as he went along, Tommy chased after him. He had an idea that was so crazy that it just might work.

CHAPTER NINE

"Hey, wait up!" Tommy called out as he chased down the mime.

The mime paused and turned around, making eye contact with Tommy, yet saying nothing. He was already deep in character.

"I have a big favor to ask of you," Tommy said.

The mime nodded in understanding as Tommy struggled to find his next words. It was difficult enough to have conversations in a foreign language, but it was that much harder when the other person couldn't talk back. "I'm a performer, just like you. I tell jokes on stage and I'm also in the movies. But I have a big problem now. That guy on the bus and his friends caused some problems at my last show and now I can't perform there anymore. I need to find a new gig or else I'm going to be in a whole lot of trouble. I want to learn to mime. Is there any way I could join in with your show?"

The mime made a series of gestures that seemed to be affirmative and then beckoned Tommy to follow him. They walked several blocks in the early morning light, taking in the sights and sounds of a city arising from its slumber. Tommy still had no idea how he was going to clear his name or get the information to the embassy, but this would at least buy him some time. Joining the mimes seemed like the perfect way to lay low for a little bit and let his trail go cold while he figured out the next step.

They eventually arrived at an open square along the banks of the Seine, where local artists were beginning to gather for a long day's work of offering their wares to tourists. A cool, refreshing breeze blew in from the water as the sound of accordions warming up could be heard in the background. If Tommy wasn't running for his life, it would be the perfect place to spend a vacation and soak up the atmosphere of Paris.

"Good morning, Paul," an elderly artist said to the mime, finally revealing his name.

The old man then turned to Tommy as he set up his easel and laid out his paintbrushes in front of a blank canvas. "My name is Marcel. You must be new here."

"I'm Bob." Tommy gave the first name that popped into his head as he reached out to shake Marcel's hand.

Marcel had a weathered face that had spent many days out in the sun, and his long grey hair was pulled back in a pony tail that seemed a tad ill-fitting on a man of his age. "There is no better place in the world to be an artist. I predict that you are going to like it here."

Paul beckoned for Tommy's attention and then handed him a black hat and a tube of white paint.

Tommy accepted the gifts and walked around until he found a public restroom, where he applied the paint to his face. He tried various poses in front of the mirror with his white face and new hat, doing his best to think and feel like a mime. He certainly looked the part. More importantly, he hoped it would make it impossible for any of his pursuers to recognize him.

Once Tommy was in costume, his attention then turned to his rumbling stomach, and he walked to a nearby food cart where he purchased four freshly baked croissants. He eagerly wolfed them all down, not certain of when he would have the opportunity to eat again. Feeling a bit bloated now, Tommy sat down to observe the artists in action as the day's first tourists began to arrive.

Taking his cue, Paul strode to the center of the square with the confidence of a seasoned performer. A small crowd gathered around him in a semi-circle in eager anticipation of his act. He opened with some of the standard mime fare, acting out such classics as being trapped in an invisible box, walking down an invisible staircase, and pulling an invisible rope. He then invited audience participation, drawing them into some more complicated stunts. Finally, he concluded with a simulated climb up an invisible Eiffel Tower and subsequent fall to the bottom. The crowd laughed and applauded with delight, leaving some generous tips in his box before moving on to examine the artwork.

When the next group of tourists walked up, it was Tommy's turn. He was nervous to work in this new medium, but he reminded himself that he was a performer first and foremost and that comedy was comedy in any language or lack thereof. He started out with the invisible box routine, imitating what he had observed from Paul. The crowd seemed to enjoy it, and Tommy heard some distinctly American voices among them, which gave him his next idea. He folded down the brim of his hat, pulled up his socks, chewed a huge wad of imaginary tobacco, and gripped an invisible baseball in his invisible glove, adopting the persona of a pitcher on the baseball diamond. He looked in towards home plate, angrily shaking off all the catcher's signals. Then he went through the greatly embellished motions of a windup, throwing a real heater to the plate.

The crowd gasped with excitement as he turned around and switched roles, now becoming the batter. He pointed to the distance, calling his shot like Babe Ruth, and then took a dramatic swing to knock one over the fence. He emphatically flipped the imaginary bat and made a triumphant trot around the bases, culminating in a head first slide into home. The crowd loved it; showering him with applause, laughter and cash. This miming business was turning out to be a lot of fun. There were certainly less enjoyable ways to spend one's time as a fugitive.

However, the fun was to be short lived. A chorus of eye rolls and groans arose from the group of artists as a short but proud-looking police officer with an immaculately pressed uniform arrived on the scene.

"Have your licenses in order and ready to inspect!" He bellowed as he strolled through their ranks with the precision and attention to detail of a drill instructor.

The officer's two much larger deputies trailed behind him, their facial expressions betraying an uncomfortable sense of embarrassment over the excessive zeal with which their superior was engaging in a very mundane task.

"That's Inspector Phaneuf," Marcel explained to Tommy. "If you've ever heard of a 'Napoleon Complex,' well they coined the phrase for him."

Moments later, the Inspector reached Marcel. "Your license, please."

Marcel rolled his eyes. "I have been painting here for forty years. Shouldn't you recognize me by now?"

Incensed by the slight, Phaneuf pored over Marcel's papers with an even higher level of scrutiny. After taking far longer than any reasonable person would deem necessary, he finally handed Marcel's papers back and then moved on to Tommy.

"Your license, Monsieur," he demanded.

Forced to improvise, Tommy made an exaggerated production of turning his pocket inside out to reveal it was empty and then helplessly shrugging. The act drew plenty of laughs from both the nearby tourists and the fellow artists.

Inspector Phaneuf was not amused. "Answer me! Where is your license?"

"He cannot answer you. He is a mime," Marcel said.

The artists laughed at Phaneuf even more as the Inspector gritted his teeth in anger. "Do not toy with me! You need a license to be a mime in my city!"

As he stared at Tommy's face, he paused with a hint of recognition. The wheels in his head seemed to be spinning, as if he was having the realization that he was not simply confronting a wayward mime, but an at-large murder suspect. His eyes drifted back and forth between Tommy and the set of papers in his hand, the suspicion seeming to grow with each glance.

Sensing the imminent danger, Tommy bolted. Every muscle in his body strained as he ran forth with the reckless urgency of a baserunner rounding third for the winning run. Phaneuf followed closely on his heels, loudly blowing a whistle to sound the alarm. The crowd began to scatter and mill in confusion, not really knowing what to make of all this. Some screamed in shock, others chattered excitedly, and still more laughed out loud, thinking this was all part of another act for their amusement.

Tommy kept running through the rows of artists, dodging, darting and tumbling his way through the serpentine path of obstacles. Phaneuf began to lag behind him, being slightly less deft in his maneuvering of the obstacles, knocking over many easels and spilling a lot of paint in the process. The angry artists made no attempt to get out of his way and some actively tried to obstruct him. Tommy lengthened his stride as he ventured out towards the open road. His heart was pounding inside his chest and his lungs were gasping for air, but the rush of adrenaline kept pushing him forwards.

Tommy looked over his shoulder as he rounded a corner and ran out onto one of the bridges crossing the river. Although he had left Phaneuf far behind, the other two officers were at his heels, quickly closing in on him. He continued to will himself forward until he saw a police car turn the corner onto the other side of the bridge and start careening towards him. The trap was now set.

With the police closing in on both sides, Tommy climbed to the edge of the bridge and looked down. His stomach felt queasy when he saw how far the drop to the water was. It was certainly survivable, but it was not going to be fun. Memories came rushing back of the first time he had jumped from a plane during airborne training. He hated heights then, and he still hated them now, but he hated water even more. He would probably rather jump into Normandy again than jump into water, but as he heard the shouts of the police officers approaching behind him, he knew he had no other choice.

Just when Tommy was about to launch himself off, he saw a large ripple in the water as a double-decked tourist boat emerged from under the bridge. Now with a much shorter way to fall, Tommy much more willingly leaped from the bridge. His legs buckled beneath him as they impacted the deck, and he landed with a thud on his rear. It wasn't the most stylish landing, but at least he was mostly intact.

The tourists on the boat scattered from their seats, circling around him and gawking at this odd occurrence. Tommy slowly stood up, his tail bone throbbing with pain, and became aware of their awkward glares. Remembering that he was still in costume, he gave an impromptu mime performance, reenacting the entire chase scene culminating with his leap from the bridge. The crowd was in stitches the whole time, and they cheered wildly when he concluded with a flourishing bow. Satisfied with his latest turn in fortune, Tommy climbed down to the lower deck, bracing himself for the next step of what was sure to be a very long day.

CHAPTER TEN

As Tommy arrived on the lower deck, he could feel the eyes of a whole new group of tourists looking his way. They had obviously heard the effects of his upstairs performance, and were curious to see what had caused the commotion. The downstairs crowd mostly consisted of aging pensioners, and they were a much less lively group than the upstairs contingent, but they seemed to expect Tommy to amuse them all the same.

With all their eyes on him, Tommy launched into a reprise of the miming performance he had given upstairs. It was becoming easier now, and he felt as if he had already gained several years of miming experience in the past few hours. As he grew more comfortable, he incorporated newer moves into the routine as well. He remembered the style of comic acting that Louis Poutine had perfected in his early silent films and mimicked it as closely as possible, finding that it translated very well to the mime genre. Once more, he finished his performance to a raucous round of applause.

As Tommy soaked in the adulation, he noticed that the captain of the boat was coming down the ladder and heading his way, presumably having left one of his crew members in charge of the pilothouse. He was a burly man with dark but graying hair, a thick moustache, and a charismatic smile, and he was wearing a double-breasted navy blue blazer with a colorful scarf. He had a jolly and easy-going nature that reminded Tommy of the friendly uncles that were ubiquitous in his old neighborhood.

"That was an excellent show!" the captain said.

He gave Tommy a hearty slap on the back and then wrapped one of his thick arms around him. "Come, walk with me, we have much to discuss."

Tommy was caught off-guard by these new developments, but he saw no other option than to just go along with it. They walked the length of the aisle between the rows of seats and then went behind a closed door to the captain's small but comfortable cabin near the stern of the boat. Tommy plopped down in a wooden chair, still very much feeling the effects of his fall to the deck. The captain offered a cup of coffee, which Tommy eagerly accepted. After a night with no sleep, he was completely dependent on caffeine and adrenaline.

Once Tommy was relaxed, the captain addressed him. "Don't think that I wouldn't recognize you with that makeup on, Tommy Malloy."

Tommy sputtered in surprise. "What...I'm not...I mean...how did you know?"

"I went to your opening show and it was superb. I've seen most of your movies as well. What can I say? I'm a big fan."

Tommy breathed a sigh of relief, amazed at the wild fluctuations of his luck. "You know, I always dreamed that one day a beautiful woman would track me down and say something like that. But I suppose that you'll have to do for right now."

The captain's stomach shook as he laughed. "You're a funny guy, Tommy Malloy. That is why I like you."

Tommy leaned back and sipped the coffee, trying to make sense of it all. "But seriously though, how did a fellow like you get snookered into watching my act?"

The captain explained, "You are a friend of Tony Vespa, Tony is a friend of Paulie Prosciutto, and Paulie is an old friend and associate of mine. Ergo, ipso facto, you are my friend."

"Ahhh, that explains it," said Tommy, who knew better than to ask any further questions about the connection. Paulie Prosciutto was a powerful and notorious figure in the New York City mafia. Among his many other ventures, he owned a series of night clubs throughout New York and New Jersey. It was in these clubs that Tony Vespa had first made a name for himself as a singer, and throughout Tony's career Paulie had often used his influence to help him advance. If this captain was a friend of Paulie's, he was probably involved in a similar line of work.

"So you performed on my boat and gave my passengers some great entertainment for free. Surely there must be some sort of compensation I can offer you?"

Tommy paused, unsure of just how much of his story to reveal. "Well, actually there is. Umm, well you see, I got into a little trouble at my last show, and umm…let's just say the police are looking for me."

The captain nodded knowingly. "Say no more."

He rose from his seat and shepherded Tommy into a small private bathroom, where some extra sailor uniforms were sitting out. Tommy washed the makeup off his face and changed his attire once more, discarding Thierry's maintenance uniform in the trashcan after he emptied the pockets. He felt terrible that he couldn't return it, but at least Thierry had gotten a free minor celebrity-worn tuxedo out of the deal. Tommy now appeared to be a member of the boat's crew, and hoped that the police would have no reason to suspect anything different.

"This cruise is nearly finished, but you are welcome to remain with me for as long as you need to, unless you have other things you need to do, of course," the captain said when Tommy stepped out.

"I really appreciate the offer, but I'm afraid I do have some other things I need to do," said Tommy. He wanted to get to the U.S. Embassy as soon as possible, and he really couldn't tell anybody why.

The captain nodded. "I understand. In that case, I wish you well. I hope that whatever you are dealing with is straightened out soon." He wrote down an address on a piece of scrap paper and handed it to Tommy. "In case it doesn't and you need a place to lie low, I own a bar called the Soleil-Royal and you can find it at that address. I will be there later tonight, as will many of my colleagues. Now, if you'll excuse me, we have to bring this boat into the dock."

Tommy thanked the captain profusely and went on to do his best job of pretending to be a sailor. As the boat pulled into the dock, he stayed behind to help the crew tie up the mooring lines while the guests walked off in a single-file line. Two police officers stood along the river bank, observing the passengers debark, and growing increasingly agitated when none of them fit the description they were looking for. When the line of departing passengers finally reached its end, the police approached the boat to ask the crew some questions. By this time, Tommy had slipped by unnoticed, carrying two large bags of garbage. He guessed that nobody would want to interrupt one who was carrying out such a task, and he was correct.

Tommy dropped the trash in the first dumpster he could find and then walked purposefully down the nearest street. His first order of business was yet another wardrobe change, as his sailor disguise made less and less sense the further he ventured from the river. After walking a few blocks, he found a little thrift shop that seemed to suit his purposes. He browsed their collection of second hand clothing, and ultimately decided to go with an erudite professorial look. He purchased a tweed sport coat, complete with leather elbow patches, to go with a plain white dress shirt, brown tie and loose fitting khaki pants. To complete the ensemble, he added a deerstalker hat and a fake pair of reading glasses.

Next, Tommy needed to gather his bearings and figure out where exactly in the city he was and how to reach the embassy. He came upon a coffee shop, and decided that it would be a good place to regroup. It was an eclectic place, seemingly designed to attract writers and artists of the avant garde, certainly not the type of place a working class boy from Philadelphia would typically go. As he strolled towards the counter, his head turning to soak up the surroundings, he collided with a rather disagreeable old man, spilling the man's coffee in the process.

"Watch where you're going, you fool!" the old man grumbled as he picked himself up from the floor.

"I'm really sorry, sir. Let me buy you another drink," Tommy said as he knelt down to help pick up the man's belongings.

"Don't bother!" The old man scowled disapprovingly and stormed off in a huff.

Tommy felt really bad, but was dumbfounded as to why the man left so abruptly without even picking up his things. He glanced down at a stack of handwritten papers the man had left behind, seeming to contain some sort of speech or remarks. He shrugged and put it in his pocket as he went up to place his order.

After Tommy received his coffee, he found a seat at a small corner table and picked up a newspaper to read. As luck would have it, Tommy's name was on the front page, right underneath the lead story about some sort of treaty negotiations over Montravia. Tommy winced at the article's cringe worthy opening lines, "Yesterday, we called Tommy Malloy the 'Clown Prince of Paris'. Today, we call him a murderer. An American businessman named Harry Thompson attended a comedy performance last night, hoping to enjoy a fun night out. Several hours later, he was found dead in Malloy's hotel room..."

Tommy's eyes glanced away from the newspaper and scanned the room. Motley-looking crews of students and philosopher types were lounged about the shop. The overworked baristas struggled to keep up with the orders. The occasional businessman would stop in and then quickly leave. He was hoping that some tourists would have left their Paris maps or guidebooks behind, but there was no such luck. From what he could gather, he had been somewhere around Montmartre when he gave the mime performance, but he had floated down the river quite a ways since then.

Tommy's thoughts were interrupted when he noticed two new men step into the shop. When they drew closer, his stomach turned into a knot as he realized he was looking at Jacques and Pierre. Pierre looked battered and bruised from the brawl on the bus, and both men appeared haggard and worn after long night's manhunt. Tommy's tumultuous fortunes had turned for the worse once more. Of all the coffee shops in all the cities in France, they walked into this one.

Tommy froze in his seat, pulling the newspaper close to his face, and desperately hoping that his disguise would hold up. His position was precarious; if he got up to leave, it would be obvious he was fleeing something, but the longer he remained in place, the more opportunity they would have to look in his direction and possibly recognize him. He remained perfectly still as his insides turned, fearing he was in a no-win scenario.

From the other side of the room, Tommy could hear one of the philosophy students standing up to address his colleagues. "My friends, we have a very special guest with us today. Dominique Dumont is one of France's greatest philosophers and writers, and one of the true pioneers of existentialism. As you all know, he very rarely appears in public, which makes it all the more special that he had generously agreed to address us here today. Please give him a warm welcome."

The other students and spectators applauded, eager to finally get a glimpse of the rarely seen intellectual. However, there was a long awkward pause as nobody rose to the podium. After a few moments of silence, Tommy began to put the pieces together. The grumpy old man he had run into earlier must have been Dominique Dumont, and the paper he picked up must have been his speech. If the old man was as reclusive as the introduction seemed to imply, then these people may not know what he actually looked like. Tommy saw an opportunity, and he seized it, boldly walking up to the podium. The students stood and cheered; at least so far it seemed to be working.

As the applause receded, Tommy glanced down at the handwritten speech. It was full of vague flowery language and philosophical terms that would have soared over his head even if they were written in English. With his limited French vocabulary, he had no hope of understanding it. He started off awkwardly reading from the page, but he could feel his comedian's instincts telling him that he was losing the audience. To keep their attention, he was going to have to dip into his skills once again for some good old-fashioned improvisation.

He cleared his throat and began, "The question of existence is one that perplexes us. Do I really exist? Do you really exist? Is any of this real? How can we be sure?"

The students nodded along and exchanged glances with each other, appearing deep in thought. They seemed to be buying it.

Tommy continued, "One day, I sat by a

campfire, wondering if I really existed or not. I then proceeded to eat an entire can of baked beans. As I sat in the latrine later that night, dealing with the repercussions of my actions, I knew for sure in that moment that I definitely existed, and that this life we are living is all too real."

To Tommy's amazement, the students applauded! Were they actually finding this believable?

He pressed on, "Many wise man have asked the question, 'Does a bear shit in the woods?' Well, we know that bears live in the woods, and we know that bears shit. But have any of us actually seen a bear shit in the woods? We can't really know for sure if bears shit in the woods or not, but using what we do know, we can make a reasonable assumption that it does in fact happen."

The students applauded vigorously as Tommy thought ahead to his next line of metaphorical bear droppings. Out of the corner of his eye, he saw Jacques and Pierre slip out the front door, moving on with their search and not wanting to stick around to hear such drivel. Once again, a combination of luck and quick thinking had saved Tommy's life. He was going to need a lot more of both to make it out of this alive.

CHAPTER ELEVEN

The remainder of Tommy's remarks exceeded even his highest expectations. It was a challenging test of his improvisational abilities, and if not for his impending sense of danger, it may have even been a fun one. After finishing the speech, he fielded a barrage of questions from the eager and enthralled philosophy students. Providing them with passable answers in his second language was arguably the greatest feat of acting in his career to date, and he couldn't decide if that said more about his skills as a performer or about the field of philosophy.

As the students began to disperse, they made it known that they were returning to their university for a party and extended the invitation to Tommy. After some brief deliberation, he decided that accepting their invitation might actually be his best option. It would prolong the use of his current cover, and put even more time and distance between him and his last known sighting by the police. Furthermore, whatever university they attended would likely be a landmark in and of itself, and would be sure to have maps and guidebooks available. With that in mind, finding his way to the embassy from there seemed pretty easy.

The remaining students walked outside to board a bus, and Tommy did his best to blend in with them. Throughout the duration of the bus ride, the students engaged in lively intellectual discussions that covered a series of topics ranging from the metaphors in Raymond LaFleur's arthouse films, to how the exchange rate between the franc and the deutsche mark affected the goat cheese market in Alsace-Lorraine. They were very eager to hear "Dominique Dumont's" opinions on these issues, and Tommy carefully answered their queries in vague and flowery generalities that left them wanting more.

The students stood to leave when the bus reached the end of the line, and it appeared that they were now at the Sorbonne, Paris's oldest and best-known university. It was an impressive sight to Tommy, who had never gone to college himself. He had considered using the GI Bill when he got home from the war, and had been accepted to Pennsylvania State, LaSalle, and Saint Joseph's Universities, but then his career began to take off and he found himself constantly on the road. But now, he would be able to honestly say that he had given a lecture to Sorbonne students.

The group made their way across the campus green and into a dormitory building. Once inside, they stepped down to a dingy and poorly lit basement, where a keg of beer was sitting in the corner. Tommy couldn't help but smile at the sight. He had learned to adapt to the glitz and glamour of Hollywood parties, but he still felt much more at home at this type of gathering. Once the drinks were poured, there was an excited murmur about playing a recently-learned drinking game called "Alouettes." As far as Tommy could tell, the game consisted of lucky volunteers standing in the middle of a circle and chugging a beer while everybody else sang a song and threw things at them. The object was to finish the beer before the end of the song without spilling, regardless of what objects may come your way.

After the first few rounds, the student who had made the introductory remarks at the coffee shop rose to speak once more. "My friends, we have a very special event to celebrate today. Right now, the legendary Dominique Dumont is going to play Alouettes with us."

The students chanted and sang, beckoning Tommy to come to the middle of the circle. Feeling like he had nothing to lose, he filled up his beer and stepped on out. He began to chug when the song started, and kept going throughout the barrage. The students threw crumpled up napkins, wads of papers, a few fedoras, and even a shoe or two. However, none of them disrupted Tommy, for it was utterly futile to challenge an Irishman to a drinking contest. At the end of the song, he triumphantly held up his empty glass as the students cheered wildly.

When the cheering finally dissipated, the student speaker, who introduced himself as Sebastien, came up to talk to Tommy.

"Monsieur Dumont, it is such a great honor to have you with us today. Is there anything we can do to make your stay more comfortable?"

Tommy mulled it over. As much fun as it would be to forget his problems and keep playing drinking games with these kids, he really should get moving. "Yes, there is. I would like a map and a bus schedule if that is possible."

"Yes, of course," Sebastien said. "I can probably find that upstairs, but why don't you tell me where you need to go? I know the city very well."

"I've been planning a lecture tour in the United States, but I need to go to the American Embassy as soon as I can to get my visa for the trip."

Sebastien's eyes seemed to light up. "I need to go there as well! I have been applying to graduate schools in the United States and I need to obtain a student visa. We can go now if you like."

Tommy shrugged. "Sure, why not?" Sebastien seemed like a nice enough kid, and the sooner he got there, the better.

Together, Tommy and Sebastien said their goodbyes to other students, then walked upstairs and back into the sunlight. A short bus ride later, they arrived at the Place de la Concorde. From there, it was a very manageable walk to the Avenue Gabriel, where the embassy was located. They found the entrance for the visa section, and stood in the back of the long line. Tommy had never had to deal with all this before, as his agent had handled all the immigration paperwork for him leading up to this trip.

The line was moving very slowly, and they gradually inched their way closer and closer to the offices where they would meet with the Foreign Service Officers on duty. The waiting made Tommy feel uneasy. He found some comfort in the fact that he was on American soil with a convincing disguise, but the longer he was left out in the open, the more chances there would be for something to go wrong.

After moving about ten feet in what felt like an hour, an American man in a suit walked around the room, as if he was scouting out just how long the line was. He then paused and walked straight towards Tommy.

"Excuse me, sir, you're going to have follow me," he said.

Tommy thanked Sebastien for the company and then followed the new man, not quite sure what to expect. The man led the way into a different wing of the building and into his small office, where he told Tommy to take a seat.

"It was very bold of you to come in here like this, Mr. Malloy," he said as he pulled the door shut behind them. He had a strong Southern accent, and the nameplate on his desk identified him as George Randolph.

Feeling safe at last now, Tommy saw no reason to lie anymore. "How did you know it was me?"

"Every American who gets in trouble over here comes straight to the embassy. We've been on the lookout for you ever since your name came up in the news. I'm actually a little surprised it took you this long to get here," George said.

"I didn't exactly take the direct path," said Tommy. "And by the way, you know I didn't do it, right?"

George laughed. "Of course I do. The problem is the local cops don't see it that way. They don't take too kindly to us Yankees showing up here and making trouble, so it's going to take a little while to convince them. But don't worry, we'll get this all smoothed over and you are welcome to stay here until we do."

Tommy felt as if a great burden had just been lifted from his shoulders. After all the running around, he couldn't wait to finally relax. He glanced around the room and took in the surroundings. George had decorated his office with standard patriotic fare, as well as some mementos from the war. Among the patches and decorations, Tommy recognized the big red one of the First Infantry Division.

"So you were at D-Day?" Tommy asked.

"Landed on Omaha Beach, first wave," he confirmed.

"I jumped in with the 82nd," said Tommy. "We didn't need any visas to get into France back then, right?"

George laughed heartily; glad to be momentarily freed of the diplomatic constraints of his job.

Something about the way George carried himself that gave Tommy a hunch that he was actually CIA, but of course he knew better than to ask. He pulled the notepad out of his pocket and decided to play the hunch.

"So look, Harry Thompson told me who he was working for and who was chasing him. I'm sure you know it was the KGB that killed him. Anyway, he left this behind for me and I thought it might be important."

George put on his reading glasses as Tommy handed him the notepad. "Operation Arctic Fox, October 25," he read aloud. "That doesn't ring a bell to me. But I'll let you in on something. Harry was actually working on loan with the British government. He's been off our books for months. This is probably something the Brits were working on; they always enjoyed this cloak and dagger stuff more than we did. But thank you for bringing this, I'll pass it along to the right people and see what comes of it."

Tommy had a long list of questions he wanted to ask, but before he could speak, he was interrupted by the ringing of the telephone sitting on George's desk.

"Excuse me, I just have to answer this," said George as he picked it up. "George Randolph...what was that...you cannot be serious...those sneaky son-of-bitches! I oughta' knock every one of them upside the head...so there's nothing we can do...not even that...well they can stick that up their ass...yes, tell them I said that, use those exact words."

George slammed the phone back down on the receiver, steaming with anger. He then turned to Tommy to explain what had transpired. "Sorry about that. It turns out that the French police have been keeping the embassy under surveillance and some of them even infiltrated the visa line. They saw you follow me, and now they're demanding that we turn you over to their custody."

Tommy was stunned. "But I thought this was U.S. territory, how do they have jurisdiction?"

"That is correct, and they do not have jurisdiction here. But unfortunately, some of the political types above my paygrade want to comply with the request for the sake of diplomatic relations," George explained.

Tommy's heart sank. It looked like he was heading for a French prison after all.

George stood up to open his office window, and then turned to face Tommy once more. "Now, let me tell you what is going to happen. Five minutes from now I am going to call those pencil pushers back and I am going to tell them that you assaulted me and escaped out the window."

It took a minute for Tommy to fully comprehend what George had just said, but he was very grateful once he figured it out. "Wow, I really appreciate this. I wish there was something I could do to thank you."

"There is, you can punch me in the face so I won't be making a liar out of myself," George said.

Tommy hesitated. "But I can't do that. I like you, George."

"Philadelphia is a dirty, nasty cesspool of a city, and the Russians should just nuke it and put it out of its misery."

Those words did the trick, and Tommy walloped him across the face.

"Thanks again, George," Tommy called out as he made the short jump out the window to the ground below.

"Anytime, Tommy," George called out after him.

Tommy took a deep breath to gather himself before he set off running. The chase was back on.

CHAPTER TWELVE

Anonymous amongst the sea of tourists, Natalia stepped off the bus and took in the morning air. There was a large stack of paperwork awaiting her back at the embassy, but right now there were more pressing matters to attend to. Dressed in a casual Western style with her hair in a simple pony tail, she appeared several years younger, and much more likely to be an art student than a diplomat or KGB officer. Comfortably nestled between two obnoxiously boisterous groups of schoolchildren, she walked through the entrance to the Louvre and embarked on a tour of the museum.

She discreetly followed along with a guided tour group until they reached one of the museum's most popular pieces, *The Coronation of Napoleon*. She smiled smugly as they walked past, remembering the crucial role played by Russia in bringing about the Emperor's defeat. The group continued on its tour, and Natalia waited until they reached the densely crowded room where the *Mona Lisa* was housed to discreetly slip away, hidden in the throngs of people.

Eventually, she found her way to a less-visited gallery, where she rested on a bench. She sat alone for several minutes until a young man arrived and sat at the opposite end. She did not turn to look, but she knew that one of her most valuable sources had arrived as scheduled. While she only referred to him by his code name, Agent Snowman, he was otherwise known as Rolfe Schrodinger, the royal steward to Prince Hans Friedrich.

Rolfe spoke softly as he slid a little bit closer to her. "The Prince's schedule is really filling up. It's getting harder and harder for me to sneak out."

"Things are going to be happening really fast this week. We need any piece of information you can give us," Natalia reminded him.

Rolfe understood. "I assume you saw my previous message? After his speech, the Prince met with Sir Alastair Thorncliffe."

Natalia had received that news, and she was greatly intrigued by it. "Were you able to overhear anything or see anything you weren't supposed to?"

Rolfe shook his head. "No, they're really careful about that. But from what I can gather, it seems like Thorncliffe is advising the Prince, but I really don't think the Prince knows the full details of whatever he's planning. He's probably just another piece in his schemes."

"Have you noticed anything in the residence that may be out of the ordinary? Any deviations from the normal routine?"

Rolfe paused to reflect for a moment. "Well, this is probably nothing, but when we first got home after the Prince's speech, Princess Sophia was sitting and talking with Sir Alastair and it really seemed like they knew each other well."

"Well you never know, that may be something. Have you noticed any other unusual behavior from her?"

Rolfe shook his head. "You know how she is, out at a different event every night. I have no idea where she is at any given moment. I've never suspected her of anything, but her maid, her cook, and her driver all have to report to me, so I could look into things if you like."

"Yes, please do that."

Rolfe sat silently at the end of the bench, leaning forward on his elbows and cupping his hands around his face. The stress of his double life was really beginning to show its toll. He first became enthralled with Marxist philosophy during his time as a university student, and he came to Natalia's attention when she searched the student communist groups for new recruits. She could tell from the beginning that he was in love with her, and she had mastered the art of giving him just enough hope to string him along and keep him loyal.

"You joined us because you believe in our cause. The Revolution needs you now more than ever. I have no doubt that you will come through for the Motherland, and for me."

With those parting words, she rose to depart, leaving Rolfe behind to properly stagger their departures. Her first stop was the last stall in the women's rest room, where she changed her outfit and donned a brunette wig and a pair of glasses. Next, she walked back outside towards the bus, switching lines at various random points and constantly performing counter- surveillance as she moved slowly and indirectly towards her next destination.

Finally, she arrived at a plain grey house in a quiet residential neighborhood that was serving as a KGB safe house. Having her own copy of the key, she let herself in, announcing her presence so as not to startle anybody inside. What she found was a house in disarray. The local French communists were running around like headless chickens, anxiously reviewing their plans before heading out in pairs to continue their field mission.

Around the corner in the living room she found Viktor, sitting in a chair by the fireplace. He had discarded his suit coat, rolled up his sleeves, and pulled down his tie. His eyes were bloodshot and worn, and his demeanor grew ever more agitated the more he pored over the official reports.

Natalia sat down across from him, not wanting to waste any time exchanging pleasantries. "What's the status here?"

He answered without looking up. "We've had some…complications."

Natalia glared at him. "I have now exhausted all my sources. I gave you Boris and the identity of his American contact. We had an excellent lead and everything was lining up well for us. Now would you like to explain to me why our best lead is dead?"

Viktor set the papers down and took a deep breath. "Everything was going according to plan. I lured Thompson to the club and sealed the exits. As we discussed, I was going to drug him and bring him in alive. But there were contingencies we overlooked. He had accomplices at the show and they helped him escape."

"Accomplices?"

"It turns out the comedian was working with him," Viktor explained, shaking his head at the absurdity of the situation.

Natalia took a moment to process this new information. While she had not yet read the newspaper this morning, she remembered seeing a story about Tommy Malloy in the previous day's edition. He appeared to be an imbecile, and a rather harmless one at that. But she had worked in the shadows long enough to know that people and things were not often what they seemed. The picture was still not clear, but they now had another name for Sir Alastair's spy ring, which was at least something to go on.

Viktor elaborated further, "They caused a disturbance in the club and slipped away in the chaos. I was able to follow them to Malloy's hotel and sneak into the room. There was no feasible way to remove a prisoner from that room, so eliminating the targets was the only option. I took care of Thompson, but Malloy got away." He handed her a copy of the newest newspaper. "And you might be interested to see this."

Natalia glanced at the headlines, realizing that this added a whole new dimension to the chase. "So the police think Malloy is the killer? You know, maybe we can work with this. Think of the local police as a force multiplier. We can only cover so much ground ourselves, but with that many people looking for him, it's going to be hard to hide. I have contacts in the police force, so I'll know about it if they pick him up."

"But that being so, what if he tries to spill what

93

he knows about us? What if the cops believe him? I'd rather bring him in ourselves and not take the chance," Viktor countered.

"What was the last you saw of him?"

"After he fled the hotel he boarded a bus," Viktor explained, "one of my men caught up to him on the bus and they had a pretty nasty brawl. Malloy got away again, and my man really got the worst of it."

She could see Pierre Brodeur sitting in an adjacent room, sporting a fresh black eye and holding a pack of ice on his shoulder, his teeth grinding in frustration. Although Pierre's level of training and capabilities was far below that of a career KGB man like Viktor, he was well-trained in his own right and certainly no slouch. If Malloy was capable of inflicting something like this, then perhaps there really was a lot more to him than meets the eye.

"Well I know that you're aware of the security risks involved here. It is diplomatically unacceptable for any of this to be linked back to us. The longer we have our people canvassing the city, the greater the risk of discovery is. Needless to say, this needs to be wrapped up as soon as possible," said Natalia.

Viktor stared back at her with a fierce determination in his eyes. "You have my word. I will find Tommy Malloy."

CHAPTER THIRTEEN

Struggling to catch his breath after his frantic run, Tommy did his best to disappear into the crowds of the Place de la Concorde. The large public square was once the sight of public executions by guillotine, but now it was mostly known as a thoroughfare for tourists. The square's most notable sights were two exquisite fountains, and a tall obelisk that reminded him of the Washington Monument. Once he realized where he was, he felt somewhat embarrassed for not realizing earlier that the U.S. Embassy was actually right next to one of Paris's best-known landmarks.

He walked down the stairwell to the Metro station and boarded the first train he saw. As the train pulled away, he stared at the map of the route on the wall, trying to think of his next move. He had done his part for his country, making sure Harry's last message got to the right people. Now, his priority was simply his own survival. Ideally, he could just go to the airport and hop on the first plane back to America. However, that idea did not seem feasible.

He would be far too conspicuous at the airport, and any attempt he made to purchase a ticket would presumably get flagged. There was also the option of taking a train ride to another European country, but that idea had its own problems. There was sure to be a significant police presence at the major train stations, and even if he managed to elude them, where would he go? He had no connections in any of the surrounding countries and spoke none of the relevant languages.

As Tommy struggled to brainstorm for ideas, his mind began to wander back to what he otherwise would have been doing that day. The Club Poutine was hosting "The Roast of Louis Poutine," a comedy event where a series of guests would make jokes and insults at Louis's expense, all to raise money for a children's hospital. Tommy was scheduled to emcee the event, and he had left a whole notebook's worth of material for it back in the hotel room.

Tommy glanced at his watch, and realized that the Roast was probably still going on. The more he thought about it, the idea of going back to the Club Poutine actually started to seem like a good one. Obviously he wouldn't perform as scheduled; public appearances were certainly out of the question. However, getting in contact with Louis seemed like his best option for the immediate future. What he needed above all else was a place to hide. Louis would be happy to provide that, as well as a sympathetic set of ears.

His mind made up, Tommy continued riding the train and made the necessary line changes until he reached the proximity of the club. When he stepped off the train, he blended unnoticed into the crowd once more before slipping away into the back alleys. He found his way to the performer's entrance, feeling greatly relieved that he somehow still had his key. It was eerily quiet in the back of the building, but he could hear the faint echoes of the event happening on stage.

Tommy made his way to the dressing room, where a wide range of emotions came rushing over him. His day would be going very differently if Harry Thompson hadn't snuck into this very room. He wanted nothing more than come back here and prepare for his next performance as if nothing had happened. It was a familiar feeling from the war, when all he ever wanted was to go back home. He didn't understand why these things were happening to him, but he knew that they were happening nonetheless and he had no other choice but to confront them.

The costume rack in the back of the dressing room had a few extra usher uniforms hanging up, and Tommy took the opportunity to alter his disguise once more. Now dressed as an usher, he took the long way around and entered the rear of the club. The seats were mostly full, and Louis was up on the stage with a row of chairs behind him. The one that would have been Tommy's was empty, and various French celebrities filled the others.

As Tommy looked on from afar, Louis was just beginning his rebuttal, the portion at the end of a roast when the subject had the opportunity to respond to the insults.

"It has often been said that the first rule of comedy is that you can never emcee your own roast," Louis announced to the crowd. "That is actually the second rule. The first rule of comedy is don't murder your audience members. Now I have to break the second rule because Tommy Malloy had a little bit of trouble with the first."

The audience broke out laughing, and Tommy had to admit that it was pretty funny. Louis then proceeded to launch into a litany of insults directed at the other participants. The event was nearing its conclusion, and it was time for Tommy to move. He slipped back into the bowels of the building and up the well concealed staircase that led to Louis's office.

The office was a spacious one, with a small window overlooking the stage and audience. There was a glass trophy case against the wall containing the many awards Louis had received throughout his illustrious career. Most of the awards were related to his film work, but there was also a Legion of Honour for his work with the French Resistance during the war.

The black and white photographs along the walls documented the highlights of Louis's career. There was one of him and Tommy at one of their film premiers, which felt like a memory from another life. Many other pictures featured Louis with more well-known stars such as Humphrey Bogart, Vivien Leigh, Gary Cooper, Errol Flynn, Ingrid Bergman, and of course, his most frequently compared-to peer, the legendary Charlie Chaplin.

There was a comfortable looking couch against the wall facing Louis's desk, and Tommy sat there to await his return. A brief while later, Louis walked through the door and reacted with a startled jump when he caught sight of Tommy.

"Tommy, where have you been? You

disappeared after the show and I read these horrible things in the news and I knew they weren't true…"

Tommy recounted as much of the story as he could as Louis gradually calmed down, leaving out some of the more secretive details.

"Well I am very relieved to see you. I was worried sick, we all were," said Louis.

"Well that's where things stand now," said Tommy, who was glad to hear that at least somebody knew about and was sympathetic to his plight. "Now all I need is a place to hide."

"I see," said Louis. "Unfortunately remaining here may not be possible. The police have been quite persistent in their search for evidence. Their detectives are actually coming here in an hour to interview me and search the premises. I could try to hide you, but it would be very risky."

Tommy felt his hopes deflate once more. "No, we'd better not risk that. "

Louis seemed saddened by the situation, and frustrated that he couldn't do more to help. "Can you think of anywhere else you could go? And is there anything I can do to help you get there?"

Tommy considered the question, his mind eventually reaching back to his conversation with the riverboat captain. "Yes, now that I think of it, there is somewhere I can go. And don't worry about getting me there, I'll be fine."

"Very well then," Louis said. "And may I ask how you plan on getting out of the building? There is still quite a crowd milling around out there, and even if you slip by them, I would have to think you would be spotted as soon as you stepped outside."

"I discovered a simple trick," Tommy said. "I'm

already dressed as an usher. I'll just grab a bag and walk out to the dumpster, everybody would simply see an usher taking out the trash and they wouldn't question it any further."

Louis shook his head and grinned, amazed by the brilliant simplicity.

"Now I just need to find some trash," Tommy said as he eyed a cardboard box on Louis's desk that was full of papers and envelopes.

Louis reached out to stop him. "Not that box. This is not trash. This is the collection of pledges and donations from the roast."

"Oh, sorry," Tommy said, embarrassed by the near disaster. "By the way, how did the roast go?"

"It would have been a lot better if you were there, but all things considered the show went very well. Most importantly, we raised a lot of money for the children's hospital." Louis flipped his way through the envelopes, opening them as he went, and jotting down totals in his ledger. "Wow, Princess Sophia was very generous in her gift."

Tommy remembered the sight of the princess at his opening show, greatly regretting that he didn't get the chance to meet her. "What's she like? What's it like to meet a real life princess?"

Louis smiled. "You would really like her. She reminds me a lot of Audrey Hepburn."

Tommy liked the sound of that. Who didn't love Audrey Hepburn?

A puzzled expression came across Louis's face as he held one of the envelopes up for closer inspection. He handed it over to Tommy. "I don't know how this happened, but it appears one of these envelopes is for you."

Confused but intrigued, Tommy reached for the envelope and tore it open. There was a handwritten note inside, and he pored over it again and again to make sure he wasn't missing anything. It read:

Mr. Malloy,

You are in mortal peril. The true killers are still out there, and they are looking for you. If you want to make it out of Paris alive, come to La Trompette at 20:00 tonight. Come alone, and trust no one. You have already performed great services for our cause and for that we are eternally grateful.

Yours Truly,

A Friend of Harry

The knots formed in Tommy's stomach as he let the message sink in. Whatever else he could say about this day, it certainly wasn't boring.

"Do you know what La Trompette is?" he asked Louis.

"Oh yes, that's a new jazz club on Rue des Lombards. Why, what's happening there?"

"There's going to be a show there tonight, and I hope it's a good one."

CHAPTER FOURTEEN

Exactly as planned, Tommy walked through the scattered crowd of remaining guests carrying a bag of garbage. They paid him no heed, seeing only an usher going about his duties. The late afternoon sun was pleasantly warm when he walked outside, dropped the trash in a dumpster, and left his red usher coat behind.

As if his situation wasn't crazy enough, the letter was adding a whole new layer of intrigue. It was found in the same box as the donations, so whoever put it there must have been present at the comedy roast and had either seen Tommy there or at least speculated that he would come back and try to get in touch with Louis.

The more he thought about it, the more he became aware of the possibility that this "friend of Harry" might actually be a trap to catch him. However, it was the only real lead he had to go on, so what else could he do? In any case, if the KGB was looking for him, they were going to eventually find him if he kept sneaking around the city, so he might as well bring on a direct confrontation.

Thanks to his wartime service, Tommy was very familiar with the twenty-four hour style of timekeeping preferred by both Europeans and the military, and he therefore knew that 20:00 meant 8:00pm. It only being the afternoon, he still had a few hours to kill before his attempted rendezvous, and he decided that they would be best spent at the Soleil-Royal, the bar that the riverboat captain had told him about. As luck would have it, it was only a few train stops away from his ultimate destination.

The Metro ride was uneventful, aside from the odd person who would occasionally glance at Tommy and make his insides jump for a brief moment until they looked away. He arrived otherwise without incident, and discovered that the Soleil-Royal was a nautical themed bar named after a historic French warship. The wood-paneled floors and walls were made to resemble the inside of a ship, the windows were shaped like portholes, the lights resembled gas-lit lanterns, and the walls were covered with maritime paintings. Tommy chose an isolated booth in the corner and ordered some fish and chips with a pint of beer for his lunch.

The bar remained quiet and mostly empty for the duration of Tommy's meal, and the food was pretty good as far as bar food went. Afterwards, he ordered another pint and slowly nursed it, waiting for the time to pass. The rest of the patrons emptied out by the posted closing time of 5:00 pm, which seemed like a ridiculously early time for a bar to close. Tommy wondered if he should leave too, but the manager gave him a smile and a nod that indicated that he was welcome to remain.

The manager was almost finished mopping the floor when a small group of men stepped inside. They were dressed in tailored suits and fine silk ties, but their mannerisms and demeanor conveyed a sense of brute roughness. No words were spoken, but all parties involved seemed familiar with the routine. The bar was closing to the outside world, but it was about to be co-opted for an entirely different purpose.

The new group of men greeted Tommy politely, and then took seats in a corner booth on the opposite side to discuss their business. Tommy had seen plenty of men just like this have them exact same conversations at many of the New York and New Jersey clubs he once performed at, and he knew better than to stick his nose in it. These European businessmen of ill repute did not seem all that different from their brethren in the La Casa Nostra back home. They could make very dangerous enemies, but they could also be very powerful friends as long as you kissed the right rings, paid the right dues, and knew when to keep your mouth shut.

A steady stream of wise guys, hoodlums and rapscallions filtered through the door as the bar quickly began to fill back up. Finally, the Captain came striding in with an entourage following closely in his wake. He had changed out of his earlier nautical attire and was now wearing a flashy three-piece pinstriped suit complete with a bright pink tie and a matching pocket square. His charismatic aura seemed to multiply tenfold now that was even more in his element. The men who surrounded him were types who would yield to no man, and yet they yielded to him out of sheer respect.

The Captain soon spotted Tommy and made a beeline towards his table. It was only then that Tommy's eyes were met with a new shocking twist, the sight of Tony Vespa following in the captain's coattails.

The Captain smiled warmly as he offered his greeting. "Tommy Malloy, I am glad to see that you found the right place. I hope you have made yourself at home here."

Tommy thanked him, remembering how much men like this liked to be flattered. "I appreciate your hospitality very much. You have an excellent establishment here. I felt safe and well-protected, and I had some pretty good fish and chips to boot."

The Captain looked pleased. "It is an honor to welcome you in my place of business." He glanced around at the men setting up a craps table and at the other various poker and blackjack games breaking out in the booths. "But now I believe you can gather the true nature of my business."

Tommy nodded, being careful not to say anything more than he had to.

"I must attend to my guests," the Captain said. "But for now, I will let you catch up with your friend. I am sure you two have much to talk about."

As the captain walked away, Tony took a seat across from Tommy, his face looking both confused and concerned. "Tommy, where the hell have you been? Everybody's been looking for you, the cops were asking me questions about it, and the newspaper reporters were too. I didn't answer any of them because I don't snitch, but it was really crazy out there."

Tommy took a deep breath, not sure where to even begin. "So, you remember that guy who was heckling us at the show? The one I allegedly murdered? Well, it turns out he did that because he wanted to make a scene to help him get away. You see, he got set up and the guys he was there with were trying to kill him. He ended up being a pretty stand-up guy, and he was actually from Philly too."

"So you mean it was part of this mob business?"

"No, it was much worse than that. He worked for the government. It was the Russian bastards that were after him."

Tony's jaw dropped. "The Russians were at our show? So what happened next?"

"I hid him in my hotel room, but when I stepped out for a smoke, the Russian punks snuck in and killed him. So now the Russians think I was working with him, the cops think I was the real killer and I'm just over here wearing disguises until this all blows over."

Tony shook his head in disbelief. "Wow, that really is something else."

As the pair sat and talked, the activity level in the rest of the bar was steadily picking up, and before they knew it, it had become a vibrant, happening place. Raucous games were breaking out all around them, and the crowd presented a veritable "Who's Who" of the shady and corrupt of Parisian society. Crooked police officers and judges, local government officials, and well-known entertainers mingled with the gangsters, demonstrating the full extent of just how much pull a man like the captain really had.

A cocktail waitress walked by bearing a bottle of high-end whiskey. Tony flagged her down and ordered two shots.

"To Tommy Malloy, the craziest mick in Paris."

After they downed the shots, Tommy wanted to ask some questions of his own. "So our friend the Captain invited you here too? How much do you really know about him?"

"Well his real name is Vittorio Malbranque, but everybody just calls him 'Le Capitaine.' That's French for 'The Captain' in case you didn't know. Anyway, he's a real big shot in the Corsican mob, and he runs the docks down in Marseille as well as the gambling rings here in Paris," Tony said.

"He mentioned he was friends with Paulie Prosciutto," Tommy added.

"They have a very strong working relationship," Tony confirmed. He leaned in closer and spoke in a hushed tone. "Le Capitaine ships drugs from Marseilles to New York, and then Paulie buys and distributes them. They have this whole system about it. They call it the French Connection."

Throughout their conversation, the card games and other activities became ever more raucous as more people continued to stream into the club, completing its total transformation from a quaint tourist trap into a wretched hive of scum and villainy. Ironically for Tommy, being surrounded by criminals was actually the safest he had felt all day.

Never one to sit still for very long, Tony stood up and beckoned for Tommy to follow. "Come on. Let's just shoot one round of craps for good luck."

Tommy was reluctant. He was going to need a lot of luck to survive the rest of his ordeal and he didn't want to waste any on a craps game. However, he eventually caved in and figured one round couldn't hurt. Tony cut a swathe through the crowd with Tommy in tow, walking up to the front of the craps table, and splashing down a large wad of cash. Tommy took the dice in his hands and closed his eyes, hoping for a lucky roll. But before he got the chance, the revelry was interrupted by the high-pitched shrill of a police whistle. In a well-drilled and methodical manner, the gangsters began to deconstruct the room, quickly converting it back into a normal bar.

Le Capitaine appeared, wrapping one burly arm each around Tommy and Tony. "My friends, there is no need to worry. This is all part of the game we play. The police have to stop by here to save face, but then they will search the premises and report that they found nothing out of the ordinary. That way they did their job and everybody is satisfied."

Tommy squirmed uncomfortably. "That's all fine, but you see, I'm wanted for murder. I can't really risk having the cops see me."

Le Capitaine's jovial expression suddenly became more somber. "In that case, follow me. Tony, stay here and talk to the police, delay as long as you can."

Walking deliberately, he led Tommy back through the kitchen, where he pushed a refrigerator aside and opened up a trap door in the floor.

"This was very useful during the occupation," he explained as they crawled their way through a dark, musty tunnel. Several meters later, the tunnel gave way to a ladder, which led to an opening in an unused shed in an alley above.

Le Capitaine shook Tommy's hand and clasped a gold coin inside it. "Any friend of mine can call on me at any time. I wish you luck, Tommy Malloy."

"Thank you." Tommy glanced at the time and stepped back out into the city, knowing that his ordeal was only yet beginning.

CHAPTER FIFTEEN

Tommy made it outside just in time for the first dark shadows of dusk and the crisp chilling breeze that came with it. He still had almost three hours to go until his scheduled rendezvous at *La Trompette*, and it was only a few blocks away, so it seemed his best option was to get there early and scope the place out.

As he walked along, a change of shifts seemed to be underway in the city streets as the working commuters of the day gave way to the social revelers of the night. The increasing bustle made it easier for Tommy to lose himself in the crowd as he followed the flow of pedestrian traffic, inching ever closer to his destination. Nobody seemed to take interest in him, yet he couldn't help but suspect them all. In his mind, every bowler hat served to conceal a pair of eyes that were watching him, and beneath every overcoat was a gun that could be drawn at any moment.

As he drew nearer to the Rue des Lombards, Tommy glanced across the street and noticed the unmistakable silver badge and pillbox hat of an officer on patrol. His heart pounded as his survival instincts kicked in once more, filling him with the urge to make flight. But he suppressed this urge for the time being, thinking it wiser to stay with the flow of pedestrians, and not betray himself with any sudden or rash movements. The officer may not have spotted him, and he may yet be in the clear. Doing his best to remain calm, he kept walking forward as if he was an ordinary person on ordinary business.

When Tommy approached the next intersection, his peripheral vision caught sight of the officer crossing the street from left to right, approaching Tommy's side of the street. He couldn't tell if he had been spotted or not, but with this new development, he preferred not to leave things to chance. As calmly as possible, he stopped and turned to walk through the entrance of the nearest storefront, hoping it would give him some cover.

Once inside, he gathered his bearings. The shop seemed to be the European equivalent of the classic Five and Dime stores from back home, carrying all your basic essentials at low affordable prices. He browsed the store's merchandise for a few moments before settling on an oversized pair of browline sunglasses. He took his place in the checkout line, standing behind an elderly man who was buying several boxes of raisins.

With all the urgency of a sloth, the old man put his raisin boxes on the counter one at a time, and then meticulously counted out exact change from his coin purse. Tommy tried his best to be patient while waiting behind him, but he felt increasingly exposed the longer he had to stand still. Several meters away, the officer had now entered the store, and was walking the perimeter as if he was a shopper. Tommy looked straight ahead, attempting to look as normal as possible, hoping once more that he hadn't been spotted. He withdrew exact change from his wallet so that he was ready to go as soon as the old man finally finished. After the purchase, he briskly walked outside and immediately put on his new sunglasses, hoping to obscure his face.

Back out on the sidewalk, Tommy glanced at the reflections in the glass windows, straining to see if he was being followed. He noticed the officer walk out of the shop, but instead of following in pursuit, he doubled back and returned to his patrol car. Tommy breathed a sigh of relief, believing he had escaped detection. However, his relief was short-lived as he looked back at the officer and realized he was making a radio call.

With an added urgency, Tommy picked up the pace of his step as his eyes scanned all around him. Mere seconds later, he could hear the wail of police sirens, echoing through the streets so that he could not tell which direction it was coming from. A new car appeared, barreling down the road to confront him head-on. He glanced back over his shoulder and saw the original car, now closing in on his heels. He was about to be cut-off and surrounded, unless he did something drastic right now.

Reaching deep inside himself, Tommy called upon skills that he had not used in quite some time; the skills that he had developed as a youth being chased by angry neighborhood dogs through the streets of Philadelphia. Like a baserunner reading the pitcher's delivery before he takes off to steal second base, Tommy waited for just the right gap in the stream of traffic to make his sudden dart out into the street. The nearest car slammed on its brakes and nearly spun out of control as it screeched to a halt inches away from hitting him. Tommy briefly flinched, but he kept on running as the other cars were forced to stop as well, becoming embroiled in a quagmire of angry honks and shouts. The police cars slowed down to avoid the near crash, buying Tommy a few desperately needed seconds.

When he safely reached the other side, Tommy faked as if he was going to run back into the street, then doubled back and turned onto a narrow side street. With the officers now out of their cars and pursuing him on foot, he had no time to lose. He swiftly ran to the nearest storm gutter and began to climb. Remembering the technique he had learned on the obstacle courses at basic training, he used the force of his legs pushing against the wall to propel himself upwards, and wrapped his arms around the pipe for guidance. He was never very comfortable with heights, but he knew the key was to keep moving and never look down. An angry drill instructor was a very effective motivator for getting over one's fears, and a police pursuit was an even better one. He could hear the shouts of the officers on the ground behind him as he pulled himself over the top and rolled over onto the roof.

With no time to lose, Tommy picked himself up and ran once more along the rooftops, nimbly leaping from building to building like a squirrel among branches. Adrenaline carried him along as the whistles and shouts of the police grew ever more distant behind him. When he spotted a soft pile of shrubbery on a grassy knoll, he knew it was his best opportunity to jump. He leaped from the roof and landed to the snaps of breaking twigs.

Uncomfortable but surprisingly uninjured, Tommy dusted himself off and looked around to get his bearings. He was now in a somewhat quieter area a few blocks away from the busy street he had just fled. On the lot directly ahead of him sat a church, one of the lucky ones that managed to survive the war with its gothic medieval architecture still intact. As Tommy walked towards it, he noticed that adjacent to the church was a complex that appeared to be a convent. When he got close enough to see the emblem displayed over top the door, he could not believe his luck. This convent belonged to the Sisters of Saint Wenceslaus, the same Catholic order that operated his old stomping grounds of St. Sebastian's Elementary School.

After a quick scan around to check if he was being followed, Tommy walked up and knocked several times on the thick wooden door to the convent. The sisters he had known back home were strict and straight-laced women who would not put up with any nonsense or shenanigans, but they were also the most kind and generous people around when they encountered those most in need.

Tommy waited in the doorway for a few moments until the door creaked open and a short elderly nun peered out, eying him with cautious apprehension. He looked down towards her with pleading eyes as he professed the most flowery piety he could muster.

"Sister, I have come to ask that this house of

holiness may take mercy on me, a mere humble sinner..."

She looked back at him with confusion as she asked him questions he did not understand. She spoke no English, and her French was a rural dialect that Tommy had never heard before. She motioned for one of her colleagues to come help her break the communication barrier with this strange new visitor. When the second nun arrived, Tommy felt a tremendous sense of both shock and relief as he came face to face with a person from his past he had not seen in many years.

"Sister Frances! Boy, am I glad to see you!"

Sister Frances Donohue was an Irish woman from a small rural town in County Mayo. She had never left her hometown until she began her journey of service to her vocation, a journey that had taken her everywhere from teaching school children in Philadelphia to nursing wounded soldiers on the battlefields of Normandy and the Ardennes. She was nearing her seventieth birthday, but she showed no signs of slowing down. She gave Tommy a look of vague recognition, knowing that she should remember him from somewhere.

"It's me, Tommy Malloy, from Saint Sebastian's! You were my third grade teacher!" He paused a moment to count the years on his fingers. "That would have been...wow, that was 1932. Where did the time go?"

The memories came rushing back to her, and she spoke to him with the authoritative teacher's voice he knew all too well. "Get inside, now."

Tommy followed her inside like a newly trained puppy chasing after its master.

"I never realized that the Tommy Malloy I heard about in the news was my Tommy Malloy. The newspapers are saying some pretty awful things about you. Am I correct in assuming that you are you coming here to hide from the police?"

Shame and anxiety washed over Tommy as he feared that she might think the worst of him. "Sister please, you have to believe me, none of those stories are true, I can explain..."

She looked back at him with calm and forgiving eyes. "I always knew you were a problem child, Tommy Malloy. To tell you the truth, I never thought you would amount to much of anything. But I don't believe for one minute that you're a murderer."

Tommy breathed a sigh of relief and could finally smile again. "Well I've murdered plenty of performances, just never people."

They walked into the cavernous lobby of the convent, where the thick stone walls shielded them from the outside world. Candles provided the only light, save for the last few rays of dusk filtering through the stained glass windows. They spoke quietly as they walked, and Tommy brought Sister Frances up to date on his adventures thus far, remembering to be intentionally vague about just who exactly Harry was and who he was working for. She understood that Tommy was in trouble through no fault of his own, and concluded that it was better for all involved if she didn't know the full details of the situation.

"We haven't done anything like this since the war, but you are welcome to remain here as long as you need," she said. "Monsignor Lloris from the parish next door is in Rome at the moment, but he would be happy to lend you some of his clothes."

She led him outside and through the well-manicured gardens of the grounds to the rectory of the adjacent parish. There, Sister Frances waited outside as Tommy entered the sparsely decorated living quarters of Monsignor Lloris, who despite his lofty title was a man of very simple tastes. Tommy rummaged through the Monsignor's closet, where he discarded his usher outfit in favor of some traditional priestly garb; a plain black shirt with a white Roman collar along with matching black trousers and a black suit coat. He topped the outfit off with a black biretta hat, with its recognizable fuzzy ball on top of its four peaks. The clothes were a little short and a little bit baggy, but Tommy just had to tighten his belt and make do. He took a quick glance in the mirror, imagining what the rest of his old teachers would think if they could see him now.

As Tommy had not yet eaten supper, Sister Frances led him back to the convent and downstairs to the kitchen, where he feasted on the leftovers of their hearty meal of roasted chicken and potatoes. A few of the sisters who passed by had quizzical glances at their new visitor, but the convent had sheltered enough refugees and resistance fighters during the war that they asked no questions. When he finished eating, they walked back towards the lobby, reminiscing about the old days as Tommy brought her up-to-date on the current whereabouts of his former classmates, some of whom didn't make it back from the war, some of whom ended up on Skid Row, and some of whom ended up being much more successful than she would have predicted at the time.

Living the busy and secluded life of a nun, Sister Frances hardly ever went to the movies or the theatre, let alone the comedy clubs, and as such she was shocked to learn the details of what Tommy had accomplished in his career. She was even more shocked and greatly flattered to learn that she was the inspiration for the main character in the film *The Boys of Saint Beatrice*. The 1949 B-movie comedy was Tommy's first foray into screenwriting, and it told the story of a strict disciplinarian nun who had to bring order to a school of unruly delinquent young men.

As the shadows of dusk gave way to the dark of night, they were interrupted by an authoritative knock on the door announcing the presence of police. Sister Frances pointed Tommy towards a nearby closet of cleaning supplies, where he hid while she answered the knock. From his hiding place, Tommy could hear and almost feel the unmistakable smugness of Inspector Phaneuf.

"Excuse me, Sister, we have been pursuing a murder suspect who was last seen in this neighborhood. Have you seen any suspicious characters or activity?"

"No, I have not."

"I see, but is it possible that you may be concealing something from me?"

She raised an eyebrow. "Are you accusing a nun of lying to a police officer?"

"I am not accusing you of anything, but I would like to search the premises all the same."

Sister Frances's Irish temper began to boil over. Young Tommy had been on the receiving end of it on more than one occasion, and he couldn't wait to see where this was going.

"This is a house of God! You dare cast aspersions on us and accuse of us of fostering a den of sins? You had better look to your own house first! Leave us at once, and go seek the Lord's forgiveness!"

Inspector Phaneuf was left momentarily speechless. When he recovered, he sheepishly bid his adieus and slipped away. Once he was gone, Tommy emerged from his hiding spot with a slow clap of applause. "Well done, Sister. That was one for the ages."

She took a deep breath to regain her composure. "Men like him are all bark and no bite. They don't know what to do when somebody barks back."

Feeling eternally grateful, Tommy sat and prayed the rosary with his former teacher until he eventually checked the time and realized that his long awaited appointment was drawing near. "Well I guess it's time I hit the road."

Before he left, Sister Frances stopped to give him a matronly hug. "Good luck, Tommy Malloy. I'll be praying for you."

He thanked her profusely as he walked out the door. He had a feeling he was in for another crazy night.

CHAPTER SIXTEEN

Tommy was still wearing his priest disguise when he left the convent and wandered back outside into the night. He was worried about how much it made him stick out, but the police had already spotted him wearing his previous disguise and nothing else was readily available. All things considered, it actually provided a pretty good cover. People usually see what they are expecting to see, and somebody who encounters a man in priestly garb would have no reason to suspect that he was actually a comedian turned fugitive.

The effects of the day's adventures were beginning to wear on Tommy as he walked the remaining kilometer or so to his ultimate destination. His legs were cramping up after all the walking and running, he had all kinds of bruises and aches from various shenanigans, and he was exhausted after missing a night of sleep. He wanted nothing more at this point than to return to his hotel room, have a nice strong drink, and then pass out for the night.

But that hotel room was now a crime scene, and the mysterious meeting he was now walking towards was the only hope he had at resolving this crazy situation.

When Tommy finally reached the Rue des Lombards, he was greeted by the glow of neon lights and the sounds of raucous revelry. A few of the partiers traversing the streets or waiting outside the clubs gave confused glances when they saw the priestly looking man walk by, but for the most part, he was ignored. At the end of the street, he finally came upon a club whose sign had a large neon trumpet over top the words "La Trompette," which even the most remedial student could tell you was the French word for "trumpet." There was no line outside to get in, as there was at some of the other clubs, but judging by the noise level coming from inside there seemed to be a lively crowd there. Tommy was gripped with trepidation as he walked up to the door. It was a similar sensation to what he felt before his performances, but with the added twist that the audience might actually kill him if the performance didn't go well.

He looked down at his watch and took one last glance at the time; he had made it there with about ten minutes to spare. He took a deep breath and stepped inside to gather his bearings. At first glance, it looked very similar to some of the smaller venues he had performed at earlier in his career. There was a stage at the front of the room where a jazz quintet consisting of a trumpet, saxophone, piano, bass and drum set was busy playing. There were tables on the floor in front of the stage which were mostly full of guests, a very busy bar on the left side of the room, and booths along the walls and in the corners.

He lingered near the entrance for a few brief moments, taking everything in. When nobody approached him, he walked over to claim a seat in the most secluded corner booth he could find. From this corner, he had an excellent vantage point to observe the rest of the room as well as anybody coming in or out of the front door. The club was slowly filling up, and the crowd seemed to be well-dressed, and mostly well-behaved. Tommy was scanning the faces, looking for anyone who might potentially be the "friend of Harry," when the waiter walked up to take his order.

"What would you like to drink, Monsieur?" If he was at all surprised to see a priest in the club, he was too professional to show it.

"How about a bottle of communion wine?"

The waiter did not react, and Tommy made a mental note that this joke probably wasn't good enough to use again.

"I'll have a scotch on the rocks."

"Yes sir, right away."

The waiter returned with the drink moments later, leaving Tommy to sit in silence. Under ordinary circumstances, his time in a club like this would be spent networking with the powers that be, doing anything he could to land auditions and performance slots. But now, much bigger things than his career were at stake. He sipped at his drink, wondering if he was about to be rescued, murdered or something in between.

As Tommy looked around the room, his eyes made contact with a rather distraught looking man who was standing by the bar. The man seemed to stare at Tommy for a few seconds before he approached the booth and sat down. He had bloodshot eyes, a thick layer of stubble on his face, and his tie was a crumpled up mess. Tommy scooted up to the edge of his seat, nervous and excited that something was finally happening.

"Bless me father, for I have sinned," the man said in badly slurred French.

Tommy looked back at him quizzically, not sure if this was some kind of test.

"I have not been to confession in many years, but I have committed many sins."

Tommy felt his excitement deflate as he realized that the man in front of him was not an international spy, but merely a wayward drunk. He did not have the time or the desire to listen to this man's problems, but he had enough Catholic guilt that he couldn't just turn him away. With that in mind, he stood up and took the man by the arm, guiding him towards the exit, and pointing him in the direction of the nearest church, hoping that somebody out there could save this poor soul.

Feeling the roller coaster ride of high tension to deflating let-down back to high tension again, Tommy slumped back down in his seat and sipped some more of his scotch. It was then that he noticed a woman slowly making her way across the floor. She had wavy red hair like Rita Hayworth, and was casually dressed in trousers and a blouse. She purposefully marched through the crowd, a look of grim determination on her face. Tommy watched her the whole way, and grew increasingly nervous as she drew closer and closer to his booth.

"What are you doing here, Father? Did you run out of communion wine?" she said as she slid into the booth sitting across from him.

He squirmed uncomfortably, caught equally off guard by her sudden approach and the fact that she used the same lame joke as him. "Well, you see...I'm not actually...I mean..."

She leaned across the table and spoke in a hushed tone. "I know who you are, Mr. Malloy. I am a friend of Harry."

Tommy took a deep breath. Now things were finally happening. It remained to be seen if she was a friend or foe, but least he was close to getting some answers. "So what's your name, friend of Harry?"

"You can call me Marlene."

"So, Marlene, how about we just get this out of the way so there's no suspense. Are you actually here to help me or are you here to murder me?"

She smiled and answered him calmly, speaking fluent English in the vaguely British-sounding accent of the European aristocracy. "I'm here to help you, of course, but I don't blame you for being suspicious after what you have been through. I am a friend of your country in addition to Harry, and we worked closely together in the same line of work for quite some time. When I found out the details of what happened, I knew right away who had to be behind it, and when I learned of your involvement, I knew they would come for you as well. I've been trying to catch up to you all day, but it has been very difficult. It seems you have had your share of close calls with both the killers and the police."

Her explanation seemed sincere enough. Tommy couldn't quite place his finger on what it was, but there was something about her that made him want to trust her. He reached into his pocket for a pen and paper and scribbled down, "Operation Arctic Fox, October 25."

"Here, Harry left this message for me, and it seemed important."

She briefly examined it and then put it away in her purse. "Thank you, this helps us much more than you may know. I hope you didn't go through much trouble to get it to me."

Tommy could only shake his head and laugh. "No, it was no trouble at all, just a walk in the park."

"Well on behalf of your country and its allies, we appreciate everything you have done. If you ever want a change of career, there is a job for you out in the field."

After everything that had happened, he could not imagine a more unappealing idea. "Thank you, but I'll just stick to telling jokes." He took a long sip from his scotch. "So now that I got you the information, what comes next? Do we have to go anywhere? Do anything?"

"The most important thing for us to do now is get you out of the country until everything blows over," she said.

Tommy understood. It was very disappointing that his much-anticipated debut on the Paris comedy scene was going to end like this, but at least he had survived his adventure and lived to tell about it. Maybe someday he could even turn it into a screenplay. But for right now, more serious concerns took precedence.

He finished the rest of his drink and then stood up. "Well before I go anywhere else, I'm going to have to go to the bathroom."

Tommy reflected on the utter absurdity of his

situation as he walked towards the bathroom. Here he was, in Paris, drinking fine scotch and listening to live jazz music with a beautiful woman. Under normal circumstances, it would have been a perfect night. Yet here he was, dodging assassins and running from the law while dressed as a priest.

When he reached the bathroom in the rear corner of the club, he found it unoccupied. There were three urinals against the back wall, and he chose the one on the right and felt the great sense of relief and satisfaction that comes from letting it go after holding it in for far too long. While he was finishing his business, a tall man walked into the room and occupied the adjacent urinal. Tommy was very annoyed at this blatant breach of etiquette, as any decent self-respecting man would know to leave a buffer zone. He finished up and went over to the sink to wash his hands, suspiciously eying the rude intruder through the mirror.

As he applied the soap to his hands, Tommy glanced in the mirror once more and saw that the man had finished up and was turning around. When he caught a glimpse of his face, he felt a sudden jolt as he realized that the urinal-crowding cretin was none other than Jacques, the tall companion of the short man he had fought on the bus. Confident that Jacques had not yet recognized him, Tommy decided to play it cool. He looked straight ahead and betrayed no emotion when Jacques walked up to the sink next to him. He simply finished rinsing his hands, turned off the faucet, and wiped his hands off on his pants. Jacques meanwhile, was busy washing his own hands, a fact which pleasantly surprised Tommy given his earlier lack of etiquette and overall classlessness.

Tommy was about to open the door to leave when he finally noticed a sudden flash of movement in his peripheral vision. Having expected it all along, Tommy quickly assumed a fighting stance and met Jacques' forward lunge with a crushing right uppercut to the jaw. The force of the impact sent Jacques stumbling backwards, and Tommy pressed the attack, moving forwards with a rapid flurry of punches. Jacques lost his balance and fell crashing into a stall, where Tommy grabbed him by the back of the neck and forcefully jammed his head into the toilet, flushing it for good measure. Tommy then ran outside, feeling mildly disgusted that he didn't have time to wash his hands again.

He ran as fast as he could back to his table and dropped a handful of francs to cover his bill. Marlene stood up quickly, sensing his urgency.

"What's the matter? Did you have an accident in there?"

In the midst of his urgency, Tommy still had to respect somebody who could make a joke at a time like this. "Well I'm doing ok, but the other guy is feeling a bit *flushed*. But seriously, we have to leave now."

She took him by the arm and led the way towards the exit.

"Just shut up and follow me."

CHAPTER SEVENTEEN

Tommy kept quiet and followed along as Marlene led him out the door. They passed the line of people that had formed at the entrance and made a sharp turn onto the sidewalk. When they were clear of the crowd, they broke into an all-out sprint, pushing Tommy's cramped legs to the limit.

"Where are we going anyway?" Tommy asked, gasping for air as he struggled to keep up.

Marlene didn't answer, but she made another turn to a side street full of parallel-parked cars. They finally came to a stop when they reached the vehicle she had arrived in; a German military motorcycle left over from the war, complete with an attached side car.

"Get in!" she ordered him, before he had the chance to ask any more questions.

Tommy had already experienced far too many absurd events to be surprised by anything at this point. He crammed himself into the tiny sidecar, his knees protruding up past his face with no room to stretch out. Meanwhile, Marlene climbed on top of the bike, revved up the engine, and peeled out of the parking spot.

Looking over his shoulder, Tommy caught a glimpse of a very irate Jacques stumbling around the corner and climbing into a black Renault. He angrily barked orders at the driver as they pulled out in hot pursuit, their tires screeching against the pavement. Marlene banked towards the right and made a sharp turn, hoping to get lost in the traffic on a busier street, and causing Tommy to bounce uncomfortably in his unsecured seat. The Renault followed closely on their tail, violently skidding as it pushed the limits of it turn radius.

Tommy craned his neck around, catching a glimpse of Jacques leaning out the car's passenger side window, aiming a rifle in their general direction.

"Watch out!" Tommy shouted over the din.

Marlene gave him a nod as she shifted into a faster gear and executed serpentine maneuvers between the lanes. They could feel the cracks in the air as bullets went whizzing by. It was a sensation that Tommy had not experienced since the war, and one that he certainly had not missed. Fortunately, the accuracy of Jacques' shooting seemed to be much closer to the movie version of Nazis rather than the actual Nazis, and the shots missed wildly. Tommy pressed low to the ground and kept his head down nonetheless, not wanting to take any chances.

As they approached a particularly busy intersection, Marlene began to slow down, gradually drawing the Renault in closer behind them.

"What are you doing?" Tommy asked frantically as the car drew close enough for him to see the driver's face.

"Just trust me."

As the traffic light changed from green to yellow to red, she displayed no intentions of stopping. The Renault followed close on their heels, charging forward with reckless disregard for the traffic laws.

"Hold on!" Marlene yelled as she slammed on the brakes at the last possible moment. The tires screeched against the pavement as the bike skidded to a halt, stopping mere inches shy of the oncoming traffic of the parallel street. Tommy's cap flew off of his head and into the street, and he greatly regretted that he would not be able to return it to the poor Monsignor he had pilfered it from.

The Renault attempted the stop as well, but with its heavier weight and much wider turning radius, it was not so lucky. It flew right past the motorcycle, narrowly avoiding a collision. As the driver desperately tried to stop, it sputtered and spun into the middle of the intersection. As the oncoming cars skidded and swerved in frantic attempts to avoid the wayward vehicle, the normally quiet city street began to resemble the Monaco Grand Prix. In the midst of the confusion, a large truck plowed through the crowd with no chance of stopping in time. With great force, it slammed into the side of the Renault. There was a loud, metallic crunch as the smaller car was sent hurtling end over end, finally coming to a rest with its roof on the ground. Black smoke billowed from the wreckage as the truck driver ran out to go help. Very slowly, Jacques emerged from the car, battered, bloodied and disoriented.

Marlene looked on with a cool detachment, then revved up the bike and peeled away, going unnoticed in the midst of the confusion.   The police would be arriving at the accident scene soon, and they needed to be well clear of it before that happened.   She quickly and skillfully maneuvered her way through the backstreets, cutting corners wherever possible, until they finally reached an out-of-the-way city park. There she turned the bike off the road, and it tore up some grass before finally sliding to a stop beneath a clump of trees.   Marlene stepped off the bike, and then finally allowed herself to exhale.

Tommy's dismount from the sidecar was less smooth, as his foot got caught on the edge and he face-planted into the dirt.   With nothing injured but his pride, he stood up, dusted his shoulders off, and quipped, "Well that ride was a *smashing* success."

Marlene looked back at him, smiled, and then began to laugh hysterically.   Tommy leaned back and collapsed against a tree, laughing as well.   Jokes that weren't normally funny had a strange way of becoming hilarious at late hours of the night, and all the more so after near- death experiences. When the laughter finally subsided, Marlene resumed her professional demeanor and motioned for Tommy to follow her as she briskly walked away.

They took a roundabout route to wherever they were going, avoiding the main streets, and constantly doubling back to make sure they were not being followed.   After what felt like at least an hour, they finally arrived at an old and unkempt tenement building in a much less expensive area of the city. They walked through the empty lobby and up a staircase to the second floor, where Marlene produced a key and unlocked the door to a small apartment.

"Is there where you live?" Tommy asked as he poked his head inside.

"Good heavens, no! I just keep this place off the books for whenever I need to lie low. It has been rather helpful in my professional endeavors."

The apartment looked like as if it would difficult for anyone to live in, let alone someone of Marlene's presumably refined tastes. The walls were plain drywall; there were no decorations and they had not even been painted. A thick layer of dust covered the hardwood floor, and the smell of mildew emanated from the corners. A worn and tattered couch with a drab grey color was the only real piece of furniture in the living room. There was a rickety dining table just outside the kitchen, and a short hallway leading to the bathroom, closet, and only bedroom.

"Well, I guess it has a certain charm to it," Tommy said.

Marlene began to walk towards the closet. "Come on now; let me show you the best part."

Tommy followed her into the walk-in closet, where she pulled the hanging string to turn on the exposed light bulb in the ceiling. What they saw inside firmly established Marlene's credentials as a master of disguise. There were outfits of all different sizes and styles of both men's and women's clothing. The collection included formal wear, casual business attire, police and military uniforms, and just about anything in between. There were also boxes on the ground, containing wigs, as well as accessories such as glasses, watches, and jewelry. It was just as extensive as the costume departments on any of the movie sets Tommy had worked on.

"You're going to need some new clothes before

we leave tomorrow," she informed him. "Help yourself to whatever you want in here."

Tommy looked through the men's section of the closet as Marlene walked back towards the kitchen, leaving Tommy more intrigued about her than ever. It seemed obvious now that her long red locks were actually a wig, and he wondered what else she may be hiding. After trying on several options, he settled on a conservative grey business suit that was close enough to his size, along with a white shirt, a black wool tie, a fedora hat, and a set of reading glasses. He set the outfit aside and walked back out to the dining table, where Marlene was sitting with two cups of tea set out for them.

"Do you have anything to eat here?" he asked, getting down to what really mattered.

"There's not much, but you can look around."

Tommy opened up a set of cabinets and found that they had been stocked with surplus military rations. Not being in the mood for beans or canned meat, he went straight for the stash of standard issue chocolate bars. While military chocolate could never compare with what you could get in a candy store, it had gotten Tommy through the war, not to mention winning the hearts and minds of children across Europe and the Pacific. With the candy in hand, he joined Marlene at the table, and she slid him a folder containing a travel itinerary.

"The arrangements are made. I booked you a ticket on the first train to Amsterdam tomorrow morning. I know what you're thinking; that seems too simple, the train stations are probably being watched. Well that's right, they are, but that is why I showed you the closet first. When we're finished with your disguise, your own family won't even recognize you. This folder also contains directions and a key to an apartment much like this one."

"Well I always did want to see what Amsterdam is like," he responded with a smile. Tommy's most notable film credit to date was a supporting role in the Louis Poutine film *Accountants of Amsterdam*, a rollicking comedy about an accountant who lived a double life smuggling tulips on the black market. Despite its namesake setting, the movie had actually been filmed in Hollywood. Tommy had actually visited Netherlands once before, but the occasion of his visit was a combat jump to help capture a crucial bridge during Operation Market Garden.

Marlene continued, "You are to remain there until further instruction. As you have seen already, the situation in Paris is becoming quite dangerous. It is best that you remain out of the country until this whole thing blows over."

Tommy read through the folder as he took it all in. Here he was, effectively putting his life in this mysterious woman's hands. Thus far, she had given him no reason to doubt her trustworthiness. While he did wonder about how Jacques managed to find him in the bathroom, he knew that if it was an intentional set-up, it would have been much more smoothly executed. Furthermore, Jacques had seemed very surprised to find him there, and Marlene had risked her life to help him escape, so he had to conclude that Jacque's appearance was just another coincidence in a day that was already full of them.

Speculating on her identity further, he remembered what George Randolph had said about how Harry had gone out on loan to the British government. Thus, it seemed probable that Marlene was working for the British as well, even though her accent and mannerisms seemed more continental. Overall, he was just really curious to know more about her.

"So where are you from, anyway?" he asked. "Austria? Switzerland?"

She nodded. "Yes, somewhere around there."

He couldn't help but laugh. "You really like to keep up the aura of mystery, don't you?"

She gave him a sly grin as she stood up from the table. "You have had a very long day, Mr. Malloy. Perhaps it is time you got some sleep."

A wave of exhaustion was washing over Tommy as his adrenaline wore off, and he realized that, of course, she was right. It had been a very long and crazy day, and the one thing his body needed more than anything right now, even more than chocolate, was sleep.

"Goodnight, Mr. Malloy," she whispered as she turned and disappeared down the hallway and into the bedroom.

"Goodnight…Marlene…if that's really your name," he said under his breath as he curled up to sleep on the couch.

CHAPTER EIGHTEEN

Before the morning sun arose, Tommy's slumber was interrupted by the high-pitched shrill of the teapot. His body ached as he reluctantly rolled off of the couch, cursing the fact that his train was scheduled to depart so early. He had grown accustomed to the comedian's schedule of late night shows and lazy mornings, and he had not seen this ungodly hour of the day since leaving the army.

"Good morning, Mr. Malloy," Marlene greeted him from the kitchen.

Tommy almost didn't recognize her at first glance. She had a different wig on today, this one a mousy brown model pulled back in a tight bun. She wore a plain beige blazer with a matching skirt and an unneeded pair of glasses.

"Top of the morning to you too," he said as he stretched and shook himself awake.

She ignored the sarcasm. "We depart in one hour. Do whatever you must do to prepare. Breakfast will be ready momentarily."

Tommy managed to drag himself into the bathroom for a much needed shower and shave. The water was merely lukewarm, but it got the job done. By the time he finished dressing in the outfit he had picked out the night before, Marlene had set out a freshly cooked breakfast of powdered eggs and canned ham. They ate in silence, and when they were finished, it was time for Marlene to work her magic. With the skill of a Hollywood artist, she helped Tommy put on a grey wig and applied a fresh set of makeup to his face. When they were through, he looked at least seventy years old.

She handed him a cane to complete the ensemble, and then they grabbed their bags and left. They walked a roundabout route away from the apartment to ensure that nobody was following, and then finally boarded a bus bound for Gare du Nord, the largest rail station in Paris. The morning rush was just beginning when they arrived at the station, and they did their best to blend seamlessly into the crowd. Several police officers were patrolling the grounds, but if they noticed Tommy's presence, they didn't show it. Everybody who observed them seemed to make the obvious assumption that they were simply seeing a daughter accompany her elderly father to his train.

With the poise of seasoned travelers, they cut through the growing crowds and found the appropriate platform. Moments later, the train began its first boarding call.

"Thank you for visiting, Papa. Don't forget to write," Marlene called after Tommy as he stepped onto the stairs.

He tipped his hat. "I'll send a postcard!"

He walked onto the third car of the train and found an open seat next to a window. With nobody sitting next to or across from him, there was plenty of room to stretch out. If all went well, he was set up for a pleasant and relaxing ride followed by a quiet stay in Amsterdam. As the departure time grew nearer, more people boarded the train, and the other seats in the car began to fill up around him. Just after the last call for boarding, an athletic blond man in a business suit walked down the aisle and motioned towards the seat across from Tommy.

"Is anybody sitting here?"

"No, go ahead," Tommy responded, disappointed that he would no longer be able to use the opposite seat as a foot rest.

The man's eyes lit up when he heard Tommy's accent. "Oh, you're American? Me too! It's always great to find people from back home, especially when you're traveling abroad like this."

"There haven't been this many Yanks in France since Normandy," Tommy quipped, his hopes of a quiet and peaceful train ride evaporating before his eyes.

The blond man offered a handshake. "My name is Vince, Vince Bennett. I'm from New York, and I'm a traveling salesman for Acme Insurance."

Tommy shook his hand, impressed by the strength of his grip. "I'm Ernie. I'm from Chicago and I work for a bank." He was surprised to hear that Vince was a New Yorker, because his accent and his friendliness to point of being annoying both seemed thoroughly Midwestern.

"I'm on my way to Copenhagen. It's a long ride, so I booked a sleeping compartment, but I wanted to sit out here for a while to get some sunlight," said Vince, eager to engage in some small talk.

"Yeah, who doesn't like the sun?" answered Tommy, wishing this conversation would end already.

Vince continued, "I'm negotiating an insurance policy with this new company in Denmark called Lego. You won't believe the kind of things they're working on; it's going to revolutionize children's playtime forever. But enough about me, where are you off to?"

"Belgium. I'm hungry for some waffles," Tommy said brusquely.

Vince laughed heartily. "Hahaha, you're a funny guy. Has anyone ever told you that? You could be a comedian!"

Tommy rolled his eyes as he reached for his copy of the morning newspaper, opening it up in front of his face. Much to his initial relief, he was not mentioned on the front page of this paper. However, he turned the page and found a prominent article on the third page entitled "Manhunt for Malloy," complete with a picture of him on stage.

"May I see that paper when you're done?" Vince asked.

Tommy forced himself to sneeze, projecting his germs all over the paper, then crumpled it up and wiped his nose with it.

"Oh, this paper? This is disgusting. You don't want this."

He leaned back in his seat and pulled his fedora down low over his eyes. With his only reading material now useless, feigning sleep became Tommy's only alternative to talking to Captain Chatterbox.

The ploy was effective for a few moments, as

Vince stopped talking, and Tommy felt as if he might actually drift off to sleep. However, just as the train began to pull away, he noticed some very concerning activity in the preceding car. It appeared that two police officers were canvassing the passengers row by row, searching for something that they had yet to find. Tommy began to fidget, trying to think of a way out of this one. His disguise had held up so far, but he wasn't confident that it would withstand careful scrutiny. His first thought was to hide in the toilet and take a really long dump, hoping they would overlook him. However, the toilets were located at the front of the train, and he would have to walk past the police in order to reach them.

Noticing Tommy's discomfort, Vince leaned forward and spoke in a hushed tone, "You can drop the charade, Mr. Malloy. I know who you are and what you're running from. I work for our government and I'm here to help you."

Tommy was stunned. He thought for sure that Marlene would have mentioned if there was going to be another agent meeting him on the train. However, nothing that had happened over the past couple days really made any sense at all, and at this point, he saw no other option but to believe this man. The two men stood up, and Vince led the way as they walked three cars back and entered into Vince's sleeping compartment. Vince closed the door behind them, and quickly searched the room for any signs of disturbance.

"I understand the past couple days have been pretty eventful for you."

"That would be quite the understatement," Tommy said.

"Well you can relax now, your role in this game is nearly over," Vince reassured him.

Taking the instructions to heart, Tommy sat down on the bed, leaning backwards to stretch out his arms and back.

"So, Vince, are you a baseball fan?" he asked, hoping to pass the time with a more interesting subject.

"I enjoy a good day at the ballpark."

"So being a New Yorker, as you said, do you support the Yankees, Dodgers, or Giants?"

"The Yankees, of course," Vince responded as he walked over to the sink to wash his hands.

Tommy grimaced. The Yankees had swept the Phillies in the 1950 World Series, the only time the Phillies had ever made it that far in his lifetime. He still wasn't over it.

"So who's your favorite player?"

After a brief pause, Vince answered, "Mickey Bellagio."

With a sudden jolt, Tommy sat up straight and moved forward to the edge of his seat.

"Who did you say again?"

"Mickey Bellagio."

Tommy began to sweat with panic. Any real American, but especially one claiming to be a Yankees fan, would know that Mickey Mantle and Joe DiMaggio were two different people. And only a communist would butcher the latter's name like that. It was now perfectly clear that this situation did not add up, and that this man was not who he claimed to be. With Vince's back turned to him, Tommy stood up and tiptoed towards the door. Sensing the movement, Vince spun around instantly, drawing a pistol from his concealed shoulder holster.

"Stop right there, now go sit back down," he commanded.

Tommy raised his hands above his head and slowly returned to his seat on the bed.

"I should have known. Vince Bennett means Viktor Bazarov. You lazy bastard, you couldn't even think of a good alias."

Viktor was not amused. "I'm not here to hurt you or kill you. I want information. The more you cooperate, the easier it will be. Your friend, Harry Thompson...did not cooperate."

Tommy took a deep breath; it was going to take some pretty good improvisation to get out of this one.

"Now, let's begin. What can you tell me about Operation Corner Kick?"

"I've never even heard of it," Tommy answered truthfully.

Viktor gave him a backhanded slap across the face. "Don't lie to me!"

Tommy protested. "No, I'm being perfectly honest. What the hell is a 'corner kick' anyway? Is that something from soccer? I'm American; we don't even play that. We play football, with touchdowns and field goals."

Viktor kicked the ground in frustration. "Stop talking, you insolent fool!"

But Tommy went on rambling as much as he could, watching Viktor get ever more frustrated, as he tried to think of his next move. Then, a sudden realization came to him.

"No, you listen to me, Viktor. The whole reason we came back here in the first place is because there were police officers outside. The only power you have to keep me here is that you have a gun and I don't. However, that advantage is actually useless because if you shot me, the police would hear it and you would have no chance to escape. Therefore, I am just going to walk out that door, and there is nothing you can do to stop me."

Starting to feel a bit smug, Tommy stood up to leave while Viktor simply seemed stunned by his audacity. However, his smugness was short-lived. Just as he reached the doorway, he felt the crushing blow of Viktor's fist connecting with his jaw. Tommy stumbled backwards, feeling disoriented. He hadn't been hit that hard since the time Dino Bronski jumped him for his lunch money in seventh grade.

With Tommy on the ropes, Viktor pressed his advantage, wrapping his hands around Tommy's neck in an attempt to strangle him. As he struggled to break free, Tommy reached for his cane and swung it wildly, finally managing to hit Viktor in the eye. Viktor winced in pain, giving Tommy the brief window he needed to wriggle his way out of his grasp. Before Viktor could react, he lunged to push the door open and spilled out into the passageway.

Without looking back, he ran full speed down the lengths of the cars, and back towards his original seat. As the passengers turned to look at this mysterious new arrival, Tommy stood on top of the seat, tore off his wig, and began to address them.

"Bonjour, everybody! It's me, Tommy Malloy here, the most wanted man in France! I'm coming to you live from car number three on the railroad line. I just took the train in from Paris and my back is killing me!"

Tommy looked around to gather situational awareness. The other passengers were all staring at him; some were laughing, and others just looked perplexed. Viktor was nowhere to be seen, and two police officers were rapidly approaching him. The train was slowing down, presumably at the officers' instruction.

"So what's the deal with railroad food?" he called out, the quality of his material not really important at this point.

The joke earned a few boos and jeers as he surrendered himself into police custody. The train slowed down to a stop as the officers placed handcuffs on Tommy and led him to the exit.

As the perplexed passengers looked on, he offered his farewell, "You've been a great audience, enjoy the rest of your trip, and remember to tip the bagman."

The officers showed no signs of amusement as they dragged him off the train and into the waiting car.

CHAPTER NINETEEN

Tommy had lost track of just how long he had been in the interrogation room. It was a small room, with concrete walls and a dank musty smell. There were no windows, and the only light came from an overhead fixture and a small lamp on the metal desk in front of him. He was sitting in an uncomfortable wooden chair with his hands handcuffed behind him. His body ached, he was ravenously hungry, and his throat was parched with thirst. Less than forty-eight hours after he last performed underneath the lights of the big stage, Tommy Malloy was confined to the lowest depths of the penal system.

His memories since departing the train were mostly a blur. First, he was carried off and placed in the back of a police car for what felt like a very long drive. Next, he was brought to this station for processing. He was booked, photographed, and informed of his charges. Since then, he had been confined in this inhospitable room, struggling in silence as the police waited for him to confess to a crime that he did not commit.

At long last, the door slowly creaked open, and an authoritative looking officer walked through, flanked by two other officers who remained near the entrance to guard the door. He was a middle-aged man with the worn and weathered face of somebody who had been around the block a few times. His nametag identified him as Inspector Cormier, and the expression in his eyes seemed to suggest that he was getting too old for all this.

As a sign of good faith, Cormier walked behind Tommy and removed his handcuffs. Tommy stretched his arms, finally feeling relieved from the hours of stiffness and aches. Cormier walked back around the table and took a seat directly across from him.

"I apologize for the accommodations. It is one of our longstanding procedures, albeit not a very pleasant one."

Tommy scoffed. "My stay here was not a satisfactory travel experience, and I would not recommend it to a friend."

Cormier motioned with his hand, and another officer walked into the room, bringing in a tray with a ham and cheese sandwich and a tall glass of water and then setting it down on the table.

"You have not eaten in quite some time. I assume you must be hungry."

Tommy didn't need a detective to tell him that. He quickly consumed the sandwich and gulped down the glass of water.

"Now, is there anything else we can provide for you?"

Tommy felt indignant. "I don't know…maybe,

my freedom? Or a plane ticket out of here?"

Cormier ignored the remark. "This has been a trying ordeal for you, I am sure. Trust me, we do not want you to be here in this room any more than you do. We simply need one thing from you; your confession of your guilt for the murder of Harry Thompson."

The nature of his predicament put Tommy in a difficult position. He knew that the French were a trusted if not an erstwhile ally in the grand geopolitical game, but he also knew that the secrets of the world that Harry and Marlene had introduced him to needed to be closely guarded. In fact, Harry had specifically warned him not to bring any of this business to the police. Therefore, providing them with the full truth was out of the question. Tommy was just going to have to proclaim his innocence and hope that the legal system would function fairly and the evidence would exonerate him.

He leaned forward and looked the detective in the eyes. "I was raised to never tell a lie. I am not going to confess to that crime because I did not do it."

Cormier produced sheets of paper with various police reports. "You have been caught red-handed resisting arrest, fleeing the scene of a crime, assaulting police officers, assaulting diplomatic officials, creating public disturbances, traveling with false documents…and that is only the beginning. Please, I am on your side. I want to make things easier for you, but you have to work with me."

Tommy remained defiant. "I did what I had to do to get away from your Keystone Cops, and you would have done the same thing in my shoes. But as for the murder, I did not do it."

Cormier looked very disappointed. "I see, very well then." He stood up to leave. "Remember, this could have been a whole lot easier."

Cormier closed the door behind him, leaving the room in an eerie silence. Tommy relaxed, alone in his thoughts once more. He was just beginning to nod off when the door flew open, crashing loudly as it slammed against the wall. The familiar face of Inspector Phaneuf appeared, dramatically marching into the room, and pausing to glare menacingly at Tommy between each step. He approached Tommy and dramatically leaned over the table.

"Would you like a cigarette?"

"Yes please."

Phaneuf lit a cigarette, slowly inhaled as much as he could and then leaned closer and blew the smoke in Tommy's face.

"I bet you would."

Tommy was more amused than offended, mostly unable to take the little man seriously.

"There are many in this world who mock me, who underestimate me because of my size. But, you see, I am like a mongoose. The mongoose is quiet and underappreciated, but the mongoose can also kill the viper. You, Monsieur Malloy, are the viper. You came to our city and created a menace, leaving a wake of death and destruction in your path. But now, the game is up, for the mongoose has caught up to the snake, and the reign of the viper is over. Now, I am only going to ask this once; why did you kill Monsieur Thompson?"

"I didn't," Tommy responded nonchalantly.

Phaneuf pounded his fist on the table. "Do not

lie to me! Do you take me for a fool?"

Unable to help himself, Tommy started to laugh. It was just a little bit at first, but it quickly became uncontrollable.

"Why are you laughing? Is this all a joke to you?"

"I can't believe you guys are actually doing the classic good cop/bad cop routine. Do you have any idea how trite and clichéd it's become? I expected better from you, Phaneuf."

Phaneuf struggled for words. He was greatly taken aback because this obviously wasn't the reaction he was expecting.

"Oh, but don't worry, that mongoose monologue was pretty good. I'll give you that one."

Desperate to regain control of the situation, Phaneuf charged forward and slapped Tommy in the face. Using one of his slapstick techniques, Tommy greatly exaggerated the effects of the slap, diving out of his seat and sprawling on the floor.

"Now what did you have to go and do that for?" he asked as he dusted himself off.

"You must learn to show me the proper respect," Phaneuf answered haughtily.

Tommy leaned back in his chair and took a deep breath, deciding that maybe he should humor him just a little bit, but only as long as he could stand it.

"So, let us go back to the night of the crime. You had a big performance, the biggest of your career. Everything is going well, until Harry Thompson interrupted it. You were angry that he ruined your big moment. It gave you a motive for revenge…"

"Oh, there's more to it than that," Tommy interrupted.

Phaneuf raised an eyebrow. "Yes?"

"We had an ongoing rivalry. Well, you see, there was a woman involved. We were rivals in love."

Phaneuf's eyes seemed to light up, anticipating the type of salacious tale that provided the lifeblood of the Paris salons.

"She was an older woman, probably old enough to be our mother, in fact, she might have even had a son around my age, but I digress. You see, Harry took this woman to the opera, and he thought they really had something going on. But then I took her out to a nice dinner and an evening stroll by the river, and she told me she preferred my company to his. So naturally, things came to blows between us."

"And what was this woman's name?"

"She was none other than the infamous Madame Phaneuf, otherwise known as your mother."

The Inspector's face turned red with anger as he balled his fists and tried to restrain himself from hitting Tommy again. "How dare you! You think this whole thing is some joke? You think we are paid to laugh at you like your audiences? Let us see how much you laugh when you spend the rest of your life in prison!"

As he began to charge forward, the door opened once more and a crowd of officers poured into the room, grabbing hold of the angry inspector and pulling him out through the door. Inspector Cormier approached Tommy to clarify the situation.

"I apologize for the escalations. We have just received a message from our Commissioner who received a message from the Foreign Ministry who received a message from…other parts of our government. You are to be released from police custody with all charges dropped. A diplomatic representative from NATO has been sent to pick you up."

It was a mouthful for the veteran cop, who was not interested in understanding the political machinations that occurred far above his paygrade. None of it made sense to Tommy either, but he was happy to go along with it. With no further ado, Cormier led Tommy out of the interrogation room and through the outside hallway to a waiting area.

"Bye Phaneuf!" Tommy couldn't resist shouting as they departed.

"I apologize again for any inconvenience you have suffered here," Cormier said when they reached the waiting room. "This gentleman here is to be your official escort."

The man facing Tommy was impeccably dressed in a navy blue Saville Row suit, a crisp white shirt with gold cufflinks, and the red and blue striped regimental tie of the Welsh Guards. He was a tall and fit man with dark hair, brown eyes, and a way of carrying himself that seemed to project supreme confidence bordering on arrogance. In many ways, he reminded Tommy of Cary Grant, who he occasionally used to run into in Hollywood circles.

"Major Richard Boothwyn, Her Majesty's Foreign Service," the man said as he offered a handshake.

Tommy shook his hand and found his grip sufficiently firm. "Tommy Malloy, runaway comedian."

Richard offered a cigarette, which Tommy gladly accepted.

"So you're the comedian who had that big show

the other night?"

"Yes, that was me. "

Richard smirked mischievously. "I heard you absolutely *killed* it."

Tommy could only laugh at that. He was pretty certain he was going to like this guy.

CHAPTER TWENTY

Tommy slept through most of the car ride to the British Embassy. It was already dark outside, giving him an idea of just how long he had been at the police station. When they arrived, Richard woke him up and led him inside. Richard flashed his identification and the guards at the gate waved them through. First, they took Tommy to a room usually used for visa screenings where he signed a few forms that he didn't care enough about to read. Then he was taken to the diplomats' residence, where he was given fresh clothes, a chance to shower, and an obligatory cup of tea. When the in-processing was finished, Richard brought Tommy across the street and down a little ways to a luxurious official residence that would have surely cost a fortune on the open market.

"This is where the real fun begins," Richard said as they walked through the marble foyer and up a spiral staircase. A massive chandelier hung from the ceiling, and the walls were lined with pastoral portraits of the English countryside. They walked through the hallway, past a medieval set of armor, and finally through a leather-padded door and into an ornate study.

Richard made the introductions as an older man rose to greet them. "Mr. Thomas Malloy, my boss, Colonel Sir Alastair Thorncliffe."

Thorncliffe shook Tommy's hand and motioned for Tommy and Richard to take the two seats facing his desk as he sat back down behind it. Immediately behind the desk was a large portrait of the young and recently crowned Queen Elizabeth II. It was flanked on either side by massive shelves full of leather bound books. The books included many classics of both fictional literature and nonfictional works of history and science, and were held in place by miniature busts of Lord Nelson and the Duke of Wellington. A liquor cart sat adjacent to Thorncliffe's desk, with a brown tinted globe sitting on top of it. The remaining walls were filled with paintings of various British battles from Rorke's Drift to Waterloo, as well as mementos of Thorncliffe's own illustrious military and diplomatic career.

"I apologize it took us this long to find you," he said to Tommy, his tone reminiscent of a wise and aging schoolmaster. "You must have many questions, and I am happy to answer as much as I reasonably can. But first, you must allow me to express my deepest gratitude for the sacrifices you have endured. At great personal risk, you have done a great service to your country as well as mine in our common struggle."

The words meant a lot to Tommy. After everything he had been through, it was nice to know that somebody appreciated it, and that some good may come of it.

"Now, if you please, it would be of great assistance if you could recount for us everything that has happened so far."

Tommy began with the night he met Harry at the show, which was shockingly only forty-eight hours ago even though it felt like a another lifetime. He retold the chain of events that had brought him to the police station, pausing frequently along the way as they interrupted him to ask questions.

When Tommy's tale was finished, Richard seemed stunned. "So you're telling me, you came face to face with Viktor Bazarov and walked away from it? How did you ever manage that?"

Tommy shrugged. "He's a tough bastard alright, but he's also pretty stupid."

Sir Alastair had a slight chuckle. "Thank you, that was very informative. I suppose now you would like some explanations." He picked up a black and white photograph from his desk and showed it to Tommy. It depicted Alastair in Berlin at the end of the war, shaking hands with a man in a Soviet General's uniform. The other man wore a patch over his eye, and his expression looked fearsome and grim.

"This is the man who has been orchestrating everything, General Igor Kharlamov. He is a powerful man; devious, cunning, and dare I say brilliant. Imagine Professor Moriarty with the might of the Soviet Union behind him." Alastair paused for a moment as he lit his pipe. "He and I go back quite a ways. In 1919, I was running an undercover operation in St. Petersburg. They call it Leningrad now, but it will always be St. Petersburg to me. Anyhow, Kharlamov sniffed it out and I barely escaped with my life. Aside from a brief interlude of cooperation during the second war, we have been plotting against each other in the shadows ever since."

He took a long draw from the pipe, blowing rings of smoke above his head as if he were a mythical wizard. "That brings us to the present day. Are you familiar with the nation of Montravia?"

Tommy nodded. "That's somewhere near Germany or Austria, right?"

"Yes, close enough. As you may have heard, we are close to signing a treaty that will restore Montravia's sovereignty as a neutral country under the leadership of their exiled monarchy. Publicly, the NATO countries and the Soviet bloc have both expressed support for this agreement. But like all things in this dangerous game of ours, both sides are covertly pursuing their own agendas. We have learned that the KGB is planning something called Operation Arctic Fox, which is what Harry's note was referring to, but we do not yet know the full details of what that entails."

"So is this where Operation Corner Kick comes in?" Tommy asked.

Alastair and Richard glanced at each other, uncertain of just how much they should reveal. Then Alastair spoke, carefully measuring his words.

"Operation Corner Kick is a covert action by the American and British governments to supply...certain technologies to the government of Montravia with the understanding that they will be used to gather information from the Soviet bloc."

Tommy absorbed this new information. It was a lot to take in, and he could hardly believe that he was here in the middle of it all.

"So where do I fit in with all this? What's next for me? Can I do anything else to help?"

Alastair shook his head. "You have already achieved far more than I could have possibly asked of you. Your part in this game has reached its conclusion."

Tommy understood, but he felt let down all the same. He had just experienced the adrenaline rush of a lifetime. While he was relieved to finally be in relative safety, it was a bit of a shock for it to be over just like that.

"So do I just leave then? Now that I'm in the clear with the cops, can I go back to doing my show?"

"I am afraid not," Alastair said. "The Soviets obviously believe you are working with us, and well, a lot of things are going to happen in Paris over the next few days. It is in your best interest that you leave the country until this all blows over. We will provide your transportation and accommodations, of course."

Richard spoke up next. "There is one further complication. Your experience on the train demonstrated that there is a mole that was aware of Marlene's travel arrangements. As such, I have asked her to book your arrangements once more. She has narrowed down a list of potential suspects and will leak a different version of the plan to each suspect. If the Russians set an ambush on one of the routes, hopefully not the one we take, then we will know who the leak is."

Tommy smiled. "Oh great, I was starting to get worried that I might be out of danger now."

With the important business out of the way,

Alastair stood up and reached for his liquor cart. "And now, gentlemen, will you join me for a drink?"

The drinks flowed freely as Alastair regaled the others with his war stories. From his days as a young intelligence officer in the First World War to a veteran spymaster in the Second, Alastair's adventures were the stuff of legends.

As the night wound down, Richard showed Tommy to the guest bedroom where he would be staying for the night. It was a much fancier room than he was accustomed to, with oriental carpets, a canopy covering the four post bed, and decorative wallpaper. In Tommy's ideal world, he could simply stay and move in here.

"There is a car park out back. Meet me there at 0700, we will depart promptly," Richard informed him. "Feel free to use the intercom system if you need anything. You know where to reach me. Good night, Mr. Malloy."

Tommy was impressed. He knew it was a classy place if they had an intercom system. "Goodnight, Dick. Can I call you Dick?"

"I prefer Richard."

*****

Only a few blocks away in an upscale bar, Natalia Petrova sat alone at a table for two, already well into her third vodka martini of the night. It had been a hectic day marked by an intense flurry of urgent messages. First, her contacts in the police force informed her that Tommy Malloy had been taken into custody. Then, there was the shocking twist that he was being released. And now, one of her most reliable agents had just passed along a travel itinerary.

Malloy had slipped through their fingers so many times, but now it appeared there would be one last chance to reel him in and finally get to the bottom of whatever Sir Alastair was plotting.

She was deep inside her own thoughts when a foolishly bold local lothario slid into the chair across from her.

"What is a beautiful woman like you doing all alone on a night like this? Can I buy you a drink?"

Natalia looked up at him with an icy glare. "If you were asking for my permission, the proper expression would be, 'May I,' but since you appear to be asking me to assess your ability to perform the task, then I can assure you that you are utterly incapable."

The Frenchman slinked away in embarrassment. In addition to her usual intensity, Natalia was also known to become something of a grammar Nazi whenever she drank, or a grammar Communist as she would prefer.

She was nearly finished the martini when Viktor Bazarov arrived and took his seat. Knowing she would be disappointed in his progress, he sputtered and spun in an attempt to offer explanations and apologies. Natalia cut him off with simply her eyes. Her glares could shoot daggers under normal conditions, but drunk Natalia took it to a whole new level.

"Viktor Ivanovich, you had one job."

He hung his head in shame, offering no retort.

"Did you at least find out anything we can use?"

He handed her a folder he had taken from Tommy. "The address and key of a CIA safe house in Amsterdam."

She tucked it away; it may prove useful someday, but it had no relevance to their current mission. She then produced a folder of her own. "Did you wonder at all how I was able to discover Malloy's plans for the train?"

Viktor shook his head. His job was to take action on intelligence, not to question where it came from or how it was provided.

Natalia explained, "There is a very valuable source I have been cultivating and I asked him to pay special attention to a particular area of his employment. And he uncovered some unusual travel arrangements made by someone in his proximity. I played the hunch and it was correct." She showed Viktor a grainy black and white photograph. "Your man indicated that Malloy fled the jazz club with a woman. Surveillance photos also indicate that Malloy was accompanied to the train station by a woman. Does she look familiar to you at all?"

Viktor strained his eyes looking at the picture, but was unable to make anything of it. Natalia showed him a second picture, this one an official formal portrait. "Now do you see it?"

Now, Viktor finally made the connection and realized that they had stumbled upon a major intelligence coup.

Natalia handed him the folder. "This discovery has major implications that we will need to address. But first, we have a more urgent mission. That same source has provided me with further travel plans to move Malloy tomorrow. We must move quickly to intercept him before he escapes from our grasp."

They then set to work drawing up their new plan. After setbacks in some areas and breakthroughs in others, the game was afoot once more.

CHAPTER TWENTY-ONE

Tommy awoke far earlier than he wanted to, once again feeling like he was back in the army, only with far nicer accommodations. However, his early rise became well worth it when he walked down to the kitchen. In the ultimate meeting of the best of both worlds, he was served a full English breakfast with the added treats of French croissants, cheeses and coffee. After breakfast, he walked down to the car park comfortably ahead of schedule. Richard was waiting for him, wearing a leather jacket, and leaning against the door of a silver Porsche 356 Speedster convertible.

"I'm surprised you're on time, I thought you Yanks always liked to arrive late," he said dryly.

It was a joke that Tommy had heard far too many times. "You Limeys are always going on about that. But you wouldn't have won the war without us and you know it."

Richard unlocked and opened the doors. "Well we fought it for three bloody years before you lot showed up."

After they took their seats, Richard handed Tommy a nine millimeter Beretta and an extra clip of ammunition. "Just in case you need it."

Tommy hadn't handled a gun since the war other than movie props, but he hoped it was one of those things like riding a bicycle. He double checked to make sure the safety was on, and then let it rest on his lap.

Richard observed his actions carefully. "Were you ever in the service?"

"82nd Airborne," Tommy said proudly. "Combat jumps in Normandy and Market-Garden."

Richard nodded in approval. "I was commissioned in the Welsh Guards. I evacuated at Dunkirk, and then I was seconded to the Special Air Service in North Africa, and all over Europe with Special Operations Executive."

No further words were needed to know that they shared the common bond of warriors. Richard put the car and gear and pulled away. As they drove on, the crowded busy streets of the city gave way to the rolling green hills of the countryside. They picked up speed as they merged onto the A1, the brand new motorway connecting Paris to the northern city of Lille. The sun was out, and the crisp autumn wind was in their face. For a moment, it was easy to forget the deadly web of espionage that had enveloped them, and just feel like two regular men enjoying the freedom of the open road.

"So where are we going anyway?" Tommy finally asked.

"We're driving north to Calais and taking a ferry across the Channel to England."

There were certainly worse places they could be going. Tommy had greatly appreciated the hospitality of the English people during the war, and it would be nice to go back and visit the small town concert halls where he gave his first performances.

As the lands around them grew increasingly rural, Tommy's eyes were drawn towards a small propeller-driven plane, flying low over the green fields. He knew he was probably imagining things, but he couldn't help but feel like whoever was on the plane might be watching them. He squirmed uncomfortably in his seat.

"Hey Richard, did you notice that plane over there?"

Richard kept his eyes on the road, seemingly unconcerned. "Yes, what about it?"

"What if it's part of the trap? What if they're up there scouting us? And what if they dive down and make a strafing run?"

Richard did not seem bothered. "First of all, it is extremely difficult to hit a moving target from a moving aircraft, so it wouldn't be a very good plan. Furthermore, imagine you are a KGB operative undercover in enemy territory. You have a vested interest in remaining as inconspicuous as possible. Flying an aircraft and using it to attack people is one of the most conspicuous things you could possibly do. If they were aware of our plans and wanted to kill us, they would simply set up a road block, or wait for us at the docks, or throw you overboard on the ferry. Do you really think they would pursue a far less reliable method simply because it would be more dramatic and frightening?"

Tommy sighed. "Alright, I guess I'm just being

paranoid." A one-in-five chance of walking into a deadly ambush tended to have that effect on people.

As the miles wore on, the conversation returned to small talk about the scenery, reminiscing about the war, and discovering the great differences between growing up in a blue collar South Philadelphia neighborhood and a Welsh country estate.

About halfway through the journey, they approached the first of several toll booths, the inconvenient but necessary downside of fast highway traveling. Richard applied the brakes and coasted to a stop. He fumbled around in his pockets as they waited behind the one car in front of them.

"Do you have exact change?"

Tommy looked through his wallet. "No, I only have hundred franc notes."

Richard cursed under his breath as he took a hundred franc note of his own in his hand. They rolled up to the window and he handed it to the toll collector. If the collector was annoyed by the inconvenience, he didn't show it. He simply accepted the note, and turned towards the register to make the proper change. Richard rapped his fingers against the steering wheel, starting to grow impatient as the collector took much longer than expected.

While Tommy looked around in boredom, he noticed that a black Alfa Romeo with three men inside seemed to be stopped in the shoulder just after the tolls. "What do you think happened to those guys?" He wondered out loud. "I guess they didn't have enough money."

Richard looked over at the car and back at the booth, growing increasingly uncomfortable the longer they had to remain exposed in one place.

After fruitlessly looking through the register, the collector told them, "I'm sorry, we do not have the proper change here. I'm going to have to call the office to have them bring some over."

Before Richard could say, "Don't bother," the collector closed the window, picked up a radio receiver, and started talking. Seemingly in response, the Alfa Romeo immediately sprung into motion, sliding in front of them as if to impede their escape. Meanwhile, the rear view mirror revealed a blue Peugeot rapidly closing in on them from behind. Richard and Tommy shared a quick glance as they reached for their pistols; they had a very bad feeling about this.

Richard floored the gas pedal and the Porsche shot forward, slamming into the broad side of the Alfa. The impact was jolting as the two cars became entangled in a twisting mess of metal. Richard and Tommy braced themselves as much as they could, and immediately after impact they rolled out of their respective doors, both turning over several times before popping up on one knee with guns drawn.

The three men in the Alfa had much less warning of the crash. After they figured out what hit them, they stumbled out of the car with rifles slung over their shoulders. They were just beginning to turn around and take aim when Richard methodically dropped them with three perfectly placed shots.

"Watch behind you!" Tommy called out.

The Peugeot was closing in on them, arriving a brief moment too late in its attempt to seal off the ambush. As it drew closer, they could see that Viktor Bazarov was behind the wheel and there was another man in the passenger seat and two more in the back.

Richard and Tommy faced the car, held their ground, and unleashed a hail of bullets.

With his plan already blown, Viktor wisely decided to cut his losses. He whipped the car around and sped off, traveling the opposite direction of traffic until he cut across to the other side of the highway. Other cars spun and skidded to avoid him, narrowly missing another catastrophic accident. Richard briefly gave chase on foot, but Viktor's car soon pulled out of range. Struggling to keep up, Tommy switched on his safety and leaned forward with his hands on his knees, trying to catch his breath.

"Are you alright?" Richard walked back and asked him.

"I'm fine." Tommy was winded, his ears were ringing, and his ribs were sore from the crash, but he was doing alright all things considered.

"Then cover me, we have one more thing to take care of."

With Tommy trailing on his heels, Richard ran back to the toll booth and flung the door open. The toll collector was sitting curled up on the ground with his hands over his ears, looking rather shocked about the whole thing. Richard grabbed him by the collar, lifted him up and pinned him against the wall.

"Who put you up to this? Who are you working for?" Richard shouted in his face.

The man was on the brink of tears. "I...I don't know...nobody...honest I'm just a toll collector!"

Richard slightly relaxed his grip and lowered his voice. "What did they tell you? How did you know to look for us?"

The man took a few deep breaths to collect himself. "It was the blond man in the blue car...he came and talked to all of us this morning…he told us he was a police detective, he had a badge and everything…he showed us your picture and told us to call it in if you passed through…I didn't know any of this would happen, I swear!"

Deciding that he believed him, Richard let go and walked away. He and Tommy trudged past the smoldering wreckage of the cars, realizing that they were now stranded in the middle of the highway. Without speaking, they walked off to the side of the road, sat down on a bank of grass, and lit up a pair of cigarettes.

CHAPTER TWENTY-TWO

Tommy and Richard sat and smoked their cigarettes off to the side of the highway, staring off into the tranquility of the countryside as they contemplated their latest near-death experience. Of the five different travel plans they had made, it appeared that their actual plan was the one that leaked through to the KGB.

"Well next time I go to the racetrack, I'm taking Marlene with me," Richard said. "She sure knows how to pick a winner."

"So do you know who the mole is now?" Tommy asked.

"Yes. I'm afraid it's rather complicated, but you'll see it play out when we get back."

Tommy wanted to know more, but he knew he shouldn't push it. "So we're going back to Paris now? How are we getting there?"

Richard pondered the question for a while, greatly regretting the destruction of his Porsche, before answering, "We'll hitchhike."

"Are you serious?"

"Do you have a better idea?"

Tommy pondered the question and concluded that he did not, in fact, have a better idea. They waited for a break in the traffic and then scampered across the highway to stand on the southbound side. A firetruck was just arriving to deal with the car crash, and it was only a matter of time before the police showed up and started asking questions. It was in their best interests to depart the scene sooner rather than later.

After a few minutes of standing on the side of the road with their thumbs in the air, a large white truck pulled off the road and stopped alongside them. The driver parked the truck and stepped out to greet them. He was a gregarious man around their age of Corsican extraction with dark hair and a friendly smile.

"You're Tommy Malloy, aren't you? I thought it was you!"

Tommy hesitated, having lost track of which cover identity he was supposed to be traveling under, and weighing the costs and benefits of how to answer the question. However, the truck driver did not wait for his response. He stepped forward and handed Tommy a copy of the morning paper.

"I am a big fan of your work! Your stand-up act is the best I've ever seen, and your movie work is greatly underappreciated."

Now Tommy was sold. That was more than enough to convince him that he liked and trusted this man.

"I couldn't believe what they were saying about you in the papers. Lies and slander, all of it!" the driver said with all the outrage he could muster. "I was so relieved to see that the truth has finally come out."

Tommy looked down at the paper, and found that buried on Page 9 was a brief article with the headline, "Malloy Cleared of All Charges." After how prominently they had featured his previous troubles, he was disappointed but not surprised at how little coverage the correction received.

"Oh, how could I forget, my name is Paulo Franzese. I believe we have a mutual friend in Le Capitaine."

Tommy could not believe his luck. Having connections to organized crime had always been incredibly helpful to his entertainment career, but now it was becoming a literal lifesaver. He reached out and shook Paulo's hand.

"Well, you know who I am, and this is my friend and colleague, Major Richard Boothwyn."

Paulo shook Richard's hand vigorously. "Any friend of Tommy Malloy is a friend of mine."

With no further ado, they piled into the truck. Tommy lost a coin flip with Richard and was forced to take the middle seat.

"So where do you need to go to?" Paulo asked as he merged back onto the highway.

"Back to Paris," said Richard, not wanting to give any more details than that.

"Oh, very good! I am stopping in Paris myself. There are packages of food in the back that I need to deliver to a restaurant."

Richard and Tommy both suspected that "food" actually meant drugs, but they weren't going to say anything about it.

"If we're going to be on the road this long, we are going to need some music," Paulo said. However, instead of turning on the radio, he began to sing, enthusiastically belting out a series of bawdy ballads in French, Italian, and Corsican. When he asked the others to contribute, Tommy chimed with some selections from the *Accountants of Amsterdam* soundtrack, all of which Paulo seemed to know the lyrics to. All the while, Richard simply stared out the window, longing for the ride to be over.

When they reached a suspicious looking restaurant on the outskirts of Paris, Richard and Tommy thanked Paulo profusely and then went their separate way, neither side wanting to be implicated in whatever the other was going to be doing. Richard recognized where they were, and led the way to the nearest bus stop. They rode a bus to another bus line and then to a Metro station. A train ride and a roundabout walk finally brought them back near the embassy.

They took the back entrance into Sir Alastair's residence, and he did not seem overly surprised to see them again.

"Returned so soon?"

Richard sighed. "It was a rough day at the office."

"Well your timing is rather impeccable," Alastair said. "You should get yourself cleaned up. We are expecting a royal visit momentarily."

Richard nodded in understanding and beckoned for Tommy to follow him into a different room.

"I'm confused," said Tommy. "What did he mean by all that?"

Richard explained, "Prince Hans Friedrich of

Montravia is due to visit Sir Alastair for an intelligence briefing. His steward Rolfe usually accompanies him. Rolfe also happens to be the mole who betrayed us."

Now the webs of intrigue appeared to be more tangled than ever. "But why would the Prince's steward know our travel plans? What does any of this have to do with us?"

"It will all make sense in due time," Richard assured him. "But there is no time to explain right now."

Richard led Tommy into the kitchen, where they pressed themselves against the wall and waited. They strained their ears to listen as Sir Alastair welcomed the Prince and his entourage into his parlor.

"Good afternoon, Your Highness, it is a pleasure to host you, as always," Alastair greeted him.

"Once again, I am grateful for your hospitality, Sir Alastair," the Prince responded.

Alastair took his seat and motioned for the others to sit as well. "Now, we have important business to discuss, but first, I invite you to join me in some lunch. There are some sandwich trays in the kitchen, please allow me to retrieve them."

The Prince spoke up, "Rolfe, would you be so kind as to retrieve the sandwich trays for Sir Alastair? You know where the kitchen is, right?"

"Yes, of course," Rolfe responded as he walked out of the room and turned the corner.

He made it a few steps into the kitchen before Richard jumped out and revealed himself, jamming a gun barrel into his ribcage. "No further, Rolfe! Keep your hands above your head!"

Rolfe froze in his tracks, looking as if he might

defecate in his pants at any moment. Richard held him in place at gunpoint while Tommy walked behind him and tied his hands behind his back. The only card remaining to Rolfe was to try to feign ignorance and outrage.

"What is the meaning of this? You are detaining the steward of a sovereign prince! And on what charge?"

Richard rolled his eyes. "Please, spare me. We were ambushed by the KGB on the road to Calais this morning. You were the only one who knew of our plans. Explain to me, how did the KGB find out?"

Rolfe hung his head, unable to come up with a suitable retort on the spot.

"So why did you do it?" Richard asked. "Did they pay you?"

"Do you still think everything we do is for money or ambition? It's 1954! Everything I did was to help bring about the revolution."

"Ahh, so you're a true believer. You read some Karl Marx at university and realized that you're one of the enlightened ones who know how everything really works, and that it's up to you to fix things for the rest of us. I knew far too many of your type at Oxford."

Rolfe squirmed uncomfortably. "I didn't think anybody would get hurt. I just wanted to make a difference, help bring about change."

Richard took a deep breath looked at him sternly. "Well, you probably should have given it some more thought. You've put a lot of lives in danger and you're probably going to spend the rest of your life behind bars. Or, of course, you could always walk free. Prisoner exchanges are a frequent occurrence in this business."

Rolfe slumped downwards, hanging his head in defeat. "What do I have to do?"

"Contact your KGB handler immediately and set up an emergency meeting. We'll take over from there."

Reluctantly, Rolfe agreed to go along with it. At least one strand of the puzzle was beginning to unravel.

CHAPTER TWENTY-THREE

Bon Appetit was the type of café that people usually envisioned when they conjured images of Paris. It was located on a quaint cobblestoned street in the Sixth arrondissement. A yellow awning hung over the entrance with the name of the restaurant written in fancy script, and potted flowers adorned the window sills. Most of the patrons sat outside at small round tables with individual umbrellas providing shade. But perhaps the best feature of the café was the cornucopia of smells; the freshly baked baguettes, the strongly roasted coffee, and the gourmet chocolates and pastries of the dessert menu.

It was the perfect place for artists and writers to find their inspirations, for lovers to get lost in romantic bliss as they stared into each other's eyes, or in this case, for KGB officers to conduct meetings with excitable young agents. Natalia waited patiently at her outdoor table, having received an urgent request from Rolfe to meet her here. It was an annoyance, to be sure, but Rolfe's information had proved invaluable thus far, so any reassurance or support he may need was ultimately worth the trouble.

*****

Across the street, Richard and Tommy stood vigil inside a bookstore, pretending to browse the selection while at least one of them maintained their gaze looking out the window towards the café.

"*Chronicles of the Canongate* by Sir Walter Scott," Richard said out loud as he perused a particular shelf. "I read a lot of this at Oxford. It provides some very unique insights into our rebellious neighbors north of Hadrian's Wall, as well as wider insights on the difficulties of counterinsurgency campaigns."

Tommy was instantly bored by the thought of Richard's academic analysis, but the book did bring up some more basic questions for him. "Now, how come I'm always seeing books and movies about Scotland, but almost never about Wales?"

This was a frequent sore point for Richard. "Because Wales is the most underrated and underappreciated of the Home Countries. It's always been that way, and it always will be."

"Here's *The Hunchback of Notre Dame* by Victor Hugo," Tommy called out as he turned his eyes back to the shelf. "You know, when I was younger I tried to read this because I thought it was going to be about football. I have never been more disappointed in my life."

Richard patted him on the back with a chuckle. "You were a very confused child. In many ways you still are. Maybe when you grow up, you can learn to play rugby."

Tommy shook his head. "You limeys and your rugby. Well at least it's better than cricket."

"Cricket is a complicated game for the thinking man. I wouldn't expect the likes of you to have the patience for it."

"I would watch cricket if they made the following changes: they wore gloves, they had four bases, they played nine innings..."

Richard cut off Tommy's ramblings and pulled him towards the window. "I found what we're looking for. Look for the blonde woman seated alone at the second table from the right."

Tommy looked in the direction that Richard told him, and was pleasantly surprised with what he saw; a beautiful blonde woman with her hair pulled back in a tight bun, sitting at a table as if she was waiting for somebody. She was wearing a light blue skirt and blazer with a pink scarf, flying saucer hat, and oversized tortoise-shell sunglasses.

"You have a really good eye for this, Dick. That is one fine fräulein. She looks like Grace Kelly, but with a little bit of an exotic foreign twist," Tommy said.

Richard sighed. "That is all quite true, she is rather beautiful, but that's not why I was pointing her out. What you need to know now is that the woman we are looking it is Natalia Petrova, cultural attaché at the Soviet Embassy. Sir Alastair once bet me ten quid that she was actually KGB, and now it appears I am going to have to pay up."

"So she's the one that the little punk Rolfe was giving information to?" Tommy asked.

"Yes," Richard confirmed. "And she thinks she's going to meet with Rolfe now, but this is where we step in and surprise her. Come, follow me."

Richard led the way as they exited the bookstore, looked both ways, and crossed the street. They walked right past the café's hostess and directly to Natalia's table. Richard boldly sat down in the seat she had been holding for Rolfe, while Tommy pulled up an extra chair and joined them at the table. Natalia sat and stared at them in stunned silence for several seconds before she finally leaned forward and acknowledged their presence.

"I see this meeting is going to be quite different from what I anticipated. And what do we have here? Tommy Malloy, the Clown Prince of Paris, and Richard Boothwyn, the Welsh Wanker. I was not expecting to see either of you, but I am pleased you could join me nonetheless."

"I prefer the Cambrian Crusader," Richard said, knowing full well that attempts to give oneself a nickname were almost always futile.

The pleasantries out of the way, Natalia stared him down coolly. "Before you try anything rash or ill considered, I remind you that I am protected by diplomatic immunity."

"Oh, we know that all too well," Richard responded. "Unfortunately, our friend Harry Thompson did not enjoy the same protections."

"On behalf of the Soviet Union I would like to express my deepest condolences for Harry Thompson's death. We would like to provide any assistance you may require in apprehending the true killer."

Richard rolled his eyes. "Don't patronize me, Natalia. Spare your false niceties for the diplomats. We have both been at this game long enough to know what really happened."

Before she could respond the waiter arrived at the table. "Gentlemen, Mademoiselle, would you like to order anything to drink?"

Richard looked up at him. "Let's have a bottle of the Cabernet Sauvignon and three glasses."

The waiter wrote it down. "Very well, would you like to open a separate tab?"

Richard shook his head. "No, put it on hers."

Natalia stared blankly ahead as the waiter walked away, unimpressed with Richard's gamesmanship. "Alright, let's get on with it. What exactly have the two of you come here to discuss?"

"A truce, of sorts," Richard responded. "The current situation between our organizations in this city has spiraled out of control. I believe it is in our mutual best interests to de-escalate things before anybody else gets killed."

Natalia wholeheartedly agreed, but she kept her true feelings concealed because the game was never that simple. "What terms are you proposing? And why is it in the best interests of the Soviet Union to accept such terms?"

"Well, first of all, you are probably wondering what happened to your friend Agent Snowman. I can assure you, albeit somewhat regrettably, that he is unharmed and that his release can be arranged."

Although she didn't show it, Natalia was relieved to hear this. For all his flaws, Rolfe had taken great risks on behalf of the Motherland, and was every bit the idealist that she had once been. She motioned for Richard to go on.

"And unless you have taken some drastic actions I am not aware of, I believe you are holding one of ours as well."

"Boris Bryzgalov," she confirmed. "He almost got away with it."

The waiter then returned with a bottle of wine and three glasses in hand. He set down the glasses, uncorked the bottle, and poured a glass for each of them.

"Would you care to place an order of food?" he asked.

Richard took a long cold stare at Natalia, then at the waiter, then back to Natalia. "No, thank you."

Natalia returned an equally icy glare before glancing up at the waiter. "No, thank you"

"Really, guys?" Tommy said incredulously. "I'll have the croque-monsieur," he told the waiter with a smile.

Natalia and Richard were both caught off guard by Tommy's sudden intervention, but they turned back to business as soon as the waiter walked away.

"I believe a prisoner exchange may be arranged," Natalia said.

Richard leaned back and rapped his fingers along the table. "Good, but we want more. The targeting of our personnel needs to cease. You must call off your pursuit of Mr. Malloy and allow him to have safe passage out of the country. Your people will be protected by this agreement as well, provided that Viktor Bazarov departs the country immediately."

"And why would we agree to this?"

Richard leaned forward and spoke in a hushed tone. "Because we know about Operation Arctic Fox."

Natalia managed to maintain a stoic expression, but her insides were beginning to panic. "You may have heard a code name somewhere or intercepted some communique, but you have no idea what it means or who is involved."

The waiter arrived again, bringing Tommy's order. The croque-monsieur was a fried sandwich on brioche bread with ham and melted gruyere cheese. It came with a side of frites, and Tommy quickly devoured it because it was absolutely delicious.

"Wow, you must have been very hungry," Natalia observed.

"I'm gobbling up this food like the Soviet Union gobbles up Eastern European countries," Tommy quipped.

Richard let out a slight chuckle while Natalia just stared blankly.

Tommy was just getting started. "I mean, you guys always seem to be *Hungary* for new territories. I'm surprised you haven't taken over Turkey yet."

After that, Natalia began to show the faintest hints of a smile. She stood up and left a pile of cash on the table. "I accept your terms. Please maintain open channels of communication so that we may arrange the details of the prisoner exchange."

Richard turned to Tommy as she walked away. "Well, that should buy us some more time at least."

Tommy took it all in; slowly, but surely, he was starting to learn this game. "Alright, so I'm protected enough now that I can finally just leave without getting ambushed. And it looks like things are going to calm down for everybody else. But what about Marlene? What is she up to now? Where does she come into all this?"

Richard's looked around to make sure nobody else was within earshot. "Marlene is safe, and they don't know where to find her. If they did, this situation would be a whole lot more complicated."

CHAPTER TWENTY-FOUR

The twilight shadows were just beginning to set in on another Paris evening when Natalia arrived at the arranged meeting point. Boris stood behind her, wearing a hood over his head and flanked by two armed guards from the French communist contingent. The place of their rendezvous was Pont de Bir-Hakeim, a bridge over the River Seine that connected the 16th and 17th arrondissements. It was a uniquely designed bridge, with a lower level for pedestrians and drivers, and a viaduct above that supported an elevated subway line. Underneath the shadows of the train tracks, Natalia and her retinue stood and waited.

On the other side of the bridge, the silhouettes appeared of Richard Boothwyn and an entourage of his own, leading a hooded figure that was presumably Rolfe Schrodinger. The two groups walked towards each other, casting long shadows in the dull glow of the street lamps. When they were only twenty meters apart, the two groups stopped and stood, facing each other.

"Alright, that's enough, no further," Richard called out.

Natalia called out the next step, "Verify the hostages."

She reached over to pull the hood off of Boris's head. After spending the past couple days in Viktor's custody, he certainly looked worse for the wear. There were bags underneath his bloodshot eyes, thick stubble covered his face, and his hair was greasy and unkempt. She didn't know the details of what he had endured, but she knew that he would have been put through the wringer until Viktor could determine just how much information he had compromised. Across from them, Richard removed the hood from Rolfe, who looked afraid and out of his element, but otherwise unharmed.

"Why did you do it?" Natalia whispered in Boris's ear. "Why did you betray the Motherland?"

He paused for a moment, struggling to find the right words, before simply answering, "You wouldn't understand, Natalia. But maybe someday you will."

Richard's voice bellowed out, "On the count of three, walk forward at a steady, controlled pace. Do not panic, and do not run. Ready…3…2…1…walk!"

Boris and Rolfe walked forward at his command, awkwardly passing each other in the middle of the bridge, and coming to a stop when they reached the opposite group. Rolfe looked at Natalia, his eyes full of relief to be nearing the end of a scenario that he felt was well beyond what he had originally signed up for.

"Are you ok?" she asked him quietly.

He nodded, eager to leave the scene. Natalia

turned to look back and locked eyes with Richard, who was standing facing forward with his arms crossed while his associates tended to Boris. There were deep thoughts expressed in the silence of their gaze. They were two silent warriors, aged well beyond their years by the loss, deceit, and betrayal of their covert war in the shadows. Richard gave a slight nod before he turned to walk away and Natalia returned it. They were relieved to be at peace, even if they both knew that peace could only be brief and transient.

Natalia guided Rolfe into the back seat of a waiting car while she sat in the front passenger seat. She looked out the window as the driver pulled away, watching the evening lights reflect along the river. It was another beautiful night in the world's most beautiful city. The chaotic violence of the past few days had taken its toll on her. She clung to the hope that this new truce could hold, even as she knew that it could not. Against her better judgment and over her objections, dangerous escalations were going to occur that would shake things up more than ever.

*****

The Bourbon Historical Society of Paris was the type of place that was seldom visited, save for undergraduate students on involuntary field trips, graduate students attempting to win the race for the most obscure research topics, the most dedicated of history buffs, and nostalgic senior citizens. It was an organization whose primary mission was preserving the heritage of France's monarchical past, and much of the building was old enough to have been there during the eighteenth century dynasties or even earlier.

The Society's meeting room was a spacious room with a parquet floor. A grand chandelier hung from the ceiling, and the walls were lined with portraits of French monarchs, dating back to medieval times and ending with Louis XVI and Marie Antoinette, the unlucky King and Queen who lost their heads to the guillotine in 1793. The room had once been grand and elegant. To a certain extent, it still was, but the dust and cracks it had accumulated with age were becoming increasingly difficult to hide.

On this particular night, the seldom-visited Society had attracted its largest crowd in years for a conference entitled, "Monarchy in the Twentieth Century: Maintaining Tradition in a Changing World." The Society's conferences usually only attracted the same core group of elderly patrons and a smattering of students. However, this particular conference was filling the room to capacity. Months ago, the Society had invited Princess Sophia of Montravia to be the conference's keynote speaker. Much to their pleasant surprise, she accepted the invitation and was now present in the room.

All eyes were on the Princess as she rose to speak. There were rows of folding chairs lined up to face the podium, which was flanked by the French tricolor flag on one side, and the white and gold fleur-de-lis flag of pre-revolutionary France on the other. She graciously thanked her hosts and the audience in the opening of the remarks before launching into the more substantive portion of the speech.

"Monarchy is one of the world's oldest traditions. It is almost as old as some of you..."

The quip drew even more laughs than she expected, and the rest of the speech went just as well. With impeccable timing and delivery, she seamlessly blended historical analysis, observations on current events, and well-placed comic relief. She concluded with her thoughts on the Montravia Treaty, and her vision of the duties and responsibilities she would soon be assuming. When the speech was finished, she left the stage to thunderous applause.

The speech was followed by a cocktail reception, where Sophia felt obligated to greet and make small talk with as many people as possible. While most of these encounters were plainly forgettable for her, she knew that many of those she was meeting would always remember the time they met a real life princess, and she felt she owed it to them to present her best face and give them personal attention. Through years of practice, she had become quite adept at projecting effortless charm.

It was in large part due to Princess Sophia's efforts that there was requisite public and governmental support in both Western and Eastern Europe for restoring the Montravian monarchy. Her public image as a Paris socialite had been a calculated decision on her part, with her father's tacit approval, to raise her family's profile and thereby raise awareness of her country's status. She acquired a platform of fame through her family name and fashion sense, but used the opportunity to effect real changes. Now, as Montravia stood poised to resume its place in the community of nations, she felt the responsibility of ensuring that the country's small but respected voice would remain influential and steady.

As the reception began to wind down, she

walked out the front entrance, feeling completely exhausted. Events over the past few days had taken her all over the city to deal with a myriad of pressing issues that had sprung up. She wanted to rest and recuperate, but she knew there was still so much left to do. She waited patiently outside the building until the valet pulled up in the black Mercedes that was meant to transport her home.

"Finally," she sighed under her breath, very eager to sit down.

The driver, a young man she did not recognize, stepped out and opened the rear door for her. She thanked him as she stepped inside, leaned back in her seat, and exhaled. The car pulled away, joining the flow of traffic back out on the street. It was only then that the blond man who had been hiding under a set of dark blankets in the adjacent seat revealed himself, brandishing a Makarov pistol. Before she could react, he flung a black hood over her head and pinned her arms behind her back. They drove for an indeterminable amount of time, and when they stopped, she was led inside a building and pushed down onto a chair. There, the blond man closed the door behind them and stood in front of her, as if to negotiate.

"Good evening, Your Highness," he said coolly.

She was stunned, struggling to think of who this man was and what his motives might be. "I don't know what you're trying to achieve here. If you want ransom, then you obviously know that my family has money, but you should also know that we have very powerful friends. Your short term gain will ultimately lead to your downfall."

The man laughed out loud. "Do you take me for

some common criminal? Can you not recognize when you have been outmaneuvered by a fellow professional?" He reached down and pulled the hood off her head so she could finally get a good look at him.

Sophia sighed, now it all made sense. "Viktor Bazarov, only you would be so bold, and so foolish. What quarrel does the Soviet Union have with a harmless, neutral country? Did Natalia put you up to this? Are you creating an international incident for the sake of her petty grudge?"

Viktor leaned forward, a menace in his eyes. "Please, I know what you really are. You thought you were smarter than us. You thought you could get away with it. You thought you could live a double life, publicly proclaiming your neutrality while you covertly work for your true friends. But you should have known better. The KGB is everywhere, and we are always watching."

Sophia objected, "You are committing a grievous violation of international law founded upon baseless accusations. I am a member of a sovereign government on a diplomatic mission…"

Viktor cut her off. "You are a tool for the NATO alliance and a spy!"

He turned and walked away, slamming the door behind him, and leaving Sophia alone in the room. She looked around to try to get her bearings. From what she could gather, they seemed to be in a residential area in what could only be a KGB safe house. The house appeared to be secure and heavily guarded. With no immediate hope of escape, all she could do was keep her wits about her, and hope and trust in her friends.

CHAPTER TWENTY-FIVE

Sir Alastair Thorncliffe leaned over his desk, hastily finishing a croissant and downing his fourth cup of tea of the morning. It was barely breakfast time, but he had already been hard at work for several hours. His office was in crisis mode, and the phone had been ringing off the hook, bringing in reports from field agents, fellow diplomats, eye witnesses, and anybody else with information of any kind. He knew intelligence was a dangerous business and that anybody involved understood the risks they were undertaking, but he still felt personally responsible for anybody under his charge. Once again, in what was quickly becoming the worst week of his long career, he felt as if he had failed.

He looked up as an aide announced the arrival of a visitor. Prince Hans Friedrich walked through the door, traveling incognito and without any staff to accompany him. He looked greatly distressed, and the bags underneath his eyes indicated that he had slept even less than Alastair. It had been hard enough on the Prince to learn that his trusted steward was a traitor, but this recent news was too much to bear.

"I think you know why I'm here," said the Prince as he took a seat. "My daughter did not return home last night."

"I was informed earlier this morning. I cannot begin to comprehend what you must be experiencing, but all I can offer is to do my utmost to help," Alastair said.

The Prince took a deep, sobering breath. "So, what do we know?"

Alastair sorted through the papers on his desk, trying to piece together his notes in a coherent fashion. "We know that last night she gave a speech at an event. She was last seen leaving the premises in a black Mercedes."

"So was it foul play by the driver? Rolfe was bad enough, has my entire staff betrayed me?"

Alastair shook his head. "No, it wasn't the driver. Local police found the driver's body a few blocks away from the premises. The estimated time of death was well before the incident."

"But what about the car, has anybody tracked it down?"

"Witnesses report that a car matching the description was disposed of at a local scrap yard early this morning."

The Prince paused as if his mind was reaching conclusions that he had suspected all along, but wished were untrue. "Do you think she was abducted then?"

Alastair nodded. "Yes, it appears that way."

"Well do they want ransom then? I will pay anything, whatever it takes."

Alastair shook his head. "No, if it was that type of abduction, we would have received a ransom request by now. This appears to be the work of professionals, of a foreign intelligence agency."

The Prince visibly winced. "You mean the KGB? Why would they want to do something like this? We are a neutral country. And I thought the Soviets were supporting the treaty."

Alastair paused, searching for the right words to explain the situation. Before he could find them, the Prince seemed to infer where he was going.

"Do you mean to tell me that she was working for you again? That she was involved in one of your spy games? You told me she got out of that business when the war ended! I trusted you! I went along with all your harebrained schemes! And look where it has gotten me!"

Alastair's voice was somber and there was sadness in his eyes. "Nothing I say right now can make things right. I have failed you as an ally, and I have failed you as a friend. But I swear to you I will do everything in my power to ensure that she is safely returned."

Prince Hans Friedrich turned his back and paced several steps, breathing deeply the whole way as he tried to compose himself. Then he turned back to face Alastair. "So what's my next step? What can I do from here?"

"You present a strong face. Be the best the leader you can be and show the world that Montravia is not to be trifled with."

"And what about the treaty? Is it still going to be signed on schedule?"

"Yes, we are going to proceed as if all things are

normal. The Soviets will deny all involvement, and we don't have enough tangible evidence to accuse them, not publicly at least. So for now, you must carry on with business as usual and let me work in the shadows."

"Very well, but I expect results," said the Prince.

The two men shook hands and then Alastair escorted the Prince downstairs and to the rear exit, where Richard Boothwyn was waiting to hold the door open and show him to his car. The Prince pulled a fedora hat low over his face and hiked up the collar of his overcoat as he departed the building, planning to return to his residence before resuming his official duties. As Richard stepped back inside, Alastair pulled him aside and they ducked into a secluded out cove behind the stairwell.

"We need to talk," Alastair said.

The hushed and serious tone of their conversation contrasted with the scene around the corner from them in the parlor, where Tommy and Boris were relaxing in front of the fireplace. Boris looked like a brand new man after getting a shower, shave, and fresh clothes, and was eager to begin his new life. Their bags were packed, and they were both scheduled to be departing the country later that day. This time, the plan called for them to take a military flight from the NATO base at Orly to an RAF base in England. Tommy was certain that they had finally come up with a plan that would not be interfered with.

As Tommy got acquainted with the Russian defector, he was greatly amused by Boris's quirky and unique sense of humor. As it turned out, Boris himself had always felt out of place amongst the stifling conformity of the Communist bloc, and he had long harbored seemingly unattainable ambitions of performing on the West's stand-up comedy circuits someday. When Tommy learned of this, he was determined to provide him whatever assistance and mentorship he could, just as Louis Poutine had once done for him.

"Now, before you even tell any jokes, the first thing you need to be aware of is your stage presence," Tommy told him. "You need to project confidence; you own that microphone and you own that stage. But at the same time, you should be relaxed. Forget that there's a big crowd out there, and just act like you're sharing jokes with your friends."

"I think I have some American material already. Do you want to hear it?" Boris asked excitedly.

Tommy leaned forward in anticipation. "Alright, let's hear it."

Boris stood up. "So what's the deal with football?" he posed in heavily accented English. "Everything is measured in yards, they should call it yardball."

Tommy smiled politely. "That's a good start, we can work with that." Boris had a long way to go, but Tommy was certain that there would be a significant niche in the U.S. market that Boris's eccentric Russian persona could fill.

Boris excused himself from the room as Richard and Alastair entered, still in the midst of their serious discussion. Tommy's mood instantly deflated as he sensed that something had obviously gone wrong.

"What is it? What happened?" he asked them.

Richard and Alastair looked at each other, as if they were debating how much they should divulge to

Tommy. "The Russians abducted Princess Sophia," Alastair finally said.

Tommy thought back to the night of his opening show, picturing the glamorous brunette in the back row. It felt like ages ago in a different life. "Those bastards! Why would they want to do that?"

Richard paused a moment before answering, "Because she has been working for us. In fact, you already met her. She goes by Marlene in the field."

Tommy thought back on his brief time with Marlene and it all seemed to make sense now; her mysterious origins, her hard to place accent, her wigs and disguises. She must have recognized him when he returned during Louis' roast, and it was her that slipped the secret note in with the donation pile.

"So how did that come about? How does a continental princess end up working for the British government?"

"It goes back to the war," said Alastair. "The Montravian royal family, like many other royals in those days, was living in exile in London. Richard and I were both serving with Special Operations Executive at the time. We in the intelligence community found it useful to pick the brains of these royals, as they often had intimate knowledge of the political happenings on the continent. I established a strong working relationship with Prince Hans Friedrich, and then, one day, his daughter stormed into my office demanding to join our team in the field."

"And you let her join, just like that?"

"My first instinct was to decline her offer. But she was young and energetic, spoke four languages fluently, had training in everything from first aid to equestrian, had powerful connections in every country in Europe, and wouldn't take no for an answer. In other words, she was the perfect operative."

Having seen her skills up close, Tommy had to agree with that assessment. "So what can we do to find her?"

"We're getting to that," said Richard. "But first, let us see how much you have learned. If the KGB had just kidnapped the Princess, where do you think they would keep her?"

Tommy thought hard about it and came up with a guess. "Probably some kind of building around here that they control, but not their embassy because they need deniability. So probably some kind of safe house?"

Richard nodded. "Very good. But do you think they would keep her there very long?"

"No, the longer they keep her there, the greater the chance that somebody might find them. They would probably have to move her, probably to Siberia or something."

"Very good, I see that you have learned quite a lot in these few days. We have learned over the years that the KGB has established a pipeline for transporting people into and out of France. Presumably this system is what they would use to smuggle out somebody they had kidnapped. We have been trying for years to find this pipeline, but we have yet to be successful," Richard said.

"We have a plan for finding this pipeline and possibly intercepting Sophia before they take her out of the country. It involves you, and it's very dangerous," said Alastair. "You are under no obligation to accept this assignment, and I would not think any less of you if you refused."

For Tommy, the question was simple. Princess Sophia had risked her life to help him, and it had possibly contributed to her capture. He felt personally obligated to help, and besides, how many guys could say that they rescued a real life Princess?

"Whatever it is, count me in."

"Alright then," said Richard. "Let's get to work."

CHAPTER TWENTY-SIX

The late hour of night was falling upon Paris, when the respectable citizens were fast asleep and the seedier side of the city came to life. On this particular night, the biggest item on the agenda for those who were up to no good was Le Capitaine's gathering of gamblers. Tommy observed these games by happenstance two nights ago at the Soleil-Royal, but tonight, he was actively seeking them out.

Because the previous games had ended in a police raid, a new venue had been chosen for tonight's round. To reach this game, Tommy had to travel to the 18th arrondissement and find a bar called the General Rochambeau, a name which he greatly appreciated. Tommy knew a fair bit about the American Revolution, having grown up in the city where it all started, and he remembered that Rochambeau was the General who commanded the French army that helped George Washington win his final victory at Yorktown. He saw this as a sign of good luck, and tonight, he was going to need all the luck he could get.

After walking around the block a couple times, Tommy finally spotted the entrance to the bar on a dimly lit street. It was below ground level, and one had to walk down a short staircase to reach the door. He paused for a moment, felt the St. Thomas medal and Chuck Klein card in his pocket, and then walked on through. He was immediately greeted by two large, oafish looking men who roughly patted him down and then allowed him to proceed after they verified that he was unarmed.

Tommy was wearing a navy blue suit with thick white pinstripes, a black shirt, a black fedora, and a purple pocket square that matched his tie. The outfit looked rather ridiculous on a skinny Irish guy like Tommy, but it also seemed to fit the setting. It was an old and dingy bar, with a permanent sticky glaze of spilled drinks covering the floor, and a stench of sweat and cigarette smoke baked into the walls. It was mostly dark, save for the dull glow of a few low-hanging lamps. The furnishings consisted of two billiards tables, a bar with a few stools, and several small round tables with high chairs. All in all, it was not the type of place that people would come to Paris to visit.

Very nervously, Tommy strode up to the bar and took a seat on a stool. He knew that Le Capitaine liked him, which gave him some measure of relief. But he also knew how quickly things could change in this underworld, and that the mob would rarely let personal feelings get in the way of violence, which was enough to keep him on edge.

"What are you having?" asked the bartender.

"Irish whiskey, on the rocks," Tommy said.

The bartender set the drink down, and Tommy discreetly left a very generous tip. He then swiveled around on his stool, observing the other people in the room, and assessing the situation. There were two games of billiards in progress, as well as several card games at the smaller tables. The crowd was the usual mix he would expect to see at such an event, with hardened criminals freely interacting with corrupt police officers, union bosses, and politicians. Tommy recognized many familiar faces from the previous gathering. However, Tony Vespa was not present this time, having moved on to Rome to continue his European concert tour.

Having surveyed the room, Tommy finally looked to his immediate left to see who else was sitting at the bar. As it turned out, the film director Raymond LaFleur was seated two stools over. While Tommy had never directly spoken to LaFleur, he could tell from his creepy vibe that he did not like him. Additionally, Louis Poutine had a very public rivalry with LaFleur that was often the talk of the tabloids. LaFleur looked down on Louis's comedies, considering them to be a lowbrow and juvenile type of humor that appealed to the uneducated masses. Meanwhile, Louis felt that LaFleur's arthouse films had no entertainment value and were only made for the self-indulgence of pretentious snobs who enjoyed the smell of their own flatulence. Needless to say, Tommy was not going to be appearing in any of LaFleur's movies anytime soon.

Down one stool further on LaFleur's left was Nicolas Barteaux, a prominent judge in the local court system. Barteaux was infamous for carelessly flouting his corruption, as he lived an extravagant lifestyle that would never be affordable on a judge's regular salary. France being France, the press and public did not find this outrageous, simply seeing it as business as usual. It was a poorly kept secret that he was on the mafia's payroll, and a better kept secret that he was on the KGB's payroll as well.

Three very different men sat together at the bar, united only by their common vices. It was those vices that gave them something to talk about, as they began a somewhat awkward conversation revolving around their tastes in alcohol and gambling.

"Tommy Malloy! I was not expecting to see you here! What brings you to our humble gathering?" Paulo Franzese emerged from a back room, a bottle of champagne in his hand and a smile on his face.

Tommy reached out to shake his hand. "Hello, Paulo. I was just in the neighborhood and figured I'd stop by for a drink."

"Oh yes, I see, but perhaps you will be staying here for the main event?" Paulo asked.

Tommy looked back at him with a confused expression on his face. Paulo leaned in closer to explain to him, "Le Capitaine will be hosting a high stakes poker game. It is only for his most honored guests, of which you are surely one. There is a 1 million franc buy in, but I am sure that is nothing for a celebrity of your stature."

"Oh ok, I'll have to see about that," said Tommy, whose actual stature as a celebrity was quite a bit lower than that.

A few minutes after Paulo, Le Capitaine emerged from the back room. He walked over and formed a small huddle with Paulo and the three men at the bar.

"My friends, I am greatly honored by your

presence here tonight. A man could have all the money and influence in the world, but if he did not have friends, he would be a very poor man," he said. Whatever the crime lord's flaws were, he certainly had the gift of making people feel valued.

"Nicolas, how is your family?" he asked Barteaux.

"They are very well, and thank you again for sending us that fresh pork roast last night."

"Don't mention it." Le Capitaine frequently showered his political acquaintances with gifts. It was a necessary price of doing business. "And Raymond, how is your new film coming along?" he asked next.

"Excellently, we start shooting next week," answered LaFleur. His new film, *Aumor du Fromage*, was some sort of postmodern allegory about love represented through cheese. The critics were certain to love it, even if the audiences would not.

"And finally, Tommy Malloy, I see your good name has been cleared. How does it feel to be a free man?"

"It feels great," said Tommy with a grin.

Le Capitaine addressed the whole group once more. "Now, if you gentlemen will follow me, we have some very important business to attend to."

He led the way as they walked to a private room in the back of the bar. A table with stacks of chips and a deck of cards was already set up for them. There were places set for four players along one side of the table, and Le Capitaine would be facing them from the other side as the dealer.

"Now, would you please purchase your chips?"

Paulo, Barteaux, and LaFleur all produced 1 million francs in cash and exchanged it for the appropriate number of chips. Looking embarrassed, Tommy approached Le Capitaine and asked to speak to him privately. They walked together over to the corner of the room.

"So about this game, I didn't really want to admit this, but I don't exactly have a million francs lying around," Tommy said.

Le Capitaine spoke in a hushed tone, but the Corsican version of quiet was still loud enough for the others to hear. "Are you asking me for money?"

"Well, no...what I'm really saying is, I should probably sit this round out. I can just stay and watch, or go back outside," said Tommy.

"That would be an insult to my hospitality. Are you unsatisfied with my hospitality?"

"Oh no, not at all, I am very satisfied with your hospitality," Tommy sputtered.

"Then I will loan you the money, but know that I expect to be paid back in full. In other words, you had better hope you win this game."

Tommy puffed out his chest and grinned with false bravado. "Don't worry, Big Money Malloy is here to play."

They walked back to the table, where Tommy paid for his chips and Le Capitaine dealt the first hand. It was a back and forth game for the first several hands, with no player gaining any clear advantage. As the game wore on, Paulo was steadily building up a lead by grinding out a game of attrition, but any other player still had as good a chance of winning. When Tommy finally received a particularly good hand, he felt the time was right to take a big risk and shake the game up.

"All in," he said confidently, looking down at the

three Jacks and two Eights in his hand. Barteaux and LaFleur both folded their hands when Tommy pushed all his chips into the middle, but Paulo stopped and considered his options for what felt like a very long time.

"I'll call," he finally said, pushing almost all of his chips into the middle as well.

Tommy put his cards on the table. "Full house, Jacks over Eights."

Paulo grinned from ear to ear as he put down his cards. "Four of a kind." The four Sevens lay on the table, mocking Tommy with their improbability. Just like that, he was out of the game.

Le Capitaine's expression became a lot less jovial as he pulled Tommy aside to talk. "That was very foolish of you."

Tommy looked down in shame. "I know, but give me a chance to win it back, I can do it!"

Le Capitaine shook his head. "That is not possible. I like you, Tommy Malloy, you know that. But unfortunately that does not always mean much in this business of ours. I am a very influential man because people respect my word and take me seriously. If I was lenient on you, I would have to be lenient on everybody else, and then I would no longer be an influential man. I'm running a business here, not a charity."

"I understand, and I'll get you your money somehow, I promise!" Tommy said, his eyes pleading with desperation.

"You have 48 hours to repay your debt in full. Otherwise I will be forced to take actions that neither of us will enjoy. Now get out of my sight," said Le Capitaine.

Tommy didn't need to be told to leave. He departed the room as quickly as his feet would allow.

"Hey, Tommy," Le Capitaine called after him.

Tommy turned around to see the mob boss clenching a fish in his hand and waving it menacingly. It was an old Sicilian message, and he knew perfectly well what it meant.

CHAPTER TWENTY-SEVEN

A large pile of unfinished paperwork was waiting on Natalia's desk at the Soviet Embassy. It was an unexpectedly quiet morning at the office, and she likened it to the eye of a hurricane; a brief respite of calm before the turbulent storm began anew. Viktor's operation had not technically violated the truce she agreed to with Richard, but she was certain there would be blowback of some kind nonetheless. With Operation Arctic Fox nearing its final stages, things were sure to become even more dangerously chaotic. But until those things happened, she was going to take advantage of the rare downtime to get caught up on her administrative duties.

Natalia was halfway through an After-Action Report when the phone on her desk rang. She was annoyed that it interrupted her momentum, but she knew she had to answer it. One of the guards from the embassy's front gate was on the other end, informing her that there was a new walk-in.

Unannounced visitors known as walk-ins were

not an uncommon occurrence at embassies and consulates around the world. Sometimes they were seeking political asylum, sometimes they came out of ideological sympathy for the Soviet Union, and sometimes they just wanted money. Some walk-ins offered valuable information, and some others were nothing more than con artists, but all of them had to be thoroughly investigated. Whoever this walk-in was, it more than likely meant the end of her quiet day.

"Who's handling the meeting? Did you contact anybody in the Counterintelligence Directorate?" she asked over the phone.

"He specifically asked to meet with you," the guard responded.

"I'll be right down."

Leaving the paperwork for another time, Natalia walked down to the embassy's basement level, through a set of doors, and into the secure holding room. It was an empty room, save for a wooden table and two chairs. The walls were painted white and the only decorations were a red hammer and sickle and a photograph of Chairman Khrushchev. The walk-in was seated at one of the chairs, accompanied by a security guard who left the room when Natalia entered. She did a double-take when she realized who the new guest was.

"Tommy Malloy, of all people I did not expect to see you here. I thought you were leaving the country."

"Well, something came up," said Tommy.

Natalia pulled up a chair and sat across the table from him. "So what is a nice All-American boy like you doing in a place like this?"

Tommy was fidgeting uncontrollably. His palms

were dripping with sweat, and his face had turned a shade of whitish-green. "I made some bad decisions last night. I was in a card game with some mobsters, and I borrowed a lot of money from them to get into the game, and well, things didn't really go as planned. Now I have to come up with one million francs by tomorrow or else I'm going to sleep with the fishes."

Natalia listened sympathetically, having already heard his story. Nicolas Barteaux was tasked with providing reports of the games he attended, as it often provided a treasure trove of information about the movers and shakers of Paris.

"I understand your position. You need the money fast, and you can't exactly walk into a bank and ask for a loan to pay this kind of debt, and those types of men have contacts in any country you would flee to. My government has provided assistance for many other people in similar situations. We would be happy to help you, provided that you had something to offer us in return."

Tommy squirmed uncomfortably. "Something to offer in return...what exactly would that be?"

"Information. You have been included in some very exclusive circles and you obviously have access to a lot of it. And please, don't waste my time. For a million francs, it's going to have to be something worthwhile."

Tommy looked around the room nervously, acting as if he feared somebody was listening in on them. "I understand you want to know more about Operation Corner Kick."

This got Natalia's attention. Could Tommy really be this desperate? If he was, her job was about to get a whole lot easier. "Go on, I'm listening."

"MI6 and the CIA made a secret deal with the Montravians. They're going to give them all kinds of new technology and weapons systems. I can give you the blueprints for the technology, the time and methods of delivery, the names of all the people involved, really anything you want, you name it."

Natalia felt like she had just won the lottery. This was everything she needed and more, all in one stroke. It was amazing what people would do for money. She leaned forward. "Let me ask you something, Tommy Malloy. Do you love your country?"

"Yes, I do."

"And you served your country in the war, and kept working in intelligence afterwards, even after you became a movie star?"

"Well, yes, that's also true."

"And yet, here you are; selling your country's secrets to your greatest adversary. Why would you do something like this?"

Tommy expression was desperate, and his eyes were on the brink of tears. "Because I got nowhere else to go!"

Natalia stood up as Tommy looked down in shame. "Do you know where the Parc des Buttes Chaumont is?"

Tommy nodded.

"Meet me there at 1900 tonight. Come alone. I'll bring the money, you bring the goods." She turned and walked away, leaving the guards to escort Tommy out.

*****

The Parc des Buttes Chaumont, located in the

19th arrondissement, was one of Paris's more underappreciated tourist attractions. At various points in its history, the land it sat on had been used as an execution ground, a quarry, and a landfill, before being converted to a scenic park in the mid-nineteenth century. There was a large artificial lake in the middle of the park, with a steep, rocky island at its center. A replica Roman temple sat atop the rocky cliff, and pedestrians could reach it by walking over a suspension bridge. It was underneath this bridge, along the shore of the lake, that Natalia sat to await Tommy's arrival.

Natalia had scoped out the area beforehand and determined that it was secure. It was a cloudy, moonless night with a brisk chilling breeze in the air. Tourists and locals alike had decided that it was not the ideal night to be outdoors. Aside from the occasional intrepid dog walker, she was more or less alone. Nobody seemed to be watching her, and there were no signs that she had been followed.

At the appointed time, Tommy emerged from the woods with a briefcase in his hands. Natalia rose to greet him, holding a briefcase of her own. "Let's see the goods," she told him.

Tommy set his briefcase down and opened it, giving Natalia the opportunity to look through the documents inside. There were blueprints for various new types of military technology, as well as transcripts of secure cables, messages, and internal memoranda. She would have to perform a more in-depth examination later, but after a cursory glance, the documents appeared to be the genuine article. Satisfied with the contents of Tommy's briefcase, she opened her own to let him see, revealing 1,000,000 francs in cash.

"So that's it then?" Tommy asked.

"Yes, that's it," she told him. It was only partially true, if at all. While this particular transaction was now satisfied, she did not know if and when he may be called upon again. The truth of the matter was, the KGB now owned Tommy Malloy, and he would be forever in debt to perform any favor they may require.

Tommy grabbed hold of the briefcase of cash and finally began to relax a little bit. "Well that was easy."

"Yes, it was," Natalia responded as she closed up the briefcase full of documents and tucked it under her arm.

"Betraying one's country has never been easier. Quite a pity, really," echoed a British voice that she was definitely not expecting to hear. Richard Boothwyn emerged from the shadows, a pistol in his hand pointed at Tommy. In a quick flurry of motion, Tommy spun around and drew a pistol of his own. The two men were now locked in a deadly standoff.

"I trusted you, Malloy! And this is how you handle things? One bad round of poker and you run off to the Russians?" Richard inched forward as he talked, closing the distance between them.

Tommy sputtered nervously. "Stay out of this, Dick. It's not what you think, I can explain."

Natalia began to peddle backwards one step at a time, hoping to extract herself from the situation while they were distracted.

"You can explain why you're giving state secrets to a KGB officer in exchange for a briefcase full of cash? I'd like to hear that one," Richard said.

"I didn't have a choice!" Tommy pleaded desperately. "They were going to kill me!"

"How badly have you compromised Operation Corner Kick?" Richard demanded. "Did you tell anyone else about it, or just her?"

Tommy quivered with nervousness before finally answering, "Just her."

"Good, that makes it easy to contain the leak then," Richard said coolly. He turned and faced Natalia, who hadn't yet made it very far in her attempt to back away. His gun was at the ready. "I'm sorry, Natalia. This is nothing personal, it's just business."

Natalia closed her eyes and winced as she instinctively braced herself for the inevitable. Her ears rang as the loud bang of a close range gunshot echoed across the park. But then, everything went quiet. She felt no pain, and heard no further shots. Regaining her senses, she slowly opened her eyes and discovered that it was Tommy's gun rather than Richard's that had fired the shot. Richard was lying face down on the ground as Tommy knelt by his side.

Tommy's face was white, and he was breathing heavily. "I...I didn't mean to do this...this wasn't supposed to happen!"

Natalia stepped forward cautiously.

"I never wanted to kill him," said Tommy. "But he was about to shoot you, and I panicked. I didn't know what else to do."

She put a hand on his shoulder to reassure him. "It's ok; you did what you had to do, and you saved my life."

Tommy picked up Richard's arms while Natalia grabbed his legs and together they heaved him into the pond.

Tommy looked lost and confused, as if nothing made sense to him anymore. "So what do I do now? Where can I go? What are my options?"

Natalia looked him directly in the eye. "If you don't want to spend the rest of your life in a prison cell, you have but one option remaining. You must defect and start a new life in the Soviet Union."

He gently nodded, seemingly unable to express his thoughts in words.

"Come back to the embassy with me," she told him. "And await further instructions."

CHAPTER TWENTY-EIGHT

The early morning hours found Tommy waiting alone on a street corner, in accordance with Natalia's instructions. He shivered in the predawn chill; one of the biggest lessons he remembered from the army was that the hour before dawn was the coldest of the day. His hands were in his pockets, and his eyes were constantly glancing down at his shoes to make sure everything was still where it was supposed to be. When a truck pulled up to deliver a stack of morning newspapers, his moment had finally arrived.

"*The Nutcracker* was Tchaikovsky's finest work," Tommy announced as he poked his head into the truck.

"I prefer *Swan Lake*," answered the driver, completing their prearranged code phrase.

Tommy took a seat in the front cab next to the driver. For the next hour or two, he followed along with the paper route, and even helped the driver unload some of the papers. When they delivered a stack of papers to a neighborhood grocery store, a milk truck was facing the opposite direction, having just made its drop-off. Without speaking, Tommy switched trucks. This time, he was forced to ride in the back, surrounded by crates of glass milk bottles. It was quite frigid inside the refrigerated compartment, and Tommy sat curled up in a ball, trying to preserve as much bodily warmth as possible.

The milk truck meandered along for what felt like hours. What made things even worse than the cold was the fact that Tommy would be tossed across the truck every time it turned. As the truck left the highways and drove on some more rural roads, those turns became ever more drastic. When the truck finally stopped, the doors opened up to reveal that they were now on a farm. Tommy walked outside and stretched his legs, enjoying a brief respite of fresh air before he was shepherded into a different truck and the journey began anew.

This time, the new truck was carrying a cargo of goats bound for a different farm. Tommy was once again confined to the back of the truck, sitting among the crated animals. The hideous stench that came along with the tightly packed goats made him wish he was back in the milk refrigerator. As the minutes slipped into hours, Tommy's mind began to wander. He wished he could be like Sherlock Holmes and know exactly where he was based on which turns the truck made, but he knew that the endeavor would be as unnecessary as it was futile. The mental exercise he eventually settled on to pass the time was creating names and fictional backstories for the different goats. The two most obnoxious ones he named Josef and Vladimir, knowing that he had to get all his Soviet jokes out his system while he still could.

Finally, the truck rolled to a stop and Tommy was ushered outside. He walked around to stretch his aching back and legs as he tried to gain his bearings. He was on another farm, and judging by the geography, it was somewhere in the south of France. The aging stone farm house sat atop a gently rolling hill. There were green fields all around where sheep and goats grazed freely. There was a village a few kilometers down the road that was just barely visible against the horizon. Under different circumstances, it would be the perfect place for a quiet weekend getaway.

As the truck driver beckoned Tommy to follow him into the house, he couldn't help but be reminded of the set of the 1951 B-movie comedy *Farm Hands*, in which two small-time crooks from the big city take jobs on a farm while on the run from a crime boss who wants them dead. Tony Vespa's main character enjoyed a whirlwind romance with the farmer's daughter, while Tommy's character was the quirky sidekick there to provide comic relief. A series of running gags throughout the film saw Tommy fail in hilarious fashion at performing various farming tasks. Overall, he would probably rank it as his second best film. *Accountants of Amsterdam* would always be hard to top.

"Good, you made it," a female voice said from behind as Tommy walked through the front door.

He was startled to turn around and see Natalia. "What? How did you get here?"

"I drove," she said nonchalantly.

"Why couldn't I just ride with you then?" Tommy asked her.

"It was too risky. I couldn't be certain that I

wasn't being followed until I got clear of Paris," she said.

Tommy accepted her explanation, but was still far from pleased with his arrangements thus far. However, the new accommodations were looking a whole lot better. The house had a charming rustic interior with stone fireplaces, candle chandeliers, and country décor. "What is this place anyway?"

"All your questions will be answered in time," she told him. "But first you must rid yourself of that foul stench."

The truck driver led Tommy up a set of stairs to the bedrooms and bathrooms on the second floor. There, he took a much needed shower, taking an excessively long time to warm himself up after the milk refrigerator and using a lot of extra soap to get rid of the goat smell. After the shower, he found that a fresh suit was laid out for him, as well as a note instructing him to report downstairs for dinner. He got dressed and walked downstairs, where he was directed to walk out the back door. There was a stone patio behind the house where a small round table had been set for two. Natalia was already sitting there, awaiting his arrival.

"Have a seat," she told him. "Now, we can finally speak freely." There was a bottle of Shiraz on the table, and she poured two glasses.

Tommy sat down across from her. His vantage point offered a very scenic view of the rolling green hills behind them. "Well first of all, where are we and where are we going from here?"

"We are in a village not far from the Mediterranean coast. Tomorrow morning you will be departing on a cargo ship leaving from the port of

Marseilles." She paused briefly to look back at the house. "As for this place, it is officially registered as a bed-and-breakfast and occasionally it even has actual guests. However, it is primarily used for purposes such as ours. The staff members you meet here are semi-retired KGB officers enjoying an easy assignment to finish their careers."

The driver of the goat truck, now also serving as a waiter, walked out to their table bearing two plates. The plates contained a regional dish called daube, which consisted of beef braised in wine with garlic, vegetables, and locally grown herbs. A freshly baked baguette was served alongside each dish. Tommy was very hungry, and he attacked the dish with gusto.

"So what's the food like in Russia?" he asked between bites.

Natalia chose her words carefully. "The food is ...very different. It will take some getting used to, but you will grow to love it in time."

"I don't suppose you have much of a stand-up comedy scene there, do you?" he asked.

She started to crack a rare smile. "No, that is one Western innovation that has yet to reach our side of the curtain. However, we have big plans for your new life in Moscow. You will be given a high ranking position in the Ministry of Culture. You see, it is a major propaganda coup for our government to have an American movie star coming to join our side. You will be given a generous budget to write your own films and star in them...subject to government approval of course."

"I never thought I'd be making communist propaganda, but I do like the idea of making my own movies," said Tommy. "How about this for an idea,

Road to Vladivostok, it can be just like those Bob Hope and Bing Crosby movies, except in Russia. Two best friends having wacky adventures as they journey along the Trans-Siberian railway."

Natalia mulled it over. "Our sense of humor is very different than yours. I am not certain of how that would be received."

"Well it would still be better than anything Raymond LaFleur is making," Tommy muttered under his breath.

Her ears perked up. "Raymond LaFleur? I actually met him recently, at an embassy reception."

"Oh really, what did you think of him?"

"He is a total creep!"

Tommy smiled; now they really had something to bond over.

The retired KGB man turned goat truck driver turned waiter returned to clear their plates. He came back once more bringing dessert; two plates of Feuilleté de Poires, pears baked into a puffy pastry with a custard sauce. He left the plates on the table, topped off their wine glasses, and then turned around and walked back inside.

"Ok, now here's a big idea, hear me out," said Tommy, already halfway through his dessert. "What if we made a dark comedy about the mundane everyday lives of office workers in a local government ministry and how they have to overcome the incompetence and corruption all around them?"

Natalia laughed out loud at the suggestion. "Now that is something almost everybody in the Soviet Union would appreciate. Unfortunately the government would never approve it, as you could imagine."

Tommy smiled, very satisfied with himself for making Natalia laugh. Throughout his career, he always viewed hard-to-impress audiences as a personal challenge to be overcome. In this case, he felt as if a massive wall of ice was finally beginning to melt. When the desserts were finished, Tommy and Natalia killed off the rest of the wine bottle and then agreed to go on a walk around the grounds.

"It's weighing on you, isn't it? What happened last night?" Natalia asked after Tommy was oddly silent for the beginning of their walk.

"I'd be lying if I said it wasn't," said Tommy. "I didn't want things to happen that way. I just got cleared of a murder I didn't do, the absolute last thing I wanted to do now was actually kill somebody."

"I understand the feeling. What we actually want makes no difference. Boris Bryzgalov was my friend for many years, and I had to turn him in. It's just the way things go in this crazy profession of ours," Natalia said.

"How did you get into this whole espionage business anyway? Is this what you always wanted to do?"

She paused for a moment, watching the mix of colors as the sun disappeared over the hilly horizon. "No, it wasn't. Since I was a little girl, I always dreamed of becoming a classical pianist."

Tommy could tell that this was something she did not admit often. "But what happened?"

Her smile was gone, and her serious glare had returned. "The war happened. I've been serving the Motherland ever since."

"I'll tell you what," said Tommy, "When I start making my own movies, you can be in charge of the soundtrack."

"Things are never that simple. You can't just decide what job you want. I can't just tell the KGB where I want to be assigned," she said.

"But I thought I was going to be high ranking at the Ministry of Culture?" Tommy insisted. "I'll just have to pull some rank. Then we can go on tour together and promote our films. What do you think about that?"

She gave a faint hint of a smile. "I think we should go inside. It has been a long day and we have an early morning tomorrow."

With no further words, Tommy walked Natalia back to her room and then retired to his own assigned room, where he collapsed on the bed, barely finding the energy to take his shoes off first. It had been a crazy whirlwind of a day. He had no idea what the next day would bring, he just hoped the plan would work.

CHAPTER TWENTY-NINE

Tommy managed to eat a quick breakfast before he left the farm. When he made it outside, Natalia was waiting for him in the driver's seat of a black Citroen. She was wearing oversized sunglasses and a scarf wrapped around her head, Grace Kelly style. There was not much to talk about on the car ride, as they both felt it was far too early in the morning for conversation. Once they were out on the highway, Tommy spun his way through the radio dial and eventually landed on a Tony Vespa song, a sign that he could only take as good luck. As Tommy had grown accustomed to by now, they took an indirect, roundabout route to ensure that they were not being followed. It was still early morning when they arrived in Marseilles.

Located on the southern coast, Marseilles was France's second largest city as well as its largest port. In eras gone by, it was the epicenter of France's colonial empire; a center of trade where a wide range of nationalities were constantly coming and going. In more recent years, communist and socialist parties had established a stronghold on the local politics. This political situation, along with the geographic location, had made it the perfect launching point for covert operations in France. Much like a sporting event where the traveling away supporters manage to outnumber the home team's fans, the KGB was almost playing on their home field in Marseilles.

Natalia parked the car on a narrow side street, and then they walked several blocks to another KGB safe house. It was an older house with Mediterranean style architecture and a red terracotta tiled roof. The house sat on a gently sloping hill and had a nice view of the waterfront. The inside was already teeming with activity when Tommy and Natalia walked into the dining room and took seats at the table. Viktor Bazarov was sitting there, along with Rolfe and two other men. Jacques, Pierre, and several local goons from Marseille's communist party stood back against the walls as guards, armed to the teeth.

Once the parties were seated, the guards marched Princess Sophia into the room. She was wearing fresh clothes, albeit much plainer than her usual style. She appeared to be sleep deprived, but otherwise doing as well as she could under the circumstances. She looked around the room, glaring daggers at mostly everyone, but she could not contain her surprise when she spotted Tommy.

"It appears you are going to have some company on your journey, Your Highness," said Viktor. "In case you hadn't heard, Major Boothwyn is dead and Mr. Malloy has decided to get on the right side of history."

Sophia said nothing in response. Viktor then

turned to Tommy and said, "You know, you could have just come with me on the train and saved a whole lot of trouble for all of us."

Tommy ignored the remark. The room then grew quiet as Natalia rose to address the crowd. Her mission briefing was short and to the point. There was a merchant ship called the *Baleine Blanche* that would be getting underway later that morning. Tommy, Rolfe, and Princess Sophia were to be passengers on this ship. It was bound to sail across the Mediterranean to Istanbul and from there through the Bosporus and into the Black Sea to its final destination of Odessa, a port city in Soviet territory in the Ukraine. She introduced the two unfamiliar men as Mikhail and Dmitri, and stated that they were responsible for escorting the passengers, both willing and unwilling, along their journey and coordinating their arrival in the USSR. Meanwhile, the rest of the group was to remain in place until further instructions were received from General Kharlamov.

When the briefing was finished, Tommy and Sophia were ushered into the upstairs study while the others discussed more sensitive material that they did not want them present for. The only door to the room was locked, and an armed guard was posted just outside of it. The only window in the room was big enough to let in some light, but too small for anybody to consider jumping out of it.

Once it was just the two of them, Princess Sophia was eager to clarify the situation. "So, Tommy Malloy is defecting to the dark side? After you allegedly killed Richard?" She leaned in close and spoke in a barely audible tone, "I believe there is a lot more to this story than it seems. Please tell me I am right."

Tommy had a mischievous grin as he whispered in her ear, "Nothing is ever what it seems, Marlene."

*****

Richard Boothwyn adjusted the knobs on his radio receiver, finding it difficult to focus with the high-pitched waves emanating from his oversized head phones. His equipment was set up on the top floor of a dusty old warehouse. It appeared as if nobody had visited the building for years, and he was hoping it stayed that way today. He walked over to the window and scanned the view with his field binoculars. It was a clear day outside, with the sun reflecting off the water and beating down on the red rooftops of Marseilles. He turned his attention back and forth between the window and the radio before he finally felt certain which house was the correct one.

Richard had concocted and carried out a large number of schemes over the course of his career, but this one had to be by far the most outlandish. So many moving pieces had to come together for this plan to work, and any one of them going wrong would have thrown the whole thing off. However, thus far the plan was succeeding beyond even his most optimistic predictions. The mobsters performed superbly, their code of honor and friendship giving them great loyalty to Tommy. And he couldn't say enough about the job Tommy had done. Every step of the way he played his role perfectly; losing the proper amount of money in the poker game to create a believable motive, managing to convince Natalia of his intentions, and remembering to load his gun with blanks. His acting abilities and Hollywood knowledge of how to stage a death scene had never been more useful.

Perhaps the most harebrained aspect of Richard's plan was the use of a brand new technology. It had been developed in MI6's secret laboratories and never before used in the field. A radio transmitter, small enough to be held in the palm of one's hand, had been implanted into Tommy's shoe. This device emitted signals that allowed Richard to track its location. While Richard rarely trusted technology, this particular innovation had functioned exactly as advertised and led him to his current location.

It had been a rather harrowing experience trying to follow the device while also driving on the highway, and he was lucky to have avoided any automobile accidents. Spending the previous night sleeping in a ditch outside a farm wasn't much fun either. But now, the chase was nearly up. He was not surprised to have ended up in Marseilles. The busy port would be the perfect launching point for smuggling people into or out of the country.

Richard turned to the window once more, adjusting the focus on his binoculars as he carefully analyzed the safe house. He stopped and stared at the second floor rear window as he could see the silhouettes of a man and a woman sitting there. After watching for a few more minutes, he was certain that these two figures had to be Tommy and Sophia. With their location confirmed, he knew it was time to take action. He was alone, and it would still be quite some time before his backup support would arrive, but he knew that this window of opportunity may not be open for long. He may be outnumbered and outgunned, but he had the element of surprise on his side, and besides, one SAS man was worth at least ten communist thugs.

He closed up the radio equipment, prepared his tactical gear, and started to march out. He was wearing black combat boots, khaki pants, and an olive green military sweater. He armed himself with a Leigh Enfield EM-2 Bullpup rifle, a Beretta sidearm, and some smoke grenades. He carried a pack with extra magazines, flares, emergency rations, and a first aid kit. He rolled out the front door, determined to close the distance between him and the safe house as quickly as possible.

Outside in the streets, Richard moved quickly in a tactical manner. He crouched behind corners, waited and observed until the coast was clear, and then sprinted ahead to the next block. Only a few short blocks away from the safe house, he peered down a back alley. It was empty, save for some piles of trash and a few scurrying mice. He stepped out and began to run, every step bringing him closer to the target. When he was about halfway through, a car turned down the alley and was quickly following behind him. Hoping against hope that it was simply some poor tourist who got lost, he pushed himself to run faster. But unfortunately, the car accelerated, rapidly closing in on him. He turned around and started to raise his rifle, but before he could fire, the front of the car slammed into him.

The impact of the crash sent Richard flying. He landed face down on the pavement, his rifle skidding several meters away from him. His ribs were badly bruised, his nose was more than likely broken, and he wasn't quite sure where he was. As he slowly regained his situational awareness, three men poured out of the car and approached him with guns drawn. Their leader stood a few steps behind them, slowly and cautiously approaching.

"Is that you, Major Boothwyn?" the leader's voice called out. "I'm disappointed. I would have thought Sir Alastair's apprentice would be better trained than that."

With great effort, Richard rolled over and looked up, catching sight of the leader's unmistakable eyepatch-wearing face. The game had just become even more complex. General Kharlamov had arrived.

CHAPTER THIRTY

A cool salty breeze was blowing in from the sea as the truck drove down to the pier where the *Baleine Blanche* was making its final preparations to get underway. Mikhail and Dmitri were sitting in the driver and passenger seats, while Tommy and Rolfe were crammed into the second row of the cab. The truck bed behind them was carrying the conex box in which Princess Sophia was being detained. Once the passengers were loaded onto the ship, she was to be given accommodations more fitting with her rank and station. However, for the time being, the KGB could not afford the risk of having her spotted in public.

Tommy craned his neck to look out the window of the cab. The sights and sounds of the docks made him feel nostalgia for the Philadelphia shipyards he had grown up around. The ships resting at their moorings, the cranes raising and lowering their cargo, the longshoreman hard at work, the seagulls circling overhead, these were the sights that connected faraway lands and made the world go around. The truck approached a checkpoint where a customs official stopped them and asked what they had to declare. Mikhail handed the official an envelope of cash, and then he waved them through with only a cursory inspection.

When they arrived at the *Baleine Blanche's* berthing, the preparations for the ship's departure were already well underway. The harbor pilot was onboard, a tugboat had pulled alongside, and line handlers were standing by to cast off the mooring lines. The only task they were waiting on was loading the final conex box of cargo. The four men exited the truck and stood by as a crane lifted the box out of the truck and slowly transferred it to the top of the pile of boxes already laid out on the deck.

Tommy's eyes were constantly shifting between his watch, the other men, and the conex box as he grew ever more anxious. He had not been able to communicate with Richard since the night he pretended to kill him; he had simply played his part and trusted that the technology was functioning properly and Richard was following him. Now, as the box came to rest on the ship's deck, he knew that time was running out. His options appeared limited, as he was realistic about the very slim odds of him being able to successfully overpower two hardened KGB officers, free the Princess, and escape without being noticed. For now, he was just going to have to wait and possibly improvise a new plan once the ship departed. In the meantime, if Richard was planning a rescue attempt, he would have to show up soon.

*****

Things had gotten a lot quieter for Natalia once

the traveling party had departed the safe house. She sat at the dining room table with Viktor, both of them silently reading reports as they sipped coffee. Jacques, Pierre, and three of the local southern French communists were also in the house, keeping their eyes out the windows as they provided security. The Frenchmen jumped to alert when they heard somebody knocking on the door. Natalia jumped up, peered out the window, and then walked over to answer the door when she determined it was safe. She opened the door to find that her commander had arrived.

"General Kharlamov, your arrival has been much anticipated."

"It has been far too long, Natalia, but you know that I aim to arrive at the opportune moment. Also, I brought you a present. Consider this a housewarming gift."

Kharlamov waved his hand and his men stepped forward, bringing a restrained Richard with them. Richard was looking rather worse for the wear after his run in with the General's car, but there was still a hint of defiance in his step. Natalia was very surprised to see him alive, but she had seen enough deception and subterfuge in her career to not be overly shocked. Richard's presence raised obvious questions about the sincerity of Tommy's defection, but Natalia realized that those questions were mostly irrelevant at this point. Tommy was currently boarding a ship to the Soviet Union, whether he was there voluntarily or not. It would ultimately be up to him to decide if he would rather cooperate and be rewarded, or resist and end up in Siberia.

Natalia turned around to face the Frenchmen.

"Jacques, Pierre, take the other three with you and escort the prisoner down to the cellar. I want guards placed around him, but he is not to be harmed."

The Frenchmen dutifully carried out their instructions, with General Kharlamov's men joining them in the effort. The seemingly excessive number of guards they assigned was a clear sign of respect for Richard's abilities. When they had left the room, General Kharlamov asked Natalia and Viktor to follow him back into the dining room, where he closed the doors and sat down. Even disguised in plain clothes without his extensive military decorations, Kharlamov cast an imposing figure. He was the type of man that commanded fear in those that opposed him and loyalty and respect in those that followed him.

"Well, here we are," he said. "Now that I can finally speak to the two of you, please update me on the current status of Operation Arctic Fox."

Kharlamov listened patiently as Natalia and Viktor recounted what had happened so far on their operations. Natalia also showed him the documents that Tommy had given her, presenting a total exposé of the opposing side's Operation Corner Kick. The General's eyes opened wide at parts of the writings, taken aback by just how audacious some of his British counterpart's ideas were.

"And there you have it," said Natalia as she finished showing the documents. "Everybody involved in Operation Corner Kick, aside from Colonel Thorncliffe of course, is now either dead or in our custody."

General Kharlamov thanked Natalia and Viktor for their presentations and then handed each of them a folder containing the details of their next assignments. They were aware of the calendar, and they therefore knew that today was October 25th, the day that the action phase of Operation Arctic Fox was to be launched. However, until now, neither of them knew the full details of what exactly the operation entailed. Natalia felt the butterflies in her stomach as she read on. The plan was highly ambitious and very much fraught with risk. Ultimately, whatever the risks, it would be a major victory for the Soviet Union if it succeeded, and that was what Moscow was paying her for.

Natalia and Viktor looked up at General Kharlamov when they were finished reading and he rose to speak, the excitement gleaming in his eyes. "For many years now, Sir Alastair Thorncliffe and I have been playing this deadly game of chess. Our agents and operatives are our pieces, and all of Europe is our board. For years we have been locked in a stalemate; for every piece we took, they took one of ours. But now, that stalemate is broken. Sir Alastair's pieces have been cleared from the board, and the time has come to put him in checkmate. Luckily for me, my two most important pieces remain; my knight, and my queen. Prepare yourselves, and carry out your missions. The Revolution and the Motherland are counting on you."

Feeling buoyed by the General's words, Natalia walked upstairs to one of the bedrooms where equipment and supplies were stashed. She looked through the closet, packing her bags with whatever she thought she might need, and then sat on the bed to make one final read- through of the latest intelligence intercepts and reports. One intercepted communique in particular caught her eye, and she paused to reread it, making sure she correctly understood it and the potential implications it would have for her mission. When she was certain what it contained, she bounded downstairs to talk to the General. A major complication had just entered their plans.

"General Kharlamov, you need to see this," she said, holding the paper out in front of her.

He stopped what he was doing and looked up at her. "What is it, Natalia?"

"It's an intercepted communique between the American and British garrisons in Montravia. It appears they have been placed on their highest alert and instructed to respond with force to any Soviet incursions."

"I see." The General did not seem phased.

"But Sir, don't we have to call off the operation now? It was a great plan if the other side wasn't expecting it, but now it appears far too risky. It appears our plan would start a war."

General Kharlamov took a deep breath as he searched for the right words. "Oh Natalia, for as long as you have been in this business, are you really still this naïve?"

Natalia was taken aback. "You mean you *want* to start a war? Over a country the size of Luxembourg?"

"This isn't about Montravia, it's about Europe, and the World," the General said. "I assume you're familiar with the current Order of Battle. Soviet conventional forces on the continent outnumber NATO's in every category. It's the largest conventional advantage we've ever had, and they wouldn't dare use the atomic bomb now that we have it too. Western Europe is there for the taking. The time is now or never."

Natalia stood in silence, unsure of just how to react to this revelation.

"At the beginning of the last war I was an unknown Lieutenant Colonel, stationed on a backwater frontier post," he continued. "By the end of the war I was one of the most powerful men in the Soviet Union. War is chaos, but in chaos lies opportunity. The current leadership in Moscow is weak and indecisive; we need stronger leadership in place. Before the next war is over, I may be running the country myself. With you as my most trusted advisor, just think how far you could go."

Natalia nodded, slowly coming to terms with what he was saying. She tried not to concern herself with the political maneuverings that occurred far above her paygrade, but even so she had noticed a lot of changes in the environment since Stalin's death.

"It's a difficult task and I need you to be onboard with it. Can I count on you, Natalia?"

"Yes, Sir," she said.

"Good, we will be remembered as the heroes the Motherland deserved."

Natalia finished packing her bags and prepared to go back to Paris. Her will was hardened, and she knew what she had to do.

CHAPTER THIRTY-ONE

Richard Boothwyn was trying very hard to make the best of his situation. He found himself tied to a chair in the cellar of the safe house; a dark musty room with a low ceiling and no windows. One exposed light bulb provided the only illumination in the room and cast dark shadows behind the rows of discarded wine barrels. His injuries from the car had grown quite painful, and he dealt with it by closing his eyes and focusing his mind on other subjects. This gave the outward appearance that Richard was slipping in and out of consciousness, a fact that he intended to use to his advantage. In his current state, his captors could not possibly expect him to answer any questions. Furthermore, they were much more likely to be relaxed in what they may discuss in front of him.

Richard counted five other men in the room; Jacques, Pierre, and the three Marseilles men. By listening to the footsteps above, the opening and closing of the door, and the cars outside, he concluded that Viktor and Natalia had left the premises. General Kharlamov's men had departed as well, presumably taking him with them. Putting these pieces together, Richard surmised that KGB plots of some sort were in action, and that Viktor and Natalia were en route to perform whatever part they were to play in it. General Kharlamov would likely be on his way to direct said operation or to take whatever actions in Moscow that were needed in conjunction. As for Richard himself, he was still alive, which in itself was encouraging. He deduced that the Soviets probably intended to hold him hostage so that they would have some form of leverage in case the rest of their plan did not work out. It remained to be seen just how necessary or how valuable that leverage would be.

He jumped up in his seat when he heard a screech of tires outside the house, followed by a thunderous clatter of footsteps and the sudden boom of the door being kicked open. Sensing where things were going, Richard violently flung himself sideways, providing enough momentum to tip the chair over and press himself to the ground. The guards scrambled to organize themselves as they readied their weapons and ran towards the staircase. Richard closed his eyes as a hail of gunfire erupted, turning the staircase into a warzone. Moments later, the room was quiet once more. When the smoke cleared, Le Capitaine was standing in the room with Paulo Franzese at his side and eight more of his best men following close behind him. They were armed with luparas, the sawed-off shotguns popularly used in Sicily, and they had left a massacre in their wake.

Le Capitaine untied Richard and helped him up.

Richard stood up and shook his hand. "Thank you, your assistance is greatly appreciated."

"Anything for a friend," said the crime lord. "And now, the bigger questions; where is the Princess, and where is Tommy Malloy?"

Richard explained everything he had overheard and deduced about the ship as Le Capitaine nodded grimly.

"I run these docks. If anybody wants to do something here, I get a cut of it. That's how it's always worked. And here, I find out the KGB has been doing this right under my nose the whole time. And not only that, but now they have taken my friends. This is a grievous insult that I do not take lightly."

"Well you are not the first person they have deceived," said Richard.

Le Capitaine consulted his port operations schedule for the day. "The *Bailene Blanche* should be underway already. I'll get my yacht underway and catch up to them in the harbor."

Richard picked up his gear and prepared to head back out. "Great, I'll meet you out there. I'm going to take the long way."

*****

Right on schedule, The *Bailene Blanche* cast off its mooring lines and blew its whistle to signify that it was now underway. A tugboat pulled at the bow, directing the merchant ship away from the pier and out into the busy harbor. Tommy looked out at the clear blue water and the scenic view of the city and felt the cool breeze in his face. It would be a beautiful day to go out sailing, if only he wasn't on a

KGB chartered ship carrying him to the Soviet Union.

Princess Sophia was still locked in the conex box. Dmitri was responsible for guarding it, and he promised to let her out for the rest of the journey once they were safely clear of the harbor. Meanwhile, Mikhail led Tommy and Rolfe below decks to the cabin that they would be sharing. There was an empty cabin adjacent to them that was reserved for the Princess, and Mikhail and Dmitri were to share a third cabin at the end of the passageway.

Rolfe spread out on the bottom bunk and Tommy threw his bag onto the top one as Mikhail went back up the ladder well to the top deck. Tommy's mind was racing as he tried to determine his next move. He had assumed all along that Richard would stage some sort of rescue operation and that he should be prepared to help out in any way he could. However, it appeared to be too late for that now, and it would be up to Tommy to get himself and the Princess out. While his minders were likely to be less guarded once the ship was further out to sea, jumping overboard in the middle of the Mediterranean did not seem like the best idea. He would have to make his move while they were still within swimming distance of land, and that opportunity would not exist again until the end of the voyage, when they would be in hostile territory. It had become clear that it was now or never for Tommy to take action.

"So, Rolfe, you're not a baseball fan, are you?" Tommy asked, trying to make idle chat with his bunkmate while he continued to formulate a plan.

"No," said Rolfe.

"Do you like any other sports?"

Rolfe shook his head. "Sports are a pointless diversion created by the elites to distract the masses so they won't speak out against injustice and inequalities."

Tommy rolled his eyes; it figured that Rolfe was one of *those* guys. Tommy then leaned over and picked up a folded blanket from the corner of the room. "Sorry to bother you, Rolfe, but you could you help me make my bunk?"

With a mighty groan, Rolfe stood up and reached to grab his end of the blanket. Tommy acted swiftly, throwing a blanket over Rolfe's head and then attacking him with a quick succession of punches and elbows, pummeling him until he lost consciousness. When Rolfe was out cold, Tommy draped the blanket over top of him and slid him under the bed. He didn't bother trying to restrain him, because by the time Rolfe would wake up, Tommy would either be long gone, dead, or locked in a box somewhere.

Tommy ran up the ladder well and emerged topside. Mikhail was making rounds patrolling the ship, while Dmitri was guarding the Princess's container, casually leaning against it with a rifle slung over his back. The ship's small crew was going about the business of getting out to sea, too busy to pay much attention to anything else. Tommy walked over to the side and scanned the horizon. They were still in the harbor, and the distance to land was a challenging yet certainly feasible swim. As Mikhail approached him, Tommy leaned over the side, acting as if he was seasick. Mikhail gave a small nod and continued on his rounds. The easy part of Tommy's plan was complete, but he had yet to figure out how to accomplish the hard part.

*****

Richard reached the end of the pier in a dead sprint. One of Le Capitaine's men had left a waterproof bag out for him, and Richard put his boots and weapons inside the bag and slung it over his back. He then dove into the water, swimming as quickly as he could to close the distance to the *Bailene Blanche* and the tugboat that was pulling it. The swimming was difficult with all his recent injuries, but at least it was easier than running.

The men of the tugboat crew were loyal to Le Capitaine, who had radioed ahead to inform them that Richard was coming. When he was within arm's reach of the tugboat, the crew took his arms and pulled him over the side. Richard stretched his aching muscles as he looked up at the dark metal hull of the ship that the tugboat was pulling. He was in the midst of figuring out how to scale it when he caught a glimpse of Tommy peering over the edge. They silently communicated with hand signals until Tommy finally figured out what Richard wanted. Tommy then disappeared and returned moments later with a life ring. He tossed the ring to Richard, who secured it on the tugboat's deck. He gripped the attached rope in his hands, dug his feet into the side of the hull, and began to climb.

When Richard reached the top, Tommy grabbed his arms and helped pull him over to the deck. As he unzipped his bag and started to look through his gear, Mikhail alertly ran towards them, eager to investigate this new arrival. He shouted questions in French and Russian as he approached. Tommy and Richard both acted confused as they let him draw closer, then they each grabbed a leg as they lifted him up and tossed him overboard.

Tommy motioned for Richard to follow, taking him to other side where the conex boxes were stacked. Dmitri was alerted to their presence, and he snapped to attention and started to swing his rifle around. Seeing this, Richard immediately dropped to his knee and fired three quick shots with his Beretta, scoring direct hits before Dmitri could get a shot off.

"Boy, am I glad you showed up," Tommy told Richard as they started to climb the containers. "I was just about to try something crazy on my own."

"I apologize for the delay," said Richard. "I got a little tied up."

The door to the conex box was secured with a padlock and chain, so Richard told Tommy to stand back as he fired a shot to blow the lock open. He pulled the metal door open and stood in the entranceway, bloodied, bruised, and soaking wet.

"Sophia, it's us, you're safe now," he said as he looked inside the container.

Princess Sophia squinted in the sudden sunlight as she slowly stood up. "It took you bloody well long enough. I was beginning to think you'd lost a step in your advanced age."

Richard was greatly relieved despite the dig. If she still had her sharp wit, then the Soviets hadn't broken her. There was much to discuss, but first, they had to complete their escape.

CHAPTER THIRTY-TWO

Tommy, Richard and Sophia navigated their way through the stacks of conex boxes and back down to deck level. When they walked around the corner, several of the crew members were standing alert, investigating what had caused all the commotion. Without speaking, they began to slowly encircle the trio.

At a loss for how to handle the situation, Tommy attempted to engage them in conversation. "Hey fellas, how's everybody doing today? Isn't this a great day to be out on the water? Well maybe some people don't like the water as much, but hey, whatever floats your boat."

The sailors looked at Tommy with a blank stare.

"You get it?" he asked them. "Whatever floats your boat…because we're on a boat…oh come on, that was good."

"They don't understand you," said Richard.

Only then did Tommy realize that there was an obvious language barrier. The sailors were from

Bulgaria, or Romania, or somewhere around there. Richard reached into his bag and tossed them several wads of cash. The sailors conferred amongst themselves and then quietly dispersed. The amount Richard had given them was seemingly adequate to make up for the loss of whatever the KGB had promised to pay them, and they decided it was in their best interests to keep things quiet and continue on their usual route.

With the final obstacle out of the way, the trio walked over to where the tugboat was attached, and one by one they slid down the lifeline and landed on the tugboat deck. The tugboat crew had already fished Mikhail out of the water and restrained him in their cabin, giving Le Capitaine powerful leverage in whatever future deal he may negotiate with the KGB for the use of his docks.

When the *Bailene Blanche* was clear of the busiest zones of the harbor, the tugboat cut loose and sent them on their way. It then turned and set a course to a point about a nautical mile offshore, where Le Capitaine's yacht was slowly drifting. The crime lord was waiting on the deck as the two boats pulled adjacent to each other and the passengers performed the very difficult task of jumping from one deck to the other as both boats rocked in the waves. When they were safely aboard the yacht, the tugboat peeled away and Le Capitaine directed his guests to go below decks as he returned to the pilot house to steer and maneuver.

The interior of the yacht had wood paneling, leather couches, and well-stocked book shelves. Tommy was very impressed; it was classy and luxurious, but it wasn't over-the-top like the yachts of

Hollywood stars that he occasionally got invited on. Sir Alastair Thorncliffe was sitting at the table when they arrived, sipping a cup of tea and wearing a double-breasted blue blazer with brass buttons. A pile of paperwork was spread out in front of him as he desperately tried to keep up with the situation and plan his next steps. Tommy and Sophia joined him at the table, and Richard grimaced and groaned as he slowly lowered himself into his seat.

"That looks pretty painful, what did they do to you?" asked Tommy.

"It wasn't really that much. They just ran me over with a car and a little interrogation, pretty standard fare. That was just today's round of course. I'm also still a bit sore from when you threw me in the lake," Richard said.

"Sorry about that," said Tommy, unable to distinguish if Richard was employing sarcasm or British understatement.

"Don't apologize, it was a bloody good performance, dare I say BAFTA worthy."

Princess Sophia spoke up, "Now I need to know what you're talking about. You two are going to have to explain me how you pulled this one off."

She listened intently as Tommy and Richard told their respective sides of the rescue plan, laughing at certain parts, gasping at others, rolling at her eyes at a few. Overall, she was very impressed that they had successfully executed such a complex plan in such a short time, and very grateful for the risks they had taken to bring her back.

"So here's my next question," Tommy said to Alastair. "What is going to happen with Operation Corner Kick? Are we still going through with it, or is it cancelled now that the Russians know about it?"

Alastair looked back at him quizzically. "You didn't actually read the documents you turned over, did you?"

Tommy shook his head. "No. Why? Were they fake?"

"Well, the documents were real in the sense that they were the actual documents of Operation Corner Kick," Alastair answered. "However, Operation Corner Kick itself would not be considered real in most senses of the word."

Now Tommy was more confused than ever. Whenever he thought he had this whole espionage game figured out, he would learn that there are even deeper deceptions and twists that he never would have guessed.

"I have already given you some of the background of my old rivalry with General Kharlamov. Well, things have gotten particularly interesting in Moscow since our old friend Stalin passed away last year. Mr. Khrushchev, who is running things now, may be an irritable fellow, but he's much less extreme than old Joe and he's been making a lot of changes. The hardliners who preferred Stalin's way of doing things have not been happy with those changes. General Kharlamov is one of those hardliners."

The old spymaster had a gift for breaking down even the most complicated situations into terms that anybody could understand. Tommy greatly appreciated it, and he listened intently as Sir Alastair got to the interesting part.

"The hardliners have been maneuvering from the start to either seize power for themselves, or force the government to adopt their positions. For somebody of General Kharlamov's talents, this would best be achieved through manipulating international events. When the Soviet government was willing to participate in the Montravia treaty, I knew that Kharlamov would not be pleased. He is not the type of man to sit idly by while the Soviets withdraw from a country that could have gone communist. I fully expected him to plan a covert operation to undermine it, but as you know, he works very deep in the shadows. Therefore, we planned a covert operation of our own as a feint, knowing he would catch wind of it and want to investigate. It was a great risk, but it helped bring him and his plans out in the open, which was our only chance at stopping them."

Tommy felt as if the jigsaw puzzle in his head was finally being out together. "So what exactly was in those documents then?"

"It was a robotics program. We planted evidence that we were conspiring with Montravia to give them robots that could be used to spy on Soviet troop movements in East Germany and Czechoslovakia. Obviously this technology does not exist, but if the Soviets want to drain their treasury trying to build it, then that's all the better for us."

Sir Alastair then turned to address the whole group. "You have all performed admirably, but there is much work left to be done. First, we return to the original note that Tommy passed on to us from Harry. Remember what it told us, Operation Arctic Fox, October 25."

"That's today!" Tommy realized.

"Thank you, I was unaware," said Richard.

"Anytime, Dick."

"My father is signing the treaty tonight," Sophia reminded them. "I am sure that whatever the Soviets are planning must have something to do with that."

"I agree with that assessment," said Sir Alastair. He reached for a blank sheet of paper and began scribbling down notes. "So, we know that the KGB is planning to launch Operation Arctic Fox today. We are fairly certain of what their target is. I have already contacted the Allied garrisons in Montravia and recommended that they place their forces on high alert and resist any Soviet incursions. But now, let us compile everything we have learned thus far about the operation. Who is involved? And what are their objectives?"

"We know that General Kharlamov himself is here in France," Richard answered. "We know that Natalia Petrova and Viktor Bazarov are deeply involved and have both recently departed Marseilles en route back to Paris. And we know that they have been using local allies, most of whom we have eliminated. But as for what they're doing next and how to stop them, I wish I had the answer to that."

"I should make an appearance at the treaty signing," Princess Sophia suggested. "They think I've been removed from the equation. If I were to make an appearance, they will know that part of their plan has gone wrong. They might call the rest of it off, or they might panic and reveal themselves."

"That sounds dangerous, but I can't think of anything better," said Richard. "She can make a public showing and then Tommy and I can attend incognito and see what we can find."

Sir Alastair stood up. "I'll go inform our Captain of our plans. We need to depart promptly if we're going to make it to Paris in time."

Tommy stood up as well and stretched, looking past the luxurious surroundings to the clear blue water outside the window. He came to France to perform a comedy show, and it was still very difficult to fully appreciate everything that had happened to him. Now, once more, he was preparing to jump into the breach with his new friends. He had only known them a short time, but he already felt willing to go to war with them.

What made the situation feel even stranger for Tommy was that he gotten to know many of the adversaries as well. He had no sympathy at all for people like Rolfe or the French communists that had betrayed their countries. He regarded people like Viktor Bazarov similarly to the German soldiers he had faced in the war; he respected them as adversaries, but they were just that, adversaries. However, it was Natalia who he had gotten to know the best, and who confused him the most. While he never knew anyone's true intentions in this business, from what he could tell, she was a genuinely decent person who happened to have the misfortune of growing up under an oppressive system. He also couldn't deny that he was very much attracted to her, but he certainly couldn't afford to dwell on that.

"So we're really winging this aren't we?" he asked.

"You should have been there for the first mission we did together during the war, back then we were really winging it," answered Sophia. "Before D-Day, we were doing reconnaissance with the French Resistance. We had no idea who our point of contact was or how to get in touch with them. It was a crazy time."

"That's how it usually was during the war," said Richard. "But we were quite the team, the three of us...the Princess, Harry Thompson, and myself; otherwise known as the Cambrian Crusader, the Duchess of Doom, and the Philadelphia Phantom." He tossed Tommy a bag of gear. "Get ready; we need a new Philadelphia Phantom."

CHAPTER THIRTY-THREE

On the day of the treaty signing, Prince Hans Friedrich's residence was a bustling hive of activity. He had yet to find a new steward to replace Rolfe, so he had to accomplish more and more tasks by himself. Earlier in the day, Jürgen Freitag, Montravia's Foreign Minister and interim Prime Minister, had stopped over to update the Prince on the latest diplomatic developments. While the Prince was the public face of Montravia, it was Freitag who was performing most of the day-to-day work of negotiating with foreign governments. Together, they were working to ensure that their constitutional monarchy was ready to be up and running when the treaty went into effect.

Freitag was a diligent and conscientious man, who was intelligent without the cunning deviousness of those on the shadier side of statecraft. He also took Montravia's pledge of neutrality considerably more seriously than the royals did, and as such was never included in Sir Alastair's schemes. After

Freitag's brief, the Prince visited his barber to trim what was left of his hair, and then his tailor to have the final alterations made to his new custom suit. The rest of the day was spent preparing his remarks for the evening, keeping up with correspondences, packing up his possessions for the move back to Montravia, and generally just trying to distract himself from worrying about his daughter.

While he may have been a monarch, the current situation made him feel frustratingly powerless. What reassured him was the knowledge that Sir Alastair Throncliffe was the best in the business and if anybody could solve this problem, it was him. The Prince knew that he had to be patient, but the wait and the lack of information were very difficult to deal with.

When the hour of departure arrived, the Prince was met in the lobby of his residence by Jürgen Freitag, a security guard, and a chauffeur. The chauffeur took his bags and escorted him to the black Mercedes convertible they would be riding in. Two police officers on motorcycles waited in front of the car, providing an official escort. The chauffeur held the doors open as the Prince and the Foreign Minister settled themselves in the back seat and the security guard sat down in the front. The car's roof was closed for now, but it would be opened later on for the celebratory victory lap after the ceremonies.

The signing ceremony for the Montravia Treaty was to be held at the Luxembourg Palace. It was a grand and historic residence in the heart of Paris that had seen its fair share of history. At various times, it had been a noble estate, a legislative capital, a museum, and a headquarters for occupying Germans.

A series of peace accords were signed there immediately after the war, and now it would be returning to that purpose once more. The signing was to be immediately followed by a cocktail reception in the Jardin du Luxembourg, the beautifully sculpted gardens on the grounds of the estate.

When the Prince's entourage arrived at the Palace, the other major dignitaries were already waiting for them. The French Foreign Minister was playing the gracious host. The British and Soviet Foreign Ministers, the American Secretary of State, and their respective ambassadors to France were all present as well. For now it was a private gathering in the Palace's library, but the official signing was going to be in a larger room and open to the press. The Prince took a moment to take everything in. He had been surrounded by grandeur his whole life, but this was one of those moments where he felt like he was truly a part of something historic.

"This is it, the day we have been waiting for," he said to Freitag as they approached the table.

"Yes it is, and it is an honor to stand by your side," said the Foreign Minister. He then asked, "Will Princess Sophia be joining us?"

"No, I am afraid she has other engagements." Prince Hans Friedrich wondered just how long he could keep that story quiet.

*****

Tommy was crammed into the back seat of a Renault for the entire seven and a half hour journey from Marseilles to Paris. Princess Sophia was in the front passenger seat, and Richard was driving, aggressively accelerating and switching lanes the whole way as if he was a Formula One driver. For the first two hours of the trip, they had an in-depth discussion reviewing everything they knew about the situation they were going into, what their strategy was, and contingency plans for every possible outcome. The remainder of the journey consisted of Tommy asking Sophia about what it's like to be a royal, Sophia asking Tommy about what it's like to be in the movies, and Richard grinding his teeth and grumbling about French drivers.

It was early evening when they finally reached the city. The local commuters were starting to go home from work, the tourists were starting to seek evening entertainment, and the city lights were turning on as the sun disappeared. Richard parked the car in a little-used garage and then they continued their journey on foot to reach the apartment where Sophia had first taken Tommy before he knew her real identity. Once there, they were to change into their appropriate attire, gather whatever supplies they needed, and then make their way to the Luxembourg Palace.

"One more thing," Tommy asked Sophia as they walked, "Do they really call you 'The Duchess of Doom?' because that may be the greatest nickname I have ever heard."

Sophia laughed, shaking her head. "Oh no, only Richard does. Richard has been trying to make that happen for a very long time, but I fear it is never going to happen."

A few short blocks away from the apartment, they turned a corner and walked down a dimly lit alley. The walls of the adjacent building blocked what remained of the sunlight, helping to conceal whatever may have been lurking in the shadows. When they were halfway through the alley, a lone figure stepped out the shadows and stood facing them, obstructing their path. Upon closer examination, it was a woman. Upon even closer examination, it was Natalia Petrova.

"Well if it isn't the Three Musketeers," she greeted them. "Exactly where I expected you would be."

The three of them were caught off guard by her sudden appearance and were not exactly sure what to make of it. They exchanged quizzical glances with each other until Richard tentatively stepped forward and responded to her.

"I don't know what you're trying to accomplish here, Natalia, but I am sure you have taken into consideration that there are three of us and only one of you."

"I am impressed with your abilities of deduction, Major Boothwyn. Did they teach you that at Oxford?"

"So are you just out for an evening stroll in a concealed alley then?" Sophia prodded. "I can't say I blame you. I wouldn't want anybody to see me in public in those shoes either."

Natalia did not appear to take offense. "I am grateful to see that you have not been harmed, Your Highness. I want to offer my most sincere apologies for how you were treated by my organization." She then addressed the whole group, "I am here because of a desperate situation that requires your assistance."

"Are you trying to fool us with the classic fake defection stunt?" asked Tommy. "I invented that, sister."

"And you certainly had me fooled," she responded. "But unlike you, I am not an actor. If you wish to stop General Kharlamov, then you must listen to what I have to say, for it may be your only chance."

"Well, go on then," Richard said after an awkward pause.

"Today, the final stage of Operation Arctic Fox is going into effect. General Kharlamov is returning to the USSR to handle the political maneuverings on his level, and the rest of the plan is already in motion. Viktor Bazarov has been assigned to assassinate Prince Hans Friedrich."

Princess Sophia visibly grimaced at the revelation. Natalia continued, "And at this very moment, the Soviet garrison in Montravia is standing by to seize control of the capitol in the ensuing confusion. They are only awaiting a radio transmission; a transmission that is to be sent by me."

"And just like that, Montravia goes communist," Richard observed. "From one professional to another, it's a brilliant plan. One quick stroke, and there's another country in the communist column, except, there's just one problem. Sir Alastair has anticipated a move for Montravia and the Allied garrisons have been instructed to meet any incursion with force. The plan has no chance of success; it would end up starting a war if anything."

"Or so it would seem. However, General Kharlamov has actually anticipated Sir Alastair's anticipation. You see, his intentions are quite different from what I initially imagined. General Kharlamov wants to start a war. He feels the war is inevitable and wants it to happen now while the

Soviet bloc has an advantage in forces. He also believes the current government in Moscow is weak and wants to make a play for power." She paused and shook her head. "All this time, I thought I was serving the Motherland, but I was really just advancing the personal ambitions of a power-hungry man."

Everybody paused and exchanged glances as they took in the full implications of what was happening. "We all lived through the last war," said Natalia. "I was in Leningrad during the German siege. Only a madman would want to go through all that again. I was going to report all this to Moscow to try to stop him, but General Kharlamov has many friends there and I don't know who to trust."

Richard nodded. "So now you're here because..."

"Because I had nowhere else to go," she completed.

"And I assume you will have to defect after this. I do not think the KGB takes too kindly to whistleblowers. That can be arranged, of course," said Richard.

That was when it truly sank in for Natalia that she had crossed a line from which there was no going back. Her old life would have to be left behind. She accepted Richard's offer, and then proceeded to explain all the details she was aware of that may help stop the assassination and provocations. Because the Soviet garrison was waiting on her signal, she could avert the seizure of Montravia by sending a different signal instructing them to stand down. Meanwhile, Viktor had been given leeway to plan how to execute his end of the mission, and therefore Natalia did not know when he would strike or what methods he may employ. But she did know that it was to happen soon and for maximum effect.

"Alright, here is what we're going to do," Richard said when she was finished. "Tommy and I will go to Luxembourg Palace and try to stop Viktor. Sophia, you will escort Natalia to send the transmission. Then you will proceed to the NATO base at Orly. A military flight has already been reserved to take Boris Bryzgalov to England. Natalia should be on that plane as well."

Sophia shook her head with displeasure. "I should be out there stopping Viktor. It is my country that is at stake and my father who is in danger. This is my fight more than anyone else's."

"Which is all the more reason why you shouldn't be there, it's too personal for you, you have too much at stake," said Richard. "And besides, what if we fail? In the worst case scenario, your country would need you more than ever. Montravia can ill afford to lose both you and the Prince."

The Princess reluctantly agreed, and she set off walking back towards the car. Natalia began to follow after her, but lingered for a moment when she locked eyes with Tommy.

"I'll have to remember to send General Kharlamov a thank you card for pushing you over to our side," he said.

"It…it wasn't just that, you know."

"Really, it was my dashing good looks as well?"

She laughed. "You helped open my eyes to new possibilities. The world doesn't have to be the perfectly ordered machine I grew up in. I want to follow my dreams. I want to create my own destiny."

"Well in America you can be the classical pianist

you've always wanted to be. Or you can be a jazz pianist, or a sleazy used piano salesman. The point is, you can do whatever you want," Tommy said.

"And what if I want to get involved with a movie star and end up in all the tabloids?"

"Then you should probably try to find somebody more famous than me."

They shared a brief laugh before they parted ways.

CHAPTER THIRTY-FOUR

After Sophia and Natalia departed, Tommy and Richard quickly got changed and provisioned in the apartment. For this stage of the mission, they were disguising themselves as members of the press. They wore plain grey suits, carried large pads of paper, and wore credential badges around their necks. Underneath their suit coats, they wore shoulder holsters to carry their pistols. They packed a bag with extra gear and changes of costume, and also took along small pocket-sized flashlights.

It was a short drive to Luxembourg Palace, and once they arrived, they flashed their press credentials and the police officer guarding the entrance waved them through. Once inside, Sir Alastair Thorncliffe was there to meet them, having arrived just ahead of them to take his place as an official member of the British delegation.

"What's the situation inside?" Richard asked as they briskly walked through the corridor.

"The delegations are en route from the library to

the main room, most of the press pool is already in there waiting," said Alastair.

Richard gave him a brief overview of everything Natalia had told them.

"I see," said Alastair. "I will stay as close as I can to the Prince and I'll make sure he knows that his daughter is safe but he is not. I'll also inform the police and have them call in reinforcements. Meanwhile, you two must find Bazarov any way you can."

Sir Alastair left them to go fall in behind the British Ambassador as the diplomatic contingent turned around the corner walking towards the larger room. Tommy and Richard entered the room from the rear and surveyed the scene in front of them. It was a room that was normally used as a legislative chamber. There was a long desk at the front where the official copy of the treaty had been laid out. Prince Hans Friedrich, Jürgen Freitag, and the representatives of the Four Powers were seated behind the table. Semi-circular rows of chairs faced inward towards the front table, and a second floor balcony in the rear overlooked the whole room.

A police officer approached them as they entered the room. "I have been instructed to assist you. What do you need?"

"We have a specific security threat. I need to seal every entrance. Nobody else gets in or out. The man we are looking for is six foot two with blond hair and a muscular build, but he may be wearing a disguise. He's Russian but speaks fluent English and French. Keep the room secure and detain anybody who fits that description," Richard ordered.

As he was speaking, the French Foreign Minister

strode to the podium to give his introductory remarks. "Ladies and gentlemen, we are gathered here tonight to mark a noteworthy achievement in the cause of international peace and cooperation…"

There was a flurry of activity as the members of the press snapped photographs and scribbled down notes. Richard craned his neck and whispered to Tommy, "I'm going up to the balcony. I can see the whole room from up there and I like my shot from that range. If I see Bazarov, I'll take him out. Now, I want you to walk up there and act like a reporter, but get a good look at who's really there. If you see Bazarov, point him out and get my attention, or just take him out yourself if you have a clean shot."

Tommy gave a quick nod and Richard quietly slipped around the corner and then bounded up the stairs to take his place on the balcony. Tommy walked down the aisle towards the packed crowd of reporters with his notepad in hand, doing his best to blend in. He had been on the other end of press conferences enough to be familiar with the scene, and he put on just the right amount of pushiness to fit right in.

As Tommy reached the press section, the Foreign Minister was just concluding his remarks. The Frenchman then walked to the table and affixed his signature to the treaty as the other representatives lined up behind him to do the same. The reporters stood up to better take in the moment, giving Tommy the opportunity to push his way through them, frantically searching for Viktor. From what he could tell, Viktor was nowhere in sight. Even if he had been wearing a disguise, every reporter Tommy saw seemed to be either too short, too fat or too skinny to be the man he was looking for.

After the American Secretary of State made the final signature, Prince Hans Friedrich rose to give the closing remarks. Tommy's heart raced as he continued to push through the crowd. Every camera could be a potential gun, and every reporter could be a potential assassin. Having been warned by Sir Alastair, the Prince kept his remarks very brief. The press shouted out questions as he stepped away from the podium, disappearing into the crowd of dignitaries who were now leaving the building through the VIP entrance they had come in through.

The gathered press then turned to leave, and Tommy went along with them, feeling nervous and confused until he caught up with Richard in the back of the room. Richard was now wearing a white shirt with a black tie and vest and a white apron over his black pants. He tossed Tommy a bag with the same outfit inside.

"Hurry up and get changed. If Viktor hasn't struck yet, that means we have to be extra vigilant at the cocktail reception. We've been assigned as servers specifically attached to the Prince's party. We'll alternate making runs to the kitchen, but one of us must be by the Prince's side at all times."

Tommy ducked into the restroom and quickly changed his clothes before heading outside where the cocktail reception was about to begin. The Luxembourg Gardens were a picturesque sight, sitting behind the Palace with their manicured lawns and flowerbeds, tree-lined paths, and large circular pool. A string quartet was positioned in front of the pool, playing classical accompaniment as the guests made their way outside. A white tent had been set up hosting a temporary kitchen from which the hors d'oeuvres and beverages would be served.

Tommy had never worked as a server before, but he had played one on the screen. In the critically acclaimed comedy *The Butler and the Baroness*, Louis Poutine portrayed an upstart butler who decided to dress up and bluff his way into the European aristocracy. In one particular scene, he took the female lead out to a fancy restaurant, where Tommy's server got their orders disastrously wrong and hilarity ensued. But now, Tommy was sweating nervously, because there would be nothing funny if he failed tonight.

As the dignitaries began to mingle, Prince Hans Friedrich took up a spot near the Medici Fountain, an ornate monument dating back to the seventeenth century. Jürgen Freitag and the British Foreign Secretary stood close by in his social circle. A Montravian security guard stood next to the Prince, and Sir Alastair was in the circle as well, watching over Hans Friedrich like a hawk. Richard assumed a position on the fringe of the circle and motioned for Tommy to go the kitchen tent.

Tommy navigated his way through the party, noticing that it was quite the fancy affair. Wealthy and influential people mingled among artistic and architectural treasures on a beautiful Paris evening. But he also knew that there was danger lurking under the surface, and it could strike at any time. He arrived at the kitchen tent to find a table at the front where the already prepared trays were set out, waiting for a server to bring them around. Tommy grabbed a trey full of canapes, small slices of bread with decorative garnishes on top. He sampled a few before he reached the guests, to ensure they were fit for consumption, of course. As a hungry man of simple tastes, he would have preferred a more traditional sandwich, but he had to admit that the canapes were rather tasty.

Tommy returned to the Prince's circle and held out the tray, where most of the canapes were snatched up and eaten. Richard gave a quick nod as he began his run to the kitchen tent. Tommy stood by, scanning the area and absent-mindedly listening as the Prince and the British Foreign Minister engaged in an animated discussion about horses. There were no signs of any potential disturbances so far, which made Tommy all the more nervous. The tensions wreaked havoc with his insides as he anxiously waited for Richard to return. He had come to Paris to perform a comedy show, but now he found himself responsible for protecting a Head of State and preventing World War III. He never wished for this burden to pass to him, but yet here we he was.

After what felt like an eternity, Richard returned; bearing a tray of crudités, bite sized pieces of carrots, celery, peppers, and broccoli with a light vinaigrette sauce. Richard held the tray out and nodded to Tommy; it was his turn once again. Tommy returned to the kitchen tent and dropped off his mostly empty first tray. He then found that the next round that had been set out for him was one of his all-time favorites; the miniature hot dogs wrapped in pastry known as "pigs in a blanket." As he stepped out of the tent, Tommy stuffed three of the snacks in his mouth, wanting to ensure that the honored guests would not be served a defective product.

Tommy paused after walking a few steps. His mouth was being assaulted by an awful, foul taste. It was difficult to ruin pigs in a blanket, but whoever the chef was had managed to do exactly that. One or more of the ingredients must have gone bad. Tommy immediately turned around to address this situation, because this food was clearly not fit to be served. He dropped the tray at the front table of the tent and then pushed his way to the back, where the chef was leaning over a table, seemingly deeply absorbed in his work.

"These pigs in a blanket are no good!" Tommy called out. "What exactly are you trying to pull here anyway?"

Slowly and deliberately, the chef paused what he was doing, looked upwards, and locked eyes with Tommy. Tommy's heart stopped when he recognized the face; now it all made sense. The chef lunged towards him, wielding a large frying pan in his hands. Tommy reached for his gun, but he was not quick enough. The last thing he saw was Viktor Bazarov swinging a pan at his face.

CHAPTER THIRTY-FIVE

Princess Sophia drove the Renault as Natalia navigated through the narrow and twisting back streets. After a long and indirect drive, they arrived at a battered and poorly lit house that was owned, but rarely used, by the KGB. Natalia slid the key in the front door, assuring Sophia that it would be empty inside. Natalia stepped in first, walking over the creaking floorboards to turn on the dim and aging lamps. Sophia stepped in after her, pushing her way through the tangle of cobwebs, and trying not to look at the insects that were likely lurking below.

Natalia led the way up a staircase of questionable stability, down a short hallway, and into the master bedroom. Inside the bedroom, there was a dusty mattress sitting on top of a rusty frame, a rotting wooden dresser, and a cracked full length mirror. Natalia slid the mirror to the side, and then removed a panel of the wall to reveal a hidden walk-in closet. Inside the closet was a secret and substantial stash of radios and other communications equipment. Natalia turned on the largest radio and handed Sophia a book of codes.

"This is today's code," Natalia told her, pointing to the appropriate page in the book. "You can follow along to verify the message that I'm sending."

Sophia followed along as Natalia reached the Soviet garrison in Montravia and transmitted the coded messages for "Mission Aborted" and "Stand Down." They waited in silence for several minutes until a Soviet military officer on the other end responded, acknowledging the order. Feeling greatly relieved, Natalia and Sophia departed the house and went back to the car. Whatever else may happen this night, they had already significantly helped to de-escalate the situation. From there, it was an uneventful ride to Paris-Orly Air Base, located a few miles south of the city.

When they arrived at the base, Sophia showed her credentials to the gate guard and they were waved through and provided with an escort to the military airfield. As they left the car and gathered Natalia's bags, they could see a single light transport jet sitting on the tarmac, and just catch a glimpse of Boris Bryzgalov climbing aboard.

"Boris will surely be surprised to see me," Natalia said as she strapped a bag over her shoulder.

Princess Sophia couldn't help but smile as she took the whole scene in. "You know, I really misjudged you. I always enjoyed goading you every time we met, because I never saw past your cold blooded killer façade. But I realize now that there is a whole lot more to you."

"I misjudged you as well," said Natalia. "All I saw was the image of a shallow and materialistic socialite, but now I know there is a whole lot more to you too."

Natalia zipped up the last of her bags, and they started walking towards the plane. "That seems like it should be a microcosm of international relations. We could have a whole lot more peace in the world if we all just took the time to understand one another," she said.

Sophia nodded. "The past few days have changed all of us, and if we can change, then I think anybody can change."

"And the funny thing is, if the circumstances had been different, if we had been born on the same side of some line on a map, we could have been great friends," said Natalia.

"We still can be," Sophia insisted. "It's never too late."

The two women hugged and promised to keep in touch and then Natalia turned to board the plane. Her new life was just beginning.

*****

The first sensation Tommy experienced when he woke up was intense, crippling nausea. Unsure of his surroundings, he tried to stand up, but was jolted back down with the realization that he was handcuffed to a steel beam. He looked all around trying to make sense of the situation, but it was only when he looked down that he finally realized where he actually was. He was sitting on a ledge, fifty meters above the ground, on the first floor of the Eiffel Tower. Of course; of course he was up on the Eiffel Tower. Where else could this absurd series of events have possibly led him? He leaned over the rail and heaved, taking a perverse amusement in the fact that if he survived this night, he would be able to tell everybody he knew that he once vomited off the side of the Eiffel Tower.

Tommy looked further down the ledge and saw Viktor Bazarov scanning the horizon with his binoculars. A high powered rifle was slung over his back with a serious-looking sniper scope attached. He turned to look when he heard Tommy moving around.

"Oh, I was not expecting you to wake up."

"Don't flatter yourself, Viktor. You didn't hit me that hard," Tommy responded.

"What I meant was that I expected you to be dead by now after what you ingested. But at least now, you get to have a front row seat to watch your friends fail," said Viktor.

The wheels in Tommy's head began to turn as the various pieces of what had occurred were finally coming together. "So you poisoned the hors d'oeuvres. They were intended for the Prince, but I ate them first. Really? That was your whole plan? What if the Prince didn't like pigs in a blanket? And what about the other people that would have eaten them? Did you even think this one out? Are you even in the KGB?"

"Are you trying to provoke me into knocking you out again? Because it would be a real pity for you to miss this show. Anyway, anybody else who ate the hors d'oeuvres would have been necessary collateral damage that would have added extra layers of confusion to the situation. And I had plenty of other contingencies in place, such as this one."

Tommy thought out loud. "The Prince's

motorcade is going to be driving by…so you're going to shoot him with the sniper rifle from up here…But I'm not quite sure how you would escape…"

Viktor nodded. "Keep going. You're on the right track…"

Tommy leaned over to vomit again and then it came to him. "You're setting me up to be the fall guy! I already got accused of one murder, so it won't be too much of a stretch. You're going to leave me up here with the rifle, and I'll be dead from the poison before anybody gets the chance to interrogate me. It will look like I was the assassin and I took cyanide so they wouldn't take me alive, and that is exactly how you will sell the story to the press. Once the story is out there, it won't even matter if it's true or not. I have to hand it to you; it's actually a pretty good plan."

Viktor smiled ever so slightly. "You have a very sharp mind, such a pity that it was wasted in losing cause on the wrong side of history."

As Viktor lifted his binoculars and turned back to scan the horizon again, Tommy reached around with his one free hand and felt inside all his pockets. Unsurprisingly, Viktor had taken his gun and all his identifying information. However, whether by intention or oversight, he had not taken everything. The St. Thomas medal was still there, the Chuck Klein rookie card was still there, and most surprising of all, the flashlight was still there. Using his body to block the sight from Viktor, he pointed the flashlight out towards the city, desperately hoping to catch the attention of anybody who might be watching.

*****

Richard's internal alarm bells were furiously ringing when Tommy didn't return from his serving run. He raced to search the kitchen tent, but by the time he got there, there were signs of a struggle, but no signs of Tommy or whomever he had been struggling with. With a few quiet words to the right people, Sir Alastair had the cocktail party shut down early. "Technical difficulties" was the official word as the various dignitaries headed for the exit, disappointed that the party was ending so soon, but still very much pleased with their diplomatic accomplishments.

Richard and Alastair escorted Prince Hans Friedrich to his waiting motorcade. They wanted to send him immediately home, but the Prince insisted on still doing the planned victory lap because people had lined up to see it and he couldn't let them down. Whether there were credible assassination threats or not, he had royal duties to perform. Against their better judgment, the Britons took their place in the motorcade, knowing full well that the Prince was under no obligation to listen to them.

Two police motorcycles led the procession, followed by a line of Mercedes convertibles. Richard drove the first car, with Sir Alastair sitting beside him and the British Foreign Secretary and Ambassador to France sitting in the back seat. The Prince's car was immediately behind them, followed in turn by the American, Soviet, and French delegations. Each car had their respective country's flag attached to the antenna, and it was all-in-all a rather impressive spectacle.

Richard kept his head on a swivel as the cars started out, constantly searching for and evaluating potential threats. Several harrowing yet largely uneventful blocks later, as they moved towards the shadow of the Eiffel Tower, he caught a sight that stopped him in his tracks.

"Look, up at the tower!" he told Alastair.

Alastair looked up, and sure enough, a small light on the first observation floor of the tower was flashing the Morse code signal for SOS. Richard gave him a nod and then turned to the two distinguished guests in the back, "Hold on to your seats, gentlemen, you may experience a bumpy ride."

As the motorcade drew closer to the Eiffel Tower, Richard peeled out of the line and slammed his foot down on the accelerator. Rifle shots began to ring out around them as they approached the tower, but Richard managed to evade them by constantly swerving and never presenting a stationary target. He closed the final distance with one last burst of acceleration and then skidded to a halt underneath the Tower, burning a lot of rubber in the process.

Richard then leaped out of the car, poised and alert with his pistol at the ready. He was directly underneath the Tower now, and whoever had been shooting at him would not be able to see him at the current angles. However, the shooter still posed a grave danger to the Prince and everybody else in the motorcade, not to mention the many innocent bystanders, and Richard had to take action to stop it.

There were two options for Richard to reach the next level of the Tower; the stairs and the elevator. He briefly deliberated, weighing the advantages and drawbacks of both options, before deciding on a course of action. With a deep breath, he pushed the button to call the elevator.

*****

Viktor cursed under his breath as he peered over the ledge, trying to figure out where the unexpected aggressive driver had ended up. He paced back and forth, anxiously looking for clues, until the evidence became startlingly obvious. The machinery powering the Tower's elevator sprang to life, indicating that an upwards elevator was inbound. Viktor gave a sigh of relief as he set the sniper rifle aside and drew his sidearm. He assumed a shooting stance and waited for the elevator to arrive, his finger on the trigger.

"It appears your friends are as foolish as they are bold," he told Tommy.

Powerless to do anything else, Tommy sat and waited, intently watching for the elevator and the seemingly imminent conflict that would determine his fate. As fast as its ancient gears could carry it, the elevator climbed the tower, loudly grinding to stop at the first platform. The moment the doors began to slide open, Viktor pounced, lunging forward and firing shots, emptying an entire clip into the open car.

Viktor paused to reload, and only then did he notice that the elevator was empty. As quickly as his tired legs would carry him, Richard bounded up the last of the stairs, spun around the corner, and fired a quick succession of shots that found the mark. After Viktor went down, Richard cautiously walked forward, kicked his gun away, and then reached through his pockets to find the handcuff key. With the key in hand, he walked over to release Tommy.

"You had me worried there. For a minute I thought you were actually stupid enough to take the elevator," Tommy said.

"Always take the stairs, better for your health and the environment," Richard said as he helped lift Tommy up.

With Richard's help, Tommy hobbled his way towards the elevator and a trip to the bottom. Before they left, they paused for one last glance to take in the view.

"That's a view to die for," Richard said.

"Let's make a deal, Dick," said Tommy. "From now on, how about I leave all the dangerous spy games to you, and you leave all the jokes to me."

CHAPTER THIRTY-SIX

It was a crisp and clear day when Tommy was released from the hospital. It took a long and painful night to remove the toxins from his system, and he lost quite a bit of weight in the process. But now, he was a free man once more, and he felt like he had already gained most of the weight back while indulging at a brunch buffet. Afterwards, he finalized his travel plans to fly back to America, and also visited Louis, who arranged for him to give one final performance on his last night in Paris.

The success of Tommy's opening shows had earned him a rather large check, and he spent a portion of it buying a bespoke suit from one of the finest tailors in town. He was wearing this new suit when he left to attend the one last big event on his schedule before his closing show. Upon arrival, he tipped his cab driver well and stepped out at the entrance to Prince Hans Friedrich's residence.

Sir Alastair Thorncliffe was standing there waiting when Tommy opened the door. "Good, you've arrived. You have a lot to catch up on."

They walked through the main hallway, where most of the decorations had been taken down. The house was lined with piles of boxes and packing material, preparing the way as the royal family transferred their official residence from exile in Paris to home rule in Montravia.

"The Treaty went through as scheduled and the royals are returning to power," Alastair explained. "Every representative of the Soviet government that we know has denied any involvement in or knowledge of the incidents. Roughly speaking, about half of them may be telling the truth. Meanwhile, our friend General Kharlamov has been recalled to Moscow to answer some questions. He has a lot of friends there, but he also has a lot of enemies. He is in for an interesting time, to say the least."

Tommy nodded, taking it all in. Before he could think of any questions to ask, they turned the corner to the parlor, the one room that still had most of its furnishings. Prince Hans Friedrich was standing in front of the fireplace, wearing his ceremonial uniform as the commander of Montravia's small but proud armed forces. Princess Sophia was standing by her father's side, looking resplendent in an emerald green gown with a tiara in her hair. The household staff stood at the back of the room, providing a small but enthusiastic audience.

Richard Boothwyn was wearing his best suit and standing alone in front of a bookshelf. Sir Alastair directed Tommy to go stand beside him, and the room grew quiet when Tommy assumed his position.

"Ladies and gentlemen, your attention please," called out the Prince. "Today I have the great honor of bestowing the Legion of Valor, Montravia's most prestigious award for gallantry, on Richard Boothwyn and Thomas Malloy. While they may not hail from our country, they have done every one of us an incredible service, and they may henceforth consider themselves to be honorary citizens of Montravia."

When he was finished, Princess Sophia stepped forward and draped the gold medals with purple ribbons around their necks.

"Shouldn't you be getting one too?" Tommy whispered to her.

She laughed. "Oh no, it wouldn't look right. Monarchy is nepotistic enough to begin with."

She then stepped back and began to clap her hands. The rest of those assembled soon joined in and made a raucous round of applause. Tommy turned to face Richard and gave him a very firm handshake.

"It was a pleasure, Thomas."

"You too, Dick."

Tommy felt a wave of emotions as the whirlwind of events of the past few days finally began to sink in.

"I'm going to miss you, Dick."

Richard gave him a hearty slap on the back. "We'll always have Paris."

CHAPTER THIRTY-SEVEN

Atlantic City, New Jersey

Every seat in the club was filled as Tommy worked the stage. It was his first performance since returning to the United States, and arguably his best one yet. It was quite an experience to play an international spy for a few days, but now he was back where he belonged; on the stage, underneath the spotlights, with a microphone in his hand.

"So I came home to Philadelphia recently, and I was told that we are locked in massive Cold War. Our side on the West is the land of freedom, peace, and opportunity. Meanwhile, to the East lies a dark land where the oppressed people cry out for freedom. These lands are separated a by great curtain, and it is one which you may never cross…"

The audience sat at the end of their seats, wondering if Tommy was making a joke or a political commentary.

"But I was thinking, come on now, New Jersey

isn't *that* bad."

The audience roared with laughter, giving Tommy the exhilarating rush he experienced whenever a joke really hit home. "Thank You, Atlantic City! You've been a great audience! Remember to tip the waitresses! Please drink responsibly and watch out for rip tides!"

Tommy walked off the stage to a standing ovation. Paulie Prosciutto, the infamous New York mob boss who owned a controlling interest in the club, greeted him backstage with a vigorous bear hug.

"That was the greatest performance of comedy I have ever witnessed," he said, his voice shaking with emotion.

Tommy had originally been worried that the publicity of being framed for murder in a foreign country would have a negative impact on his career. However, it turned out that he had nothing to fear. Le Capitaine had contacted his transatlantic associate Paulie with an explicit request to promote Tommy Malloy any way he could. Paulie took the message to heart, booking Tommy at all his clubs and also putting in a good word with his contacts in Hollywood. Tommy thanked Paulie profusely for all his help and then walked outside to the boardwalk to feel the cool salty breeze blowing in from the ocean. Tommy's family and many of his friends had made the drive over the bridge and down the highway from Philadelphia, and he was anxious to go back inside and greet them. But first, there was somebody else he had to see.

He walked a short distance down the boardwalk and into a neighboring club that was mostly empty that night. Posters around the entrance advertised the major concert that was going to be held there the following night with the tagline, "A Night to Remember: Tony Vespa sings the classics, featuring Natalie Peterson on piano." The two featured musicians were rehearsing on stage, but they stopped when they noticed Tommy approaching.

"I killed it, it was even better than Paris!" Tommy told them.

"That's great, Tommy, I'm happy for you. But it's still going to be small potatoes compared to our concert tomorrow," said Tony.

Tommy sighed, "You musicians and your egos. You just can't accept that sometimes the audience just wants to laugh."

"Anyway, Tommy, you have a lot of explaining to do about Paris," said Tony. "All this time I was worried about what you were getting into, thinking you might get arrested or killed. But it turned out that you were really just running off with this dame here. That's a big part of the story to leave out. And, by the way, she is one incredible dame. I most wholeheartedly approve."

Tommy and Natalia shared a smile, knowing that they would never be able to tell anybody the full details of her real identity, or the real story of how they actually met.

"So, Natalie, I never actually asked you, where are you from?"

"Saint Petersburg," she answered.

"Saint Petersburg, Florida," Tommy specified.

Natalia folded up her music books and Tommy helped her down from the stage. She took his arm as they walked towards the exit.

"So I know you've been through a lot, but you

are about to meet your greatest challenge yet," Tommy told her. "You are about to be introduced to every living member of a Philadelphia Irish-American family."

"I have had a lot of training and experience. I believe I am adequately prepared to handle that," she said.

Tommy laughed. "Oh, you have no idea…"

"Tell your mom I said hi," Tony called out. "She'll remember me."

"And tell yours that despite her best efforts to raise an upstanding gentleman, she has truly and utterly failed," Tommy responded.

The boardwalk was bustling with activity when Tommy and Natalia walked outside, the vibrant night life standing out against the peaceful calm of the moonlight reflecting off the ocean.

"Hey, why don't we stop for ice cream," Tommy said as they waited for the Malloy clan to meet them.

Natalia took a long look down the boardwalk. "I see four different stores to buy four different kinds of ice cream. How do you even decide?"

"We'll just have to try all four then."

"But why would we do that?"

Tommy grinned from ear to ear as he wrapped his arm around her. "Because we're in America now."

ABOUT THE AUTHOR

James Dudley is a massive fan of spy fiction and stand-up comedy who finally figured out a way to combine them. He attended Villanova University and served in the U.S. Navy. He is a native of Delaware and a Philadelphia sports fanatic.

32988813R00184

Made in the USA
Middletown, DE
25 June 2016